Special thanks to the following people for helping breathe life into the Godsverse:

Amba Nevell, Andrea Johnson, Anij Fallows, Ashley, Beth Barany, Brad Com, Burnel Smith, C, Caledonia, Cat Fleming (MadCatter), Catherine Leja, Chad Bowden, Chris Call, Christina Lopez, Christine Chandra, Christopher Stillwell, Cristian Dinu, Daniel Groves, Dave Baxter, David Irgang, Dr.Salt, Earl Weiss, EconKelly, Elizabeth Noel Bennett, Emerson Kasak, Emily, Emily, Eric Williamson, Erica, Erica Hecker, Erica Jordan, Eva Jayet, Garry James Watts, Gavran, Genevieve Perosa, Gerald P. McDaniel, GMarkC, goodmancoming, Greywolfe, Isaac "Will It Work" Dansicker, James Kralik, Jason Crase, Jason 'XenoPhage' Frisvold, Jeff Frisone, Jeff Lewis, Jeremy Reppy, John "AcesofDeath7" Mullens, John Idlor, JohnDoe, Joshua Bowers, Joshua McGinnis, Juanita Nesbitt, Katrina Kunstmann, Kenny Endlich, Laura Ann Moylan, Lia, maileguy, Manic, Martin Nehmiz, Matthew Johnson, Maxi Organ, Melissa Showers, Michael Di Salvo, Nathaniel Adams Jr, Nick Smith, Paul Nygard, Paul Rose Jr., Pavlos Chatzipantelidis, Peter Anders, Peter Tarasewich, Randy Graham, Rebecca Carter, Rebecca M. Senese, Rhel ná DecVandé, Robert Brown, Robinflight,Rowan Stone, Ryan Scott James, Scantrontb, Scott Chisholm, Scott Kilburn, Shannon Carlin, Sil, Snir Kolodni, Stephan Szabo, Stephen Ballentine, Sunny Side Up, Venron, Victoria Nohelty, Walter Weiss, Winter, and Xavier Hugonet.

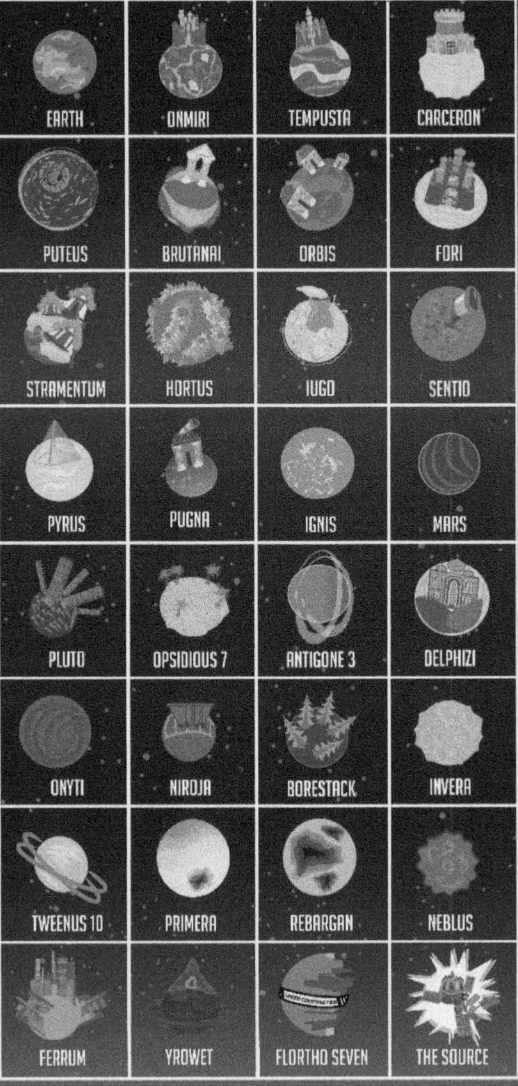
GODSVERSE PLANETS
EARTH
ONMIRI
TEMPUSTA
CARCERON
PUTEUS
BRUTANAI
ORBIS
FORI
STRAMENTUM
HORTUS
IUGO
SENTIO
PYRUS
PUGNA
IGNIS
MARS
PLUTO
OPSIDIOUS 7
ANTIGONE 3
DELPHIZI
ONYTI
NIROJA
BORESTACK
INVERA
TWEENUS 10
PRIMERA
REBARGAN
NEBLUS
FERRUM
YROWET
FLORTHO SEVEN
THE SOURCE

1000 BC – BETRAYED (HELL PT 1) /PIXIE DUST

500 BC – FALLEN (HELL PT 2)

200 BC – HELLFIRE (HELL PT 3)

1974 AD – MYSTERY SPOT (RUIN PT 1)

1976 AD – INTO HELL (RUIN PT 2)

1984 AD – LAST STAND (RUIN PT 3)

1985 AD – CHANGE

1985 AD – MAGIC/BLACK MARKET HEROINE

1985 AD – EVIL

1989 AD – DEATH'S KISS (DARKNESS PT 1)

2000 AD – TIME

2015 AD – HEAVEN

2018 AD – DEATH'S RETURN (DARKNESS PT 2)

2020 AD – KATRINA HATES THE DEAD (DEATH PT 1)

2176 AD – CONQUEST

2177 AD – DEATH'S KISS (DARKNESS PT 3)

12,018 AD – KATRINA HATES THE GODS (DEATH PT 2)

12,028 AD – KATRINA HATES THE UNIVERSE (DEATH PT 3)

12.046 AD – EVERY PLANET HAS A GODSCHURCH (DOOM PT 1)

12,047 AD – THERE'S EVERY REASON TO FEAR (DOOM PT. 2)

12,049 AD – THE END TASTES LIKE PANCAKES (DOOM PT 3)

12,176 AD – CHAOS

ALSO BY RUSSELL NOHELTY

NOVELS
My Father Didn't Kill Himself
Sorry for Existing
Gumshoes: The Case of Madison's Father
Invasion
The Vessel
The Void Calls Us Home
Worst Thing in the Universe
Anna and the Dark Place
The Marked Ones
The Dragon Scourge
The Dragon Champion
The Dragon Goddess
The Obsidian Spindle Saga

COMICS and OTHER ILLUSTRATED WORK
The Little Bird and the Little Worm
Ichabod Jones: Monster Hunter
Gherkin Boy
How NOT to Invade Earth

www.russellnohelty.com

HEAVEN

Book 4 of The Godsverse Chronicles

By:
Russell Nohelty

Edited by:
Leah Lederman

Proofread by:
Katrina Roets & Toni Cox

Cover by:
Psycat Covers

Planet chart and timeline design by:
Andrea Rosales

BOOK 1

CHAPTER 1

Kimberly

I'd finished picking the lock to the door and stepped inside the demon's apartment. The brimstone smell immediately overpowered me. Demons moved often, usually following the night as it moved across the world, taking their scent with them. But this one, Ch'ri'yl, had stayed put long enough that every surface of her apartment reeked of battery acid and sulfur.

"Be on your guard," I told Molly as she followed behind me.

Molly was my wife. We married the first day it was legal, in a big ceremony at San Francisco city hall with hundreds of other gays who had waited to marry the loves of their lives for years—or, in our case, decades. We had lived together since the 90s, so marrying her didn't change much, except that it changed everything.

"It stinks in here," Molly said as she broke away from me, moving toward the kitchen to make sure there weren't any body parts in the refrigerator. She opened the door, and another scent crashed into the brimstone: rancid food and spoiled milk. "Holy good god. That is foul."

"Rotten meat?" I asked, turning my attention to her.

"Some maggots, too." She slammed the fridge closed. "Don't think it's human."

"Well, that's good, at least. Means he's probably not dead yet," I said. "Anything else?"

She held up a blue Post-it note. "Just this stuck to the fridge. Mean anything to you?"

I walked over and looked down at the note. Ten numbers and a name. *Horace Carlson.* "You don't see that name often."

"I'll run it through our database," Molly said.

I bit the inside of my cheek. "I don't think you'll find anything. I'm going to stay here and keep looking for a clue."

She kissed me on the cheek, and I swerved to connect with her lips. "Okay. Love you."

"Love you, too."

It was good she left. She distracted me. We worked well together, but I felt myself always looking over my shoulder to protect her. One day she would die, and I was going to have to learn how to exist without her. She would never have that problem. The years were showing on her face even as mine stayed as youthful as the day we met. Her reflexes diminished exponentially with every birthday. I much preferred her back at the apartment where I knew she was safe.

Besides, I thought better alone, and I needed every bit of my faculties to find out where Ch'ri'yl had taken Geordi. His mother came to me yesterday after taking a flight from Vancouver down to San Francisco, scared out of her mind because he hadn't come home in a week. He was an eleven-year-old with a rebellious streak, but he had never stayed out all night before. It had been three weeks since she had seen her son. If I found him, I had a feeling he wouldn't be doing it again.

I had a special affinity for protecting magical creatures, and while his mother didn't have an ounce of magical blood in her, she assured me that her son was touched by the gods. If this was true, it made him a very rare breed indeed. I took the case, which led me across the country up to Canada, and finally to Fresno, where I caught the trail of the demon named Ch'ri'yl. She had stayed hidden for a quarter of a century.

I followed a hallway to a locked door at the end of it. I knocked, hearing the ting of metal. The door was thick. It wouldn't give, even when I pressed my weight against it. It was possible for me to use my powers and teleport into the room, but without having seen within its walls to direct my coordinates, I risked losing myself in the abyss forever.

There was no need for something so drastic. People who spent a lot of money on metal doors often conveniently forgot that their walls were made of flimsy drywall. I drummed my knuckles on the wall next to the door, and sure enough, it was hollow. I tapped around some more, looking for studs. Confident that I wouldn't hit anything solid, I took a running start and smashed my shoulder against the wall, tumbling through to the other side.

I hopped up and brushed myself off before flicking on the light in the dark, dank room. What the red light showed me was disappointing. It wasn't a prison to store the boy; there were no chains, no bed, no boy. Just dozens of trays filled with chemicals and pictures hanging on clotheslines to dry.

The front door creaked open. Instinctively, I went for the pair of daggers on my belt and crept to the hole in the wall. A tall, brunette woman with olive skin walked into the kitchen and put down two duffel bags with a huff.

"Gross," she said, opening the fridge and pulling out the maggoty meat. "Check your fridge before you leave for the weekend, Cheryl." She tossed the meat into the trash as her face changed into an onyx demon with long, fire-red hair and two long orange horns coming out of her head. She stepped into the hallway, and I got a look at her blood-red eyes just as she caught me peering through from the hole in her wall.

"What the hell?" She marched toward me, inspecting the damaged wall. "You know I have to pay for that, right?"

I stepped out of the room, leveling my daggers at her. "Where is Geordi?"

She held up her hands. "Are you kidding me? Who is Geordi, and who are you?"

"I'm here to find Geordi. I know you have him. Where have you taken him?"

"Are you crazy? I don't know any Geordi. I was on a trip to Napa for the weekend…with my boyfriend…and also, you're in my house pointing frigging daggers at me!" She pulled a phone out of her pocket. "I'm calling the cops."

"I don't think you want to do that, demon. Not unless you want them to know what you're doing in that room back there."

"You mean my dark room? Where I process film? For my job, as a photographer!" She dialed. "Yes, I would like to report an invas—"

I sliced the phone in half as she spoke. "No cops. Not until you tell me where Geordi is."

She glared. "Okay, so this is bananas. If I had Geordi, whoever that is, why would I call the cops on you? Jesus, you are stupid." She smacked her forehead. "Think for two seconds. Just because I'm a demon doesn't mean I'm evil."

"It doesn't mean you're good."

She scoffed, placing her hands on her hips. "That's racist. I have been up here twenty years and haven't caused one single problem, and yet, you guys can't stop harassing me for every little damn thing."

I opened my mouth to speak, but I couldn't find the words. *Had I made a mistake?* Just then, my phone rang. It was Molly. I put one of my daggers away and kept the other one pointed at Cheryl. "Don't move."

"I know the drill," Cheryl said, crossing her arms across her chest. "This is bull, though."

"What is it?" I said into the phone. "I'm in the middle of something."

"That number was for a bed and breakfast in Napa," Molly replied. "Apparently, they rented a room there this weekend to a Horace Carlson."

"Hang on," I said, putting the phone against my chest. "What's your boyfriend's name?"

"Like I have to tell you!"

"Please," I said.

She sighed. "Horace Carlson."

"Shit," I said to Molly. "I think we made a big mistake."

***

I wrote Ch'ri'yl a check for $50,000 to repair her wall and pay for the photographs I'd ruined, which got her to calm down. She even offered me tea after I told her I was a bit of an art collector.

"I don't like that name, you know," she said. "Ch'ri'yl is my slave name. I like Cheryl better."

"I like Cheryl better, too," I said, sipping the cup of black tea.

"Me too," she said, taking her own sip. "I know some of us are awful, but most demons are just trying to get along in the world. It sucks that people are trying to scapegoat us for their awful crimes. Don't mistake me, this is horrible. It sucks that this kid is missing. People that steal children are the worst kind of people."

"I agree."

She smiled. "It's funny what we could agree on if you looked past the horns on my head."

"I don't want to seem indelicate, but is there anyone else you could think of that might want to—"

She shook her head in a snit. "You just can't do it, can you? You can't comprehend that I'm not a criminal, and I don't know criminals."

"Everybody knows criminals," I said. "That's one thing I've learned in my life."

"Well, I am very glad I don't have your life because I have no interest in being around, or associating with, criminals." She drained her cup. "I think you should go."

I slid the check over to her. "My number is on the check. If you think of anything, please give me a call."

"If I do, I will, but I won't, so I shan't."

I took my leave of her with a rock of guilt swirling in my stomach. She was right, of course. By the most aggressive standards, most demons I met weren't a danger to themselves or others. Even if they came up to Earth with evil intentions, that bloodlust left them over time, and they ended up working jobs as taxi drivers or accountants. They became upstanding citizens and productive members of society.

***

I slammed Atticus's head into the table of the very nice Embarcadero restaurant where I'd asked to meet him. It wasn't my intention to slam his face into the table, but his face was so slammable, smiling at me so smug.

Blood smeared the white tablecloth as he slid to the floor. "What was that for?"

"You fed me bum information, Atticus. I should rip your face off. Getting your head smashed is a courtesy because we're old friends, or at least we used to be."

"It's not my faaaaault!"

He situated himself in his chair once more, ignoring the other patrons who stared at us unabashedly. I turned to the waiter who stood two tables away, an aghast expression on his face.

"Sorry about that. Can you tell all these nice people their meal is on me? Thanks." That seemed to settle everyone in the restaurant, and I handed the waiter my credit card with a curt smile. "Add a nice tip for yourself as well."

"You gonna pay for my meal, too, Kimmy?" Atticus held a napkin to the cut on his forehead. "Least you can do."

"Who are you protecting, Atticus?" I said, ignoring his request. "And don't lie to me, not again."

He looked around, then whispered, "You don't want to mess with these guys. They are no joke."

"I literally hunt demons for a living. It takes a lot to scare me."

"I know it does, so believe me when I tell you that you have reason to be scared of these people. I was trying to protect you."

"By sending me to harass an innocent demon?"

"Better her than me!"

"Who took Geordi? Give me a name," I snapped. "I'm a big girl and can handle myself."

"Not against these guys you can't. They are bad news."

"Ten seconds." I sat in silence, refusing to budge and staring daggers at him. Atticus squirmed in his chair, refusing to catch my eyes. "Three, two, one."

"Okay!" he shouted. The restaurant patrons all turned their attention to us for a second time. "You're gonna get me killed."

I leaned toward him. "Better than me killing you, which is what will happen if you don't tell me what you know right now." I grabbed him around the throat. "The only reason I allow you to keep your awful operation going is because you feed me the information I need, no questions asked."

"Okay, okay, okay," he squeaked as I crushed his larynx. "They're called the Blue Trident."

He gasped for air after I released him. "That sounds like a healthcare plan," I murmured.

"They aren't. They are bad news, and they're planning something big."

"You're not lying to me, are you, Atticus?" The threat in my tone was obvious.

"Of course not," he replied. "Though you should hope that I was lying because if there's one group you don't want to mess with, it's the Blue Trident."

"What do they want with Geordi?"

"I don't know!" His voice cracked. "But they're being real secretive about a lot of things these days."

"Thanks, Atticus," I said. "Find out everything you can on where they took the kid and call me when you have something."

"Are you serious? Do you think I have a death wish?"

"No, I think you very much want to live, which is why you'll help me." I stood up as the waiter brought the bill to my table. He had given himself a $1,000 tip. "I thought I told you to be generous," I said to him, smirking. I added a zero to it, making it $10,000, and signed it. "Thank you for your service."

CHAPTER 2

Angelica

Standing before a thousand staring faces used to cause my entire body to tremble, but now I could address the general assembly of Forche like I was singing to myself in the shower. It had taken a long time to win their respect, and the ones that didn't at least tolerated my presence due to my connection with Queen Margaret.

"And in the next quarter, we expect to open up relations to Nuralia and Endosp, increasing exports by thirty percent and cementing our trade routes for generations to come."

Neither Margaret nor I were from Onmiri, but we had done the hard work of integrating ourselves into the world when Margaret's uncle opened a portal with her blood and sent us here. It didn't hurt that she was a member of the royal family and the only one left to ascend to the throne after we killed her father and imprisoned her brother for crimes against the people.

"I look forward to working with all of you on the next budget proposal." There was a boisterous laugh across the chamber. "I know it's never fun to discuss our fiscal solvency, but what is the parliament for, if not to make sure we live within our means?"

It had been a shaky proposition, moving Forche from a monarchy to a constitutional democracy, and I was just a kid when we started the process. It ended up pretty good in the end, I thought. There were still people loyal to the old king even now, 25 years after his demise, but we worked hard to rebalance his power back to the people. Other countries took notice. Where once we ruled with an iron fist, now we did so with a white glove.

Most days, I wished we could just jam through whatever crazy proposal we had without having to fight tooth and nail for it. Even then, though, I have never thought about reinstalling the monarchy. The people deserve a voice, even if it was a pain in the ass to give it to them.

"Thank you," I said. "And may the gods shine on Forche for many years to come."

There was thunderous applause when I walked out of the chamber. My assistant, Gible, was waiting for me just outside.

"Great speech, ma'am," she said, pounding her tiny legs along the floor to keep up with me. I walked briskly to avoid the throng of reporters descending on us. "The delegates seem to have really loved it."

"Did they? Or were they just excited I was finally done?"

"I do—"

It was a rhetorical question, so I didn't bother listening to her response. "Tell the communications team I don't want to do any more speeches over thirty minutes long for at least another year."

"I told them already, miss. I told them last time, too."

I let out an exasperated sigh. "Then why do they insist on making me drone on and on for hours?"

"Miss Anjelica!" a bubble-faced reporter hollered as the flash bulbs started going. "What do you have to say about your missile strikes on the Forchean settlements?"

“No comment,” Gible yelled over her shoulder. We rushed down the stairs of the grand parliament building toward my car waiting outside. “We’ll be available for press questions in the conference room in an hour back at the residence.”

The settlements. The bane of my existence. We had given them freedom after the king’s passing and allowed them to self-govern, but that wasn’t enough for them. They wanted to break off from Forche to form their own government, and they had taken to bombing government buildings to show their dissatisfaction with the current structure. *How could they expect us not to bomb them back?*

“Perhaps we should prepare a statement,” Gible suggested when we were safe in the limo back to the palace.

I placed my hands on my head. “There is nothing else to say. Peace talks are ongoing, but the settlements are being intransigent. They have no leverage except blind faith in their cause, and yet they refuse to yield.”

The black divider between the driver and the back of the limo rolled down, and I heard a familiar voice. “Were you any different when you came here?”

Director Frente smiled at me from the front of the limo. She had grooved wrinkles on either side of her mouth, and thick bags hung from her eyes to the tip of her nose. Gray hairs overtook the brown in the mod cut she had kept since we met nearly three decades ago, but she was still the same optimistic do-gooder that she had been when we wrested power from the king.

“Director.” I was not pleased to see her. “I thought I told your office I wasn’t available today.”

"Today, yesterday, this week, this month, this year. Every time I contact you, it's always the same."

"Because I am always busy."

She chuckled. "There was a time you would rely on me to make every decision."

"Before I learned you were unreliable."

"Because I side with the colonies?"

"Because you side against Margaret and the crown, yes."

"Listen to yourself!" Director Frente threw her hands in the air. "You sound just like the previous king."

"Don't you dare," I growled. "I am still the Grand Advisor. Insulting me is to insult Queen Margaret herself. Remember that, Director."

"Oh, I remember it. You'll never let me forget it."

I snapped my fingers. "Gible, make a note that the director isn't to have access to me for any reason until further notice. If she violates this order or gets within thirty feet of me after this ride, see that she's arrested."

"You can't avoid this fight forever!" Director Frente was still shouting as I pushed up the separator and locked it into place.

When I turned back to Gible, her mouth was pursed shut.

"Anything to add?" I spat.

She shook her head but didn't speak, which I appreciated. Even if she disagreed with me, she kept quiet until the appropriate time, and this was not the appropriate time to discuss such nasty business as succession. If we allowed that, we would seem weak at a time when we needed to be strong. Democracy still rested on the head of a needle, threatening to tumble if we didn't keep a firm grasp on it.

***

"How was your speech today?" Queen Margaret asked at dinner. No matter what else was going on with our lives, we always ate together at least once a day, usually dinner. The banquet table was set for thirty, but tonight it was just us. We sat next to each other, sloughing off our responsibilities and sitting like old friends instead of queen and advisor.

"You didn't watch?" I asked.

She laughed. "Oh god, no. It's all so dry. I mean, I don't have to tell you that, right? You were there."

I took a sip of my tomato soup. It wasn't exactly tomatoes, but it was close enough on this foreign world. They called it *visuri* here on Onmiri. "I've begged them to cut my speeches down to thirty minutes. There is so much bluster in them. But my team insists every word is vital to the effort." I made a slurp. "What did you do today?"

"Met with the generals about the unpleasantness in the colonies, like every other day. They think it will lead to civil war across all Forche soon if we don't squash it in the coming weeks."

"How can we squash it without destroying the colonies completely?"

"I'm not sure we can. But if they get the support of Uyin, there could be trouble."

I furrowed my brow, thinking about our tenuous allies to the north. I had negotiated a peace treaty with them a decade ago, but it was always on the verge of falling apart.

"You can't possibly think we should annihilate our own people."

"Of course I don't!" Margaret said, setting her cup down loudly. "But in a democracy, it's not what I want, it's what the people want, and we're starting to lose the public's patience. If it were up to me, I would cut them off like a bad limb. If they're so sure they could exist on their own, then I'd like them to prove it. They'll be back in six months begging for our help."

I downed the last of my soup and gave her a hard look. "We can't do that either. Half the world thinks we're going to crumble any second, and the other half is waiting to pick over the remains when we do."

Margaret sighed. "Remember how we thought we were going to change everything?"

I nodded. "And we did."

"Maybe, but the more things change, the more they stay the same." She took a long drink from her wine glass. "At least there's wine."

"*Bicho*," I replied, tilting my glass to hers before the exhaustion of the day hit me. They didn't have grapes in Onmiri, and what they made wasn't wine exactly, but it did the job. I finished what was left of my wine before standing. "On that note...I have a busy day of being yelled at by bureaucrats tomorrow."

She sighed. "And I have a long day of pretending people aren't talking about me behind my back. Until tomorrow, tomorrow."

I kissed her hand. "Goodnight, my love."

She pulled me close to her and kissed me full on the mouth. "Goodnight."

We had kept our relationship secret for a decade, even as we worked to give all people the right to marry who they loved. Not because we were ashamed, but because the idea of Queen Margaret's chastity and virtue was the one thing we could count on for positive public opinion.

Even if she could marry or date, it wouldn't be with me. I was one of the most hated figures in Onmiri, the punching bag for the entirety of the government. Every bad decision was luffed off on me. It might look powerful from the outside, but my position was little more than a scapegoat for everything people felt was wrong with the world.

I slid into bed after washing my face and brushing my teeth. I took one deep sigh and turned off the light. Nights like these, I wished I could lay my head on Margaret's chest and listen to her sleep. We had to be careful, though. Our enemies were everywhere, especially with tensions so high, and were looking for anything to tip the delicate balance into anarchy.

"Good evening, Lady Anjelica," a voice from my past spoke from the dark room. "I'm sorry to come to you like this."

I wasn't surprised to see Araphael, god of death, emerge from the shadows. In fact, I was almost glad that perhaps my long life would be finally over.

"Please tell me you're here to kill me, Araphael."

He shook the hood from his head, his bright eyes staring out blankly. "It is not your time, I'm afraid."

"Then why are you here?" I propped myself up on my elbows. "It can't be good."

He sighed deeply. "I'm afraid your mother has passed. As her friend, I promised to deliver this message to you. Her funeral will be held tomorrow on Earth, and she requested your attendance."

I stared back at him for a long moment before finally saying, "Of course. Let me get my things."

***

I hadn't seen my mother in decades, not since the day I was kidnapped by demons to sacrifice my body to open a portal to Hell. Luckily, it didn't work. In order to protect her, though, I had no choice but to go into hiding. Kimberly took me to a safe house after she and Ollie saved my life, or at least they thought it was safe. Little did they know I would befriend a witch from another planet, or that she'd open a portal back to her world that sucked me through along with it.

There was one moment, in the abyss of death, that Araphael brought my mother and me together to say a sort of goodbye before I decided to stay on Onmiri and build a better world for the future. I often wondered if I had made the wrong choice. Yes, I would have been a nobody on Earth, but I would have been a happy nobody. I wouldn't have Margaret, and yet maybe I could have found somebody to be happy enough with most of the time instead of blissfully happy in tiny, hidden moments.

I would have been closer to my mother, that was for sure. Maybe not immediately, but eventually, the heat would have died down on me, and I could have seen her again. Now, I would never have that chance again.

It surprised me how emotional I was when Araphael led me into the funeral home, and I saw the body. I had negotiated deals with princes and held my own against generals without breaking, but taking one look at my mother's peaceful, dead face was enough to send me to my knees, wailing an ugly cry that turned my face a beet red.

A kindly old man in a black coat rushed in, but when he saw my condition, he didn't say anything. He simply dropped a handkerchief at my side and walked off. It was a full half-hour that I bawled my eyes out before I could pull myself up to see my mother's serene face one last time.

Funny, I never thought of her as a peaceful person. Her body was never at rest. Part of the reason she worked so much was because of the nervous energy she bottled up. Another shift was eight more hours she didn't have to confront the darkness within her. That darkness was all she would have for the rest of eternity.

"Was she happy?" I asked the shadows, knowing Araphael was inside of them.

"I will not lie to you," he replied. "She never found true happiness. There were moments when the guilt of her past didn't crash upon her when I think she found peace or the closest a ship at sea can find."

"Ah," a voice behind me said. I turned to see the old man shuffling up to me. "It is a dreadful thing to lose the ones we love. Were you close with the deceased?"

"I was her daughter."

"Oh," he said. "I wasn't sure you would be coming. Will you be saying something at the service?"

"I…I don't think I knew her enough to speak at her funeral." The words crushed me when I spoke them out loud, sinking my stomach down into my feet. It didn't make them any less true.

"I understand. Well, the viewing will begin in an hour. You are welcome to be alone with her until then. If you change your mind and wish to speak, let me know."

I had spoken in front of friends and enemies alike, thousands at a time, but the thought of speaking at my mother's funeral filled me with a dread I hadn't felt in decades.

"I won't, but thank you." I turned back to the casket as the old man left and looked down at my mother's face. "I want to see her again."

"You are seeing her, right here and right now," Araphael replied.

"No, I mean I need to go into the underworld and say a proper goodbye to her. I need to make my peace."

"That's not advisable," Araphael said, emerging again from the darkness.

"I don't care if it's advisable. Bring me to Hell. I know you have the power."

"You will not like what you find there."

"I don't care. I need to see her again. Make it happen."

Araphael was silent for a long moment. "No."

"Fine," I snapped, spinning away from the coffin. "Then I'll do it myself. Thanks for nothing."

CHAPTER 3

Lizzie

Heaven was boring. Not just a little boring, either, like watching a nature documentary about tortoise migration boring. Wait, actually, that wasn't not boring at all. I would kill to get the nature channel here. No, this was more like C-SPAN, all day, every day.

Not only were there very few people in Heaven, but they were all duller than dishwater. Apparently, only super boring people could fit through the eye of the needle. I met plenty of people in my travels across the country to know there were plenty of amazing, interesting, fun churchgoers. Clearly, none of them got into Heaven.

I had checked. I knocked on every door to every apartment in Cloud City and really tried with these people, from the ancient to the…well, slightly less ancient. Perhaps it would be easier to make friends with them if we had literally just one single thing in common. And there hadn't been a new person in Heaven for several hundred years.

Even the ones who would have been interesting hundreds of years ago, like Joan of Arc, ended up having all the fun sucked out of them in the droll doldrum and repetition of Heaven. On Earth, at least you had to eat, sleep, and poop, which chewed up most of even the most banal day. We didn't have to do any of that in Heaven, which meant there was nothing to look forward to or dread.

I ended up spending most of my time parting the clouds to watch people on Earth. I tried to keep the privacy of people I knew and instead chose to watch philandering husbands and felonious women all day. Even the most interesting life was boring most of the time.

It was hard not to turn my attention to Veronica. She was growing up so fast. I watched her join the volleyball team, get her black belt, graduate high school, and start working at a delivery company in town. She had friends, and even a nice boyfriend, Dennis. I couldn't help thinking he was holding her back, keeping her chained to Overbrook instead of traveling the world and having incredible adventures.

It was hard to fault her decision to remain in one place, though. That was all I had ever wanted: a quiet life on the farm with my parents. My life had been the opposite, having run away at sixteen and traveling the country for a decade. I still regretted it. I had been trying to avoid my destiny…a destiny that caught up with me anyway and left me dead, swallowing my parents along with me before the end.

"I found them." Gabriel blinked into existence in front of me as I watched a cruise liner move over the ocean, hoping for some bit of intrigue that never came.

I popped my head up. "My parents?"

For the price of embracing my destiny to save the world, God promised that my parents would be able to get into Heaven along with me. I had been waiting fifteen years for the angelic guard to follow through on that promise and return them to me. It had been almost twenty years, and they still weren't with me.

I kept pestering, and they kept responding with placations and platitudes. Eventually, I gave up, assuming that it would never happen and trying to make my peace with being lied to by an all-powerful being. I wasn't the only one.

"Yes," Gabriel responded. "They should be here any time now. Come with me."

I followed Gabriel toward the Golden Gates of Ascension at the entrance to Heaven. I had been waiting for this moment for so long that butterflies bounced in my stomach as I hopped along the clouds. With the magnitude of the situation, I wished that I could do something more than bounce along like a child on a trampoline, but it was the most efficient way to move across Heaven, especially since only archangels received wings. Bouncing was fun for the first ten minutes, but after that, it just gets annoying.

"Where were they?" I asked as I tried to keep up with Gabriel. "And why did it take you so long to find them?"

"I'm not sure if you've looked in on Hell recently, but it's nothing if not unorganized."

"And whose fault is it that they were sent to Hell in the first place?"

"I didn't have anything to do with it," Gabriel grumbled. "Since they were dead before you came to us, I couldn't put in the necessary paperwork to make sure they ended up here. If you recall, I even had to traverse Hell to find you the first time you died."

Oh, I remembered. The first time I died, I wound up in a huge line, hundreds of miles from the Gates of Abnegation, where millions upon millions waited to be judged. It was a complete mess down there.

"Seems like something God could have figured out, what with being all-powerful and all-knowing."

"God doesn't sully his attention on such matters. Besides, he and Lucifer have an accord. If Lucifer needs his help, he needs to come to him. Otherwise, God has agreed to stay out of the management of the underworld."

We reached the gates, and after a moment, they creaked open. Gabriel and Peter gave each other a thick, side-long glance as we moved past. They didn't get along very well.

"It took us a while to get the necessary paperwork together and for God to sign off on it, especially seeing as he has a whole planet to run," Gabriel continued once he broke off his gaze from Saint Peter. "When we eventually did, it was a matter of searching millions of souls to find the right ones."

"But you found them. You really found them?" I hadn't dared to hope for a long time, but I found that it tugged on me, and I wanted so badly to let it in again.

"We did." He snapped his fingers, and two puffs of clouds exploded in front of me, causing me to jump back. Nothing so surprising had happened to me in many years. "I present you your parents, Carl and Junebug."

The dust cloud dissipated, and my heart dropped. The man and woman standing there in front of me looked nothing like my mother and father. They were younger, for one, but even in their youth, my father had darker skin and my mother lighter. Even if I wiped the soot and dirt from their faces and squinted, they barely held a passing resemblance to my parents.

"These people are not my parents." I wasn't even angry, just disappointed.

"Don't say that, honey." The woman smiled, but her eyes filled with panic. "Of course, I'm your mother. Don't you remember that house in"—her eyes darted back and forth, trying to summon the right answer—"Missouri, where you were born…?"

I sighed. "I was adopted by Carl and Junebug. And I was born in Wisconsin."

"Umm," the man chimed in. "That's what she meant. We're your biological parents."

I looked over at Gabriel. "Then why did he say you were Carl and Junebug?"

The man and woman looked at each other, flushed with dread, before the woman turned to me. "Come on, kid. Don't make us go back there. Please. I'm begging you."

"I want these two in Heaven as well," I said to Gabriel.

There was a stern look in the angel's eyes. "You know I can't do that."

"This is your screw-up, and I'm not going to have these two people's eternal torture on my hands."

"You won't," he snapped his fingers, and the two souls went away. "It's on mine. I'm very sorry about this. I really thought we had found them that time."

I stepped forward on wobbly legs. "If you let me go into Hell, I could find them myself."

He shook his head. "Only archangels are allowed to leave Heaven."

"Then make me an archangel!"

Again, he shook his head, more vehemently this time. "You have to do something truly incredible to become one of us."

"Oh, and saving the whole world, maybe the whole universe, isn't enough?" I raised an eyebrow. "What did you do that was so deserving?"

"I have been an archangel as far back as I can remember. On this planet alone, I protected the first humans as they searched for meaning, appeared to Daniel to save him from the lions, and appeared to the Virgin Mary to announce the birth of Jesus."

"So, you're a messenger? I could deliver messages if that's all it takes."

"It's impossible right now."

I was so close to him now that I could smell the brimstone left over from his trip to Hell. "You owe me. Figure out how to fix it—and quickly. I'm sick of waiting. This is supposed to be paradise, but it's so boring, and I'm so filled with worry, every day is a nightmare."

"There is a way. Show me how to get to the Time Being. I can go back and—"

"No." This was a tactic he had used before, many times. I was one of only two people on Earth that had ever met Talinda, the goddess of time, who controlled the flow of the universe. The other was trapped in Hell, her mind warped and twisted to uselessness.

Gabriel told me that if I helped him find Talinda, he could simply go back and make sure he put in the proper paperwork to get Carl and Junebug sent to Heaven, but time didn't work like that.

I explained it once again. "She doesn't want to see anyone else. She doesn't want to help anyone else. If she did, she would show you how to find her yourself." I crossed my arms across my chest. "If you want my help, make me an archangel. Otherwise, figure this out. Leave me alone until you do."

This was Heaven. I shouldn't be constantly disappointed. If there was one place in the universe where I should be able to count on things going my way, it was in frigging Heaven. And yet, more often than not, it felt like Hell, just a different kind of Hell.

***

I had mapped out several interesting storylines down on Earth. There was a mother in Minneapolis desperately trying to keep her child from turning into a right-wing internet troll. There was a cop in Rio De Janeiro attempting to hide the fact that he was corrupt from his partner. Meanwhile, the prime minister of Italy was doing his best to convince people he wasn't a womanizer. There were a half dozen others that I flipped between like TV channels when I was feeling bad about myself.

However, I didn't go to any of those after I left Gabriel and reentered the golden gates. Instead, I made my way to the cloud cover over Oregon to spy on Veronica. She was calling herself Connie now, something her dad insisted on after he took her in. Kimberly wasn't wrong about him being a hard man, but I don't think anyone would have predicted how much bitterness he held against his ex-wife, or how much Veronica would have reminded him of her. There was very little love in his heart for his daughter, and eventually, it made Connie strong. Powerful, too. It pushed her to be better and taught her to see the flaws in manipulative people.

"I'm sorry," Gabriel said behind me.

I don't know how long I had watched Connie on her route, biking away without a care in the world, but it was long enough for day to turn into night down on Earth.

"Go away," I said. "I don't want to see you."

"I know," he said, walking toward me anyway. "There's something you should know, though. God isn't omniscient. Neither am I. We're old, so we've seen a lot, but God is also prideful. He had the Metatron spin a tale bigger than he is." Gabriel sat down next to me. "I know that doesn't make it better, I just thought maybe if you knew that, you would be a little more understanding of our mistakes, maybe cut us some slack."

I leaped to my feet. "Cut you some slack? It's been fifteen years, and you haven't done anything at all to find my parents. I mean, even the sun shines on a dog's ass some days, but it's never shined on mine. Have you actually tried to find my family? Do you even care how unhappy I am here?"

"Of course we do!" Gabriel said, his hands held out. "What kind of Heaven is this if we can't provide for the people here?"

"Not much of one," I spat back. "Go away. I don't want to see you."

"Fine," he said, deflated. "But just remember—"

I bounced away from him before he could finish and didn't stop again until I was behind a cover of clouds several hundred yards away. He flew away, and I wiped the tears from my eyes. No matter what, I would never let him see me cry.

"Aw, pet…what's wrong?"

A hulking, soot-covered man in tattered clothes stood nearby. His hair was messy, and he grinned at me with malice on his face. The smell of brimstone and sulfur permeated off him even stronger than it had from Gabriel.

"What—what do you want?" I stepped back, trepidation in my voice.

I looked down at his hand, where he held a crooked knife with a big gem on the end. "Just to have a chat," he said.

I turned away to run, but he grabbed my arm. The heat from his hand burned into my skin, and I whimpered in pain. When he pulled me to him, I balled up my fist, using the momentum to clock him across the face. He barked in pain and let go.

He recovered quickly, though, and yanked my hair as I tried to flee, pulling me down to the ground. He could have ended me there with the knife, but he held back, instead smashing me in the face with his other hand, again and again, until I bled. I hadn't tasted the acrid tinge of blood since I was on Earth.

"Surprised you could still bleed, pet?"

I was wobbly on my feet. "Everything bleeds."

"Tell me what I want to know, and you can go."

"Eat sh—seersucker suits." I really hated that you couldn't curse in Heaven.

The ugly man pulled back his upper lip, revealing a row of baked bean teeth. "Oh, you already have." He charged me with the knife.

"*Flagellum aqua*," I shouted. I hadn't used my water nymph powers since I died, and wasn't sure they would work now that I didn't have a body. Fortunately, water leeched from the air and formed into a whip in my hand. I snapped my wrist, wrapping it around his knife. I yanked hard, but he was stronger than me and instead pulled me toward him.

I slid my body under his hulking frame and grabbed his forearm, slamming it hard against my knee until his arm bent in the wrong direction. He gave up trying to stab me and howled in pain, dropping the knife.

I kicked him off me and went for the blade. He charged again, this time barehanded, and I had just enough time to spin toward him as he lunged. When we made eye contact, he let out a small scream. I felt something wet against my skin. The knife had embedded in his stomach, and green blood oozed from his mouth.

"That's not how this was—" he started, coughing green blood onto my face and looking down at his hands. They disappeared into dust. I was able to make out a blue trident on my attacker's arm before he disappeared in a million particles of dust, like the embers of a fire, leaving me with nothing but his blood on my white toga and the gnarled knife as proof of the attack.

CHAPTER 4

Ollie

Computerization killed the ports. Back when everything was done by hand, a dock manager could conveniently lose a bill of lading or swap the customs forms on two containers in minutes—seconds, even. Now that everything was done by computers, and those computers were tied to servers and nodes all over the world, it took a doctorate in computer science and a full day to hack their programs. I hadn't found a truly out-of-this-world hacker since Phil, and he was literally an alien.

Cliff was good enough, but he was chatty. And expensive. He was worth it but listening to his jibber-jabber while he worked was not my idea of a good time.

"Did you know there are some fungi that can enter your nervous system and take it over, making you a zombie?" He loved to mumble about nothing.

I shook my head, cleaning out a container of lo mein. "No, Cliff, I didn't know that or any of the other hundred facts that you've rattled off today."

"There's this one called Ophiocordyceps that infects ants, and after nine days, the ants are complete zombies. They force the ants to find nice moist soil where they thrive, and then force the ants to kill themselves and use their bodies as compost."

I sat up on the leather couch in Cliff's bedroom. He was fastidious about his room and hated when I lay on his couch, which made it all the more satisfying when I did. "That's actually kind of interesting."

"I know," he replied. "That's why I said it."

Cliff was cocky about his skills, but at least he could back up that cockiness. He was the only one who could still slip into the Port of Oakland undetected, though it seemed to be getting harder and harder each time.

"Are you almost done yet?" I asked. "I've had enough interesting facts for the day, and I use that term very loosely."

"As I told you before, this is delicate work. Every time I find a window into the port, they plaster over it, and I've gotta find a new way into their system. There are mercifully few of those, which means I have to create them as I'm going, and"—suddenly, his computer blinked green—"oh, and there we go. In like Laura Flynn Boyle!" He spun his chair toward me. His face was pasty, and his arms were lanky and thin. He didn't make much of a hero, though, in the age of the internet, a hero could be anyone, I guess. "What was the name of that container?"

I pulled my phone out of my pocket and opened the notepad. "329J4382N."

He typed furiously on his computer. "And you want it to be lost, right?"

"No, I want it never to have existed." I leaped off the couch and leaned over his shoulder. "Get its location first, though. I don't want to search every container like last time."

"That was a one-time thing. Jeez, will you ever forgive me for that?"

"Not as long as it gets under your skin," I said with a smile. "Is that it?" I pointed at the screen as the map narrowed to a single container in the middle of a hundred others.

"That's our baby."

"Not our baby, or even my baby. It's Bi'ri'thal's baby. The port just doesn't know it yet. Send the GPS to my phone, so I can find it."

"Done," Cliff said, and in the same second, my phone vibrated. He typed a flurry of keystrokes and then slammed his hand on the enter key. "Aaand it's a ghost. You're good to go."

I patted his shoulder. "You did good. Before I get to Bi'ri'thal's warehouse, make sure you get that container's new shipment history and renumber it with the information I sent you. You still have his email?"

"I do. I'll get it over to him in the next ten minutes," he said. "Just leave the money on the table, and clean up after yourself before you go—"

I didn't wait for him to finish before I walked out the door. For $35,000, he could hire a maid to clean up my mess…or put it on my tab.

***

I didn't like being involved firsthand in any illegal work. I was a facilitator. I brought people together and connected dots so that deals could happen. I was happy being a middleman, but lately, more and more clients expected me to be involved in the job to make sure it ran smoothly. We were living in a brand-new world. With the internet, it was easier than ever for criminals to find each other and make their own deals. Between the dark web and Bitcoin, cartels could funnel money to each other without the need of a middleman. My business was dying.

Luckily, I still had a set of skills, and connections at ports and harbors around the country, which made me invaluable to the right organizations—ones that didn't like to get their hands dirty—but it meant that my hands were dirtier than ever. I used to justify working with criminals by saying I didn't actually commit the felonies. That was becoming less true. Recently I had come precariously close to getting caught more times than I cared to admit. I wouldn't do well in jail, being an immortal and all. They could convict me of multiple life sentences, and I could actually carry them out. It was just about time for me to hang up my shingle and ride off into the sunset…not quite yet, though. Not while I still found joy in the work.

I drove Lucy, the Barracuda I'd kept in mint condition since the 80s, across from Highland Park to Fruitdale, where Bi'ri'thal had a bustling warehouse just outside Oakland. He had gotten into business to rob a few banks and ended up with a shipping empire that stretched across the country. Over 90 percent of his clients were on the up and up, but he was still a demon and couldn't deny getting his beak wet in the criminal underworld. He ran everything from guns to drugs for syndicates up and down the west coast.

I liked Bi'ri'thal, not because he was nice or anything, but because he was an old-school criminal. He kept his boots on the ground and made handshake deals. His word meant everything, and it was as good as bond as long as yours was as well. You always knew where you stood with him, unlike most of the new guard of criminals who spoke out of both sides of their mouths.

"You're early," Bi'ri'thal grumbled as I walked into his warehouse. Every part of him was thick, from his neck down to his fingers and toes. He always wore a three-piece suit, even when he was moving boxes, and always shook your hand tightly, looking you directly in the eyes when he did.

He kept my hand clenched tightly as he spoke. "I hate when people are early. It makes me antsy, like I have to change my whole day to suit their needs."

My hand finally fell free, and I tried my hardest not to rub the sting away. "You have to be the first and only client who would rather me show up late than early."

"Late, I understand. We all have things to do," Bi'ri'thal said. "Early? That's a whole different matter." He pointed to a semi-cab. An older Black man with a white mustache hung his arm out of it. "Luckily, I knew you would be early. You're riding with Gary today."

"He reliable?"

"Of course. Gary's the best. Real tight-lipped."

"Good. This shouldn't take long."

"See that it doesn't." He handed me a wad of cash. I didn't bother to count it. Bi'ri'thal was never short. "Half now. Half on delivery."

I hopped into the cab with Gary, and we started down the road. "Take the third street entrance. I know somebody there."

"Will do." Gary didn't ask questions. I liked that. He wasn't a criminal, that much was clear, but when Bi'ri'thal said to jump, you asked "how high" or you wound up dead.

"Did Bi'ri'thal give you a folder for me?"

He slid a manila folder over to me, turning his head away as I looked inside and found a new container number, bill of lading, and other information for our new shipment. It was flawless. *Great work, Cliff.*

We didn't talk on the way to the harbor. There was no reason for either of us to know or care about the other. Just the way I liked it. Too many people breezed into my life over the years, and they always left sooner or later. The older I got, the fewer people I gave the time of day.

There was a line several trucks deep at the entrance to the port. I smiled when I watched the pug-faced woman with a backward baseball hat moving from truck to truck. When she got to our truck, I waved her over and stepped out of the cab.

"Haven't seen you in a while," she said.

"Good to see you too, Justine. How you liking your new job?"

"Better than bookkeeping, I guess. Thanks for the recommendation."

I shrugged. "No problem. It's what I do. Besides, it's never a bad idea to have friends inside the port."

"I guess this is you calling in that favor, then?"

"Who's counting favors, Justine?" I replied with a smile. "Friends do for others. We're friends, right?"

"You don't have to put on an act with me. This is a job, and I know my place. Don't get me in trouble, and I'll help you out. Just keep your head down."

"Atta girl." I pulled my phone out of my pocket and showed her Cliff's last text message with the new inventory number. "We're picking up this container. Can we drive in and pick it up?"

She pulled a tablet out from under her arm and typed the number into her system. After several minutes of buffering, where she apologized profusely for the technology snafu, her tablet binged. "Yup, I see it here. You sure this isn't going to get me into trouble?"

"I can honestly say this won't get you in trouble."

"Don't tell me anything else; just get in and out as quickly as possible."

***

It didn't take us long to find the container with Cliff's GPS coordinates, and as soon as I replaced the container information with the ones he'd made for me, we were on our way out. What people appreciated about my work was that it came without a body count. There were plenty of criminals cheaper than me, but few of them used their heads, and even fewer of those were willing to get their hands dirty. We were a dying breed. I was immortal, though, which meant I could combine old-school techniques with the stamina of youth.

Back at Bi'ri'thal's warehouse, Gary pulled the container into the loading dock and stepped out of the cab, nearly running to his truck. One of Bi'ri'thal's people was waiting for him there with an envelope full of cash. He clearly didn't like this type of work, but the pay was hard to pass up.

I waited until I saw Bi'ri'thal cross the dock before I made my way out of the cab and over to him. He was walking with two beautiful, statuesque men, both with silken hair and fair complexions.

"And as you can see, gentlemen, Oleander has already delivered the goods as promised."

It only took one look into their crisp, ice-blue eyes to know they were archangels. Aside from one bar in Scotland, angels and demons were never seen together, at least not in public. While the Devil didn't care, God was quite strict on the movements of his chosen protectors.

"It's nice to meet both of you."

“You didn’t meet us,” one of them said in a thick Scandinavian accent.

“Right.” They certainly didn’t want it getting around that they were cavorting with the enemy, and while it raised just so many questions, I knew better than to open my mouth.

Bi’ri’thal cleared his throat. “Ethel has your money in the office. Meanwhile, boys, let’s take a look at your haul. As promised, completely under the radar from both God and Satan.”

In the office, Bi’ri’thal’s kindly secretary handed me a manila folder filled with money. I was on my way back to Lucy when I noticed the cadre of orcs and goblins unloading the palettes. Each one of them was branded with a blue trident—both the monsters and the palettes. I had never seen that symbol before. I wondered what was inside, but everyone in the warehouse eyed me with a look of suspicion, so I turned the other way and kept my interest to myself. Information was everywhere, and those in power valued their privacy more than ever.

CHAPTER 5

Lizzie

I killed somebody. *In Heaven.* This was supposed to be a place more perfect than Disneyland, and I sullied it with somebody's blood. And not just any blood—demon blood. I mean, it had to be demon blood, right? I looked at the green stains on my hands. It was sticky and smelled of rust and sulfur.

Oh my god. Blood—it was definitely blood. This was way over my paygrade.

I needed to find Gabriel. He would know what to do. He would tell me I wasn't a murderer. *I wasn't, was I?* How could they let a murderer into Heaven? Great Zombie Jesus, would I be kicked out of Heaven for this?

I waited for my stomach to drop at the thought, but it didn't. Honestly, being expelled from Heaven didn't seem so bad. At least it would be an adventure. *No, Lizzie. That's stupid.* It was boring in Heaven, but it was a right bit better than Hell. Then again, the person I killed was a demon, and demons shouldn't be in Heaven. Somehow, he'd gotten in, and I stopped him. Screw being expelled from Heaven. I was a hero.

That was the type of energy I needed walking—well, bouncing—across Heaven covered in green demon blood. I was a hero. Hold your head high, Lizzie. Maybe you'll get your wings yet.

I looked down at the dagger in my hand, jagged and dark save for the green blood caked on the burgundy hilt. A red gem that looked like a polished demon eye stared out at me from the center of the handle, and I couldn't help wiping the blood off it so it could shimmer in the light of the sun.

"What happened to you?" I heard from behind me. Saturnius, a third-century playwright with a long, bushy beard, bounced up to me. "I missed you this morning at prayer circle. I waited to see if you wanted to play shuffleboard."

The last thing I wanted to do was play shuffleboard, but Saturnius was kind, sweet, and simple, so I placated him, hoping that if I hung around with him enough, I would grow to like him and this place. He was my vaccination, a small bit of Heaven that would inoculate me to the rest of it. Except that it wasn't working. Every time I saw him, instead of growing fonder of him, I despised him more.

Even in the best of circumstances, I didn't want to talk with him, and this was certainly not the time to draw his attention. I moved faster, pretending I hadn't seen him. If there was one thing I was an expert on, it was avoiding confrontations. I'd spent ten years traipsing around the USA, always leaving right before shit hit the fan. I had a sixth sense for it, and my spider-sense was tingling.

Unfortunately, no matter how fast I bounced, Saturnius kept pace, waiting for an answer.

"Did you not hear me?" he said, leaping in front of me to stop me in my tracks. "If not, I shall shout louder so my voice might carry to your ears. WHERE WERE YOU THIS MORNING, GOOD ELIZABETH?"

"No, I heard you, I'm heading somewhere, and I'm late."

He gave me a dubious look.

"I had to leave early this morning," I added, still bouncing.

"Where to?"

There were no secrets in Heaven. "It's just—Gabriel thought that he had found my parents in Hell, and he came to get me early in the morning."

"Ah, good. I know you've been waiting on them for a long time." He smiled at me. "And how was your reunion?"

"Well, like I said, they *thought* they found my parents, but they were wrong. It was pretty disappointing."

"But this is Heaven," he replied, confused. "They don't make mistakes here."

"So they keep telling me." I watched Gabriel fly past in the other direction and spun around to catch him. "I'm sorry, Saturnius, but I have to go."

"No worries," he replied. "Probably need to get that goop off yourself. Where did you get so dirty anyway?"

I didn't answer him. Instead, I bounced forward to catch up with Gabriel. "Goodbye, Saturnius."

***

"Dead people don't just disappear, Lizzie," Gabriel said when I caught up with him flying across the Elysian Fields.

"Then how do you explain all of this?" I pointed down at the green goop caked on my hair and toga. "This is his blood. I'm telling you, somebody attacked me." I handed him the dagger.

"And you killed him?" he asked, examining the dagger. "You know that's not allowed in Heaven, Lizzie."

"He was trying to kill me!" I screamed. "What did you expect me to do? Feed him cupcakes?"

Gabriel's voice dropped to a whisper, and his face fell. "You need to lower your voice." He placed his hand on the small of my back, guiding me along. "I think we need to find somewhere more private to talk." He didn't wait for me to answer. "Come with me."

"Seriously?" I replied, though I didn't give much of a struggle. "What is more private than this? I don't see anyone for a mile in any direction."

"I think it's time to show you a side of Heaven we usually keep from residents." His voice was low, grumbling, and full of frustration. "However, since you insist on being a nuisance—"

"A nuisance? I'm trying to help—did you miss the part where somebody attacked me?"

"Yes, so you keep saying. Now, shut up."

"This is totally fu—flubbed up." *Damn it.* I kept forgetting you couldn't curse in Heaven by decree of his royal stick in the mud. Some situations called for it.

***

I followed Gabriel across the plains until a plume of clouds blocked our way, rising like a mountain. It wasn't the first time I had come across the mound, but I had never paid it any attention before.

"Do you think it's odd that there is a cloud cover blocking this section of Heaven?" Gabriel asked, watching me closely.

I shrugged. "I figured that was just the end of it all, like in a video game."

He laughed. "This isn't a video game, far from it. We have eternity to work with. Why would we block people's access to Greenland and the Scandinavian countries?"

I started to speak but faltered. He was right. In my peeking around on Earth, I had never been able to see anything in Greenland, Iceland, Northern Europe, or the North Pole. At one point, I had wanted to find out whether Santa was real, but my interest petered out when I wasn't able to locate the Arctic circle. Finally, I simply said, "Honestly, no. I try not to think about things too much up here."

He placed his hand on a piece of cloud, and it slid open for him. "That's good advice in most situations, but it's specifically your dogged determination to find your parents, never taking no for an answer, and continuing to ask questions that brings us here today."

He slid his arm between the clouds and yanked it to the left with all his might. A flood of white light washed over me. It dissipated, and a city filled my vision, with hundreds of ancient, columned buildings rising high into the air. Thousands of demons and cherubs moved between the buildings.

"What is this place?"

"This is how anything gets done on Earth," Gabriel replied. "Behind you is the staging area where we keep the residents, but this is where all the magic happens. Welcome to the nerve center of Heaven."

CHAPTER 6

Ollie

Why were angels and demons working together? Aside from that bar in Scotland, I had never seen them mingling together in all my years. I guess they could have met there and then eventually, over the course of centuries, thawed to each other until they were friendly enough to do business.

Except that having a drunken chat with somebody was a far cry from going into business together. Angels and demons were on opposite sides of the eternal struggle. Their aims were antithetical, so why would one help the other?

"*Porth i Los Angeles*," I said, focusing my energy into my yew wood wand. A portal back to Los Angeles opened. Yew was an important wood to my mother, who had a natural connection to Wales. When she was kicked out of Heaven, she began her life on Earth there, though she immigrated to America after things soured with my demon father.

It was the same reason I learned spellcasting in Welsh instead of the more common Latin. As long as you had a strong reverence for the words, the language didn't matter. I could have spoken them in English if I wanted, but it was such a bastardized language, amalgamating and twisting so many other tongues that I risked conjuring the wrong incantation if I wasn't careful.

Some years before it was trendy, I bought a small bungalow on the Venice canals south of Santa Monica and watched prices rise when it gentrified. My portal spat me into Cerritos, in one of the vestiges of undeveloped land in the city. It used to be easy to find nooks and crannies to teleport into, but Los Angeles had developed to the point that it was almost impossible for a magical girl to move around without detection.

It wasn't a short drive back to my house, but I wasn't in any rush to return to the mountain of work waiting for me there. It used to be that people came to me looking for hard-to-find pieces, and that was how I made the majority of my money. The internet made it easy to get those, sometimes even multiples, with just a few clicks, which meant that my job became finding the impossibly rare object or the things that people purposely hid.

Yes, there was still a share of my life that was about working with ports, massaging egos, and greasing the right palms, but those clients were drying up more quickly than ever. My powers of teleportation used to be extremely valuable. Now there were things like Facetime so that anybody could talk to anybody with the click of a button. My connections were nearly worthless when people could find things themselves.

I relied on people like Bi'ri'thal who did things old school, though the new technology was forcing even the dinosaurs to adapt. Technology was a necessary evil, so I tried to be on the cutting edge of whatever was new and popular. I bought into Bitcoin early and often, though I didn't need the money, and funneled some of that money into Oculus. I made a killing when it sold to Facebook last year.

It wasn't about the money for me, not anymore. Burning through money was a boring way to spend a life. I had money dating all the way back to the 80s, and I could have given up—hell, I did give up—dozens of times. I retired to Thailand, then moved to Morocco, and hopped all over the world, acquiring rare objects and having fantastic adventures. The life always called me back. If one day I couldn't do this job anymore, I would survive, but what kind of life would it be without the thrill of the hunt?

That's what I loved—hunting down rare treasures and finding them. I loved bending the law to my will just enough that it worked for me, and not enough that anyone would catch me with my hand in the cookie jar. If somebody wanted to pay me for it, all the better.

There was nothing quite like being in a Mexican standoff with two rival cartels, wondering how you were going to get out alive. I had another reason, too, buried in the depths of my soul. I hoped that maybe, one day, all of these connections I made would pay off, allowing me to do some good in the world.

It took an hour in traffic to make it back to my Venice bungalow. Lucy's headlights shone in the driveway to reveal a woman sitting on my stoop. She wasn't aggressive. I knew those types, the kind waiting with a baseball bat to teach me a lesson. This one had her head in her knees and only sat up when she saw the lights.

Security flood lights replaced my headlights when I stepped out of the car, and the woman rose to her feet. She stood powerfully, wearing a red dress, and walked over with a regal gait as if we were old friends. By the look on her face, I knew that we were. One of my curses was to see the truth about a person. It took only a second for my eyes to shift focus and see the demon beneath the woman's false face. Under her disguise, she had only aged a couple of years.

"Anjelica?"

"It's good to see you again, Ollie," she whispered. "I'm sorry for stopping by so late, but I don't have any American money, and this was the only place I remembered in the city where I might find some help."

"Anjelica?" I said again, stunned.

She smiled. "That's right. I was worried you had forgotten about me."

I rushed forward and wrapped her in a tight hug, trying to stifle my tears. "You grew up." I hadn't seen her since Kimberly, and I saved her from a demonic cult trying to use her blood to open a portal to Hell. She was only sixteen then. "What's it been, twenty years?"

"Almost thirty actually," she replied, pulling back from me. "Though it's kind of hard to tell after where I've been."

"What do you mean?"

"Maybe it's better that we talk inside," she said.

"Of course." I walked past her to unlock my house. "I think I might have some chili if you want."

"I thought you didn't eat," she said, chuckling. "Wasn't that your thing?"

"Oh, I—yeah, that was stupid. I learned to love it. I've gotten pretty good at cooking. Eating, too."

"Sounds lovely," she said. "I haven't eaten in ages."

I led her inside and pulled a Tupperware full of my world-famous chili from the fridge. I poured her a big bowl and heated it up before sitting down next to her to watch her eat.

"Aren't you going to have any?" She took a big spoonful. "This is really good, by the way."

"I like to eat, but I don't have to eat if you catch my drift. Right now, I'd rather watch you enjoy it. I do have quite a few questions, though, if you'll indulge me."

“I guess I can’t vanish for thirty years and not expect you to have a few questions for me. Shoot.”

“What happened to you? I tried to ask Kimberly about it a few times, but she always told me it was none of my business.”

“You still talk to Kimberly?”

“I’ve seen her a few times over the years. We’re not exactly close.”

“Oh.” She looked down at her food, and her nose crinkled. “You know, it turns out I’m not that hungry, either. It’s really good, though. I haven’t had chili—not like this—as far back as I can remember. They don’t really have tomatoes where I’m from.”

“Where did she put you? Antarctica?”

Anjelica told me what had happened to her. She told me how she had met a girl, Margaret, and somebody used her blood to open a portal to another planet, where she fought a king and killed him, then became a royal advisor to Margaret, who had become the new ruler. They’d been there for the last thirty years, trying to keep peace in a country that had only known war. I stayed silent, absorbing the information, and only asked the most pointed questions for clarification. When she was finished, there was one thing weighing on me.

“Why come back now?”

“My mother died.”

“Oh, I’m sorry. I looked in on her from time to time for a while, but then…well, I stopped. My condolences.”

She nodded and bowed her head. “Thank you. That’s actually why I came to see you. I need your help.”

"How can I possibly help you at this point? You have a whole nation under your thumb."

"In Onmiri, but not here. Here, I am nothing, but you…you still work with demons, right?"

"On occasion," I responded, my tone coy.

She acted sheepish for a moment, then took a breath and sat up straight. "I need to see my mother again, and since we both know she's in Hell, I need you to help me find her."

It was the last thing I expected her to say. "I risked my life to keep you out of Hell, and now you want to waltz back in there?"

"That's right," she replied, straightening her shoulders. "I'm not the naïve little girl you saved all those years ago. I learned how to use my powers and defend myself." She looked directly at me. "Now, as for payment. My mother didn't have much when she died, but anything she has is yours if you help me."

I waved away the suggestion. "Please, I don't need your mother's loose change. But I have to ask, are you sure you're not overwhelmed with grief and…well, not thinking clearly?"

"Of course, I'm overcome with grief!" Her tears flowed freely, and I realized that she had been holding them back for my benefit. "And no, I'm not thinking clearly. I'm back on this planet for the first time in thirty years, and the only person who I can think to help me is someone I knew thirty years ago for only 24 hours."

Less than that. I had stolen the car she was trapped in around midnight, and she was gone by the time the sun rose the next morning. No use splitting hairs.

"I can call Kimberl—"

"No," she said quickly. "You know she won't approve."

"And I will?"

She raised an eyebrow. "You once told me you weren't a good person. I need somebody like you to do a not-good thing and help me see my mother one more time. I know you don't owe it to me, but please, I need this favor. I haven't seen her in thirty years, and I need to see her one more time. I can't leave until I do."

"What if I don't help you?"

She looked me in the eyes. Even though her eyes were puffy and red, there was a determination in them that I knew too well. "I know how to kill myself."

There was no wavering in her. She would not give up. If I didn't help her, she was going to hurt herself. At least with me, she could find her mother safely.

"Okay," I said, leaning back in my chair with a sigh. "But we do this safely, and we do it my way."

CHAPTER 7

Kimberly

The Blue Trident. Finding information on them was nearly impossible. Molly and I followed every thread we could find, and each one led to a dead-end, often quite literally, as the people behind the screen names we tracked down ended up dead by mysterious or brutal circumstances.

"You're making me antsy," Molly said as I paced behind her. "Maybe you need to get out in the field and do some leg work."

I had been stuck in the house for longer than I enjoyed, and while Molly was a home body who was quite happy never leaving the confines of our 2,000 square foot penthouse condo, I got more out of people in person than by stalking them on the internet.

"Are you trying to get rid of me?" I asked.

"Yes," Molly replied with a smile. "I thought it would be obvious. Look, if you don't have any leads, then take a walk, or at least go outside and sit in the sun. You're a ball of nervous energy right now. I need to concentrate."

"Fine." I leaned forward to kiss her. "I love you."

"I love you, too."

"Even when I get on your nerves?"

"Especially then. As long as you're at least a thousand feet away from me."

***

The minute I exited my building and the fresh salt air from San Francisco harbor hit my face, I felt better. It was as if a full day of nerves escaped at once. It wasn't that I hated being inside, per se, but I was helpless with a computer, even after all this time.

There was nothing tangible about all those ones and zeros. At least a book was something you could touch and feel. Pulling a stack of books and going through them one by one felt like something. It meant taking notes and photocopying pages, which took deliberate time and effort. You could watch your stack growing and shrinking, breathing in and out like an organic life form.

It was then it occurred to me how I could help the investigation without crimping Molly's style. I flashed to the great red dragon's cave in the Swiss Alps. It had been a long time since I visited Aziolith's lair—I used to head over there when I was low on cash. Our money was making its own money at this point, and I didn't need to look through his things to find a priceless token to pawn or some bouillon to melt down and sell on the open market.

Aziolith had built a horde of treasure before he fell to the fairy Akta's blade over three thousand years ago. I only knew him because a bloody cult used my mentor Julia's blood to summon him to Earth. After she defeated the cult, they became friends.

Before Julia died back in the 80s, she introduced me to Aziolith and asked him to look after me, which he did. Our bond was as close as family, and, just like family, we could go years without seeing each other, but our bond never broke. Even though he kept houses all over the world, he preferred the solitude of his cave. There, he didn't have to pretend he wasn't a dragon; he could just be himself.

The mounds of gold and treasure filled every inch of the frigid cave, enough to make Scrooge McDuck green with envy. Aziolith easily had enough wealth in his cave to rival the fortunes of a medium-sized country. Really though, he sought simple pleasures: he just wanted to be left alone.

The most valuable part of his treasure trove was a collection of books from before antiquity, a library delving into the dark arts, mythology, and mysticism that rivaled the Library of Alexandria. The truths of the universe were contained in Aziolith's collection, and I used it often to search for demonology and mythology lost to the ages.

After hours of searching through the stacks, my eyes were bleary and dry, and I felt no closer to an answer, even if I had a sense of accomplishment from doing the type of research that only came with my nose stuck in a book. There was a shuffle of coins followed by footsteps.

"Aziolith!" I yelled as I rushed over to hug him. "You're looking as youthful as always."

"Hello, my dear," he replied, returning my hug. "People tend to favor beauty and youth, so I use that to my advantage when I negotiate with humans." He didn't much like the human form, but to interact with the civilized world, he had no choice but to tolerate it.

"Where were you this time?" I asked.

"Arranging funding for some internet startup or another. It's hard to even tell these days."

He turned his attention to a collection of sticks he had just finished building in the middle of the room. The flames he blew out of his mouth caught on the thatch, turning into a bonfire in a matter of seconds. Satisfied, he stretched himself from his human form into a twenty-foot-high dragon with a long neck and enormous jaw, which he lengthened with a yawn that bellowed across the whole of the cavern.

"That's so much better. I do hate that potion. Not only does it turn me into a human, it tastes terrible." He smacked his lips together. "I don't know why I even bother."

"Because you're lonely, Aziolith. I get it. Everyone needs companionship sometimes, even reclusive dragons."

"Piffle." He yawned. "So, what brings you here?"

"Looking for a book."

"You're supposed to say you're here to see me, silly girl." He shook his head in mock disappointment. "What book?"

I scratched my head. "It's the one about all the cult symbolism we used on that job back in '94. Remember that weird one, with the guy's oxen being cut in half?"

"Don't remind me. Our adventures tend to leave me with unsettling dreams."

"That's funny, coming from someone that's literally the stuff of nightmares."

"Rude."

"You know it's not like that, but look at you, and look at humans. I mean, there's a reason that you take a different form when you visit them, right?"

"They do tend to scream and run from me," he mused.

"And yet…you still change your form when you need something from them."

"Humans are basically unevolved, primitive monkeys with access to nuclear weapons. You are damn right I'm cautious." He took a moment to calm himself. "What symbol are you looking for?"

"It has to do with a blue trident. It's probably nothing."

His eyes fluttered for a moment and shuddered from what could only be described as terror. "I'm sorry. Did you say blue trident?"

"Yeah, why?"

"That…is a very bad symbol. Very, very bad."

I blinked. "Why specifically is this so bad?"

"The Blue Trident was Lucifer's weapon of choice when he was an angel. When he fell to Earth, it was lost. It's said that the Blue Trident will unite Heaven and Hell, and brothers who were once enemies will walk together as family once again. It's an omen to the end of the world. The last, great omen before God opens the seventh seal and Hellspawn reign on Earth once again. If you are hunting the Blue Trident, then this truly is the end of times."

CHAPTER 8

Anjelica

Apparently, doing things "safely" and "my way," according to Ollie, meant a séance at the home of a voodoo witch where we would contact my mother in a controlled environment. We spent most of the next day acquiring the ingredients necessary to contact a soul in Hell.

"Best case scenario, you get five minutes," Ollie said as we walked down the aisles at the grocery store. "Ooh, grab those Cocoa Pebbles."

I pulled a box of the cereal from the shelf. "How could this possibly be used in a séance?"

She grabbed the box and put it in the cart. "It won't be. I just really like them."

I rolled my eyes and followed her to the butcher. I never had Ollie's gift for seeing people's true form, so to me, he just looked like a rather hairy, lazy-eyed Asian man.

"Usual?" the man asked Ollie.

"Yup. A quart, please."

"Coming right up."

"He's a bunyip," she said when the man disappeared behind the counter. "You don't see many here in America, but I helped him get his immigration papers in order a few years ago, so he owes me." She turned the cart toward the check-out. "Come on."

"Don't you need to wait for your blood?"

She shook her head. "That's not something you get over the counter."

We loaded up the car and pulled around to the loading dock, where the bunyip was waiting with a jar of blood. It sloshed in my hand when he gave it to me, causing a shiver to crawl up my spine. I never had much of a stomach for viscera. As the acrid, metallic smell of the blood seeped from the sealed jar, my stomach turned in knots.

We dropped off the jar along with the groceries, then headed to a gem shop in Hollywood to pick up six garnets. Next was East LA to collect some finely chopped cedar. Finally, on our way back home, Ollie asked me my mother's favorite food.

"I haven't seen her in thirty years, remember?" I thought for a few moments. "She used to really love bibimbap when I was in high school."

"Interesting," she replied. "I know just the place."

We drove to a little hole in the wall in Koreatown, where I had some of the best Korean BBQ of my whole life. It was another thing we didn't have on Onmiri. There was plenty of delicious food there, and chefs in the palace had gotten very good replicating some of my favorite dishes, but it wasn't the same as the real thing.

We left with a take-out container of bibimbap and made our way back to Venice to pick up the pig's blood from Ollie's fridge, then drove back across the city to Miracle Mile just as the sun was setting. LA, as I remembered it, was seedy and covered in a thick haze of smog. The city I came back to was clean and modern, despite the potholes and cracked streets. It had lost its edge since I traveled across the universe. The tinge of danger that once lurked around every corner was replaced by high-rise luxury condos and vegan restaurants.

Not that I was complaining. I quite liked being able to drive through the city without worrying I would be mugged, shot, or worse. No, it wasn't bad, just different, and that made me sad. A part of me hoped that if I ever returned to Los Angeles, the city would have waited for me, frozen in amber.

I expected the witch to live in a dilapidated hovel, so I was surprised to see us pull up to a posh apartment complex behind the Westfield Shopping Center in Century City. Ollie punched in a code to let us in, and we took the elevator up to meet the "voodoo witch." She wasn't what I expected, either, with her shiny, straight, black hair and thick, black, horn-rimmed glasses. Her pink shirt read "Ask Me about my Feminist Agenda" in block letters across her chest, and she wore black yoga pants without socks or shoes.

"Take your shoes off," she said, turning away from the door and back into her apartment. "I don't want you tracking mud on the carpet."

We were carrying a jar of blood which I could only assume we would be painting over her floor. However, I did what I was told and threw off my shoes before walking into her place.

It was sparsely decorated, with a clean, white aesthetic. A large, flat-screen TV was mounted on the wall, and her glass coffee table was strewn with copies of *The New Yorker*, *Wall Street Journal*, and *The Economist*. Every magazine was marked with several small Post-it notes.

She pointed to the marble counter. "Put it all there."

I placed the jar of blood on the counter, and Ollie followed with the other items. The woman circled them for a moment, cocking her head one way or the other as she stroked her chin.

"You have a lovely home," I said.

"I know," she replied. "Jesus Christ, Ollie. How much blood did you think we would need? I said a vial, not a vat."

Ollie shrugged. "This was how much my guy gave me, Christina."

Christina did not sound like the name of a voodoo witch. It sounded more like the interior decorator you hired to redesign your brand new, high-rise condo.

"Whatever, Oleander."

"Don't call me that."

Christina reached for a piece of cedar with a sigh, then dipped an art brush into the blood. She painted a circle with a dot inside of it on the cedar and several other chips of the wood.

"What is that for?" I asked finally after a few long minutes of silence.

"Do you want me to explain, or do you want to talk to your mother again?"

"Both…I guess?" I said. "I was just trying to make conversation."

"Christina's not much of a talker," Ollie said. "But she's brilliant. If anyone can find your mother, it's her."

"If I can find her," Christina added. "Hell is a mess right now. Let's just hope your mother has a unique name." She looked over at me. "What is it?"

"Theresa McDonnell."

Christina returned to painting with another sigh. "Not all that unique, but not too common, either. When did she die?"

"A couple of days ago."

She shook her head. "Not nearly specific enough."

"Sorry." I reached for my phone to pull up a pdf of the death certificate and showed it to her. "Better?"

"Much," she replied, grabbing another piece of cedar. "That should be all. Come with me."

I followed Christina to a reclaimed wood table, where several bowls formed a circle in the center. She placed a piece of cedar in each bowl, along with a piece of garnet, and then sat down at the head of the table.

"Sit," she said, "and we will begin. Did you bring the offering?"

Ollie grabbed the bibimbap from the counter and opened the container, placing it in the center of the circle before she sat down. "Here you go."

"Interesting," Christina said with a smile. "I think I like your mother already."

She pulled out a torch lighter and lit all the cedar chips, blowing on each one until it started to smoke before moving on to the next. "This will keep your mother inside of the circle, and make sure she doesn't get lost in the ether. Spirits let out from Hell tend to wander off if you don't keep them contained."

"Do you have to keep saying it? Can't we just pretend like she went to Heaven?"

Christina cracked a smile. "Oh, you sweet summer child. There hasn't been a soul worthy of Heaven in a long time." She must have seen the look on my face because she held up her hands in passive submission. "Saying she's in Hell isn't a condemnation of your mother, it's just the state of things."

"She's right," Ollie said. "They let one girl through after she saved the universe, but it was a unique case. Otherwise, that gate has been shut for centuries."

"I'm not God and cannot hope to know his mind. Maybe he knows things that we don't and has a grand plan for us all." She caught eyes with Ollie, or at least the best you could with her in sunglasses. "Then again, maybe he's just a drunk."

"I'd put money on the latter," Ollie chuckled. "But that's a story for another time."

Christina ignored her and turned to me. "Hold out your hands and close your eyes. Think of your mother. Focus on her coming to us. Imagine her in the center of this prayer circle, every bit alive and well. The more real you can make her out, the easier it will be to find her in He—the underworld."

Closing my eyes, I was flooded by images of my mother so crisp that it made me want to break down and cry. I fought my emotions and focused on a single image, making her more real in my mind with every breath.

Christina squeezed my hand, talking in a whisper. "Good. I feel her energy inside of you. Now, I will reach out to the depths to search for her." She began to hum to herself. "Theresa, your daughter, who you love so and loves you in kind, wishes to speak with you. She wishes to connect with you for one last time, to tell you all the things that she never could while you were alive. Come to us, Theresa. Come back to us, this one last time."

She sat humming for several minutes, repeating the chant over and over. "Come to us, Theresa. Come back to us."

I kept myself focused on the circle and my mother. I repeated the mantra inside my head, growing more forceful as the minutes ticked by. After a long while focused intently on remembering every groove of my mother's face, Christina's murmuring stopped, and she let out a deep sigh.

"You can open your eyes. I don't think she will be joining us tonight."

I blinked, watching Christina pour water over the cedar chips. "What are you doing?"

"It's been an hour of chanting and searching, but I did not see your mother, which means I could not bring her into the light."

I pushed back my chair and stood. "I thought you were the best." I turned to Ollie. "I thought you said she was the best."

"She is," Ollie said, rising with me. "And if Christina can't find her, your mother can't be found."

"I don't believe that." I gritted my teeth. "If she can't bring my mother to me, then I'm going to find her myself."

"That's not—"

"We tried it your way, the safe way. I played by your rules"—I gave Christina a side-long glare— "and they failed. Now, I'm going to Hell to find my mother. You can help me, or you can turn your back on me, but I will find a way, whether you like it or not."

She sighed. "This is a really bad idea. You're not thinking clearly."

"I can't stop you, but I agree with Ollie." Christina slid the bibimbap across the table and took a bite of spicy pork. "Just know, if I can't find her, it means she's under the protection of the dukes."

"The dukes?"

"Powerful demons, more powerful than any in Hell save Lucifer and his kin. Ollie is right. This is more dangerous than you can possibly know. I doubt your mother would want you to risk yourself like this."

"That's right," Ollie added. "Since everything's gone to shit in Hell, the dukes are trying to seize power. They're fighting for the souls of Hell. It's chaos, and they thrive on it."

"Thank you for your concern, but don't forget, I'm half demon. I think I'll be okay."

"You think wrong," Christina said, her mouth full of food. "But it's your funeral."

"I'm just trying to protect you," Ollie said.

"I'm not sixteen anymore," I snapped. "I can take care of myself."

Ollie stared at me for a long time before saying quietly, "No, you can't. But you're too blind to see that."

"Are you going to help me or not?"

"No." She stormed to the kitchen and pulled a notepad off the refrigerator. "Maybe Kimberly can talk some sense into you."

"She's not going to help me either, and you know it." I rushed to her, holding my hands out and pleading.

Ollie scrawled a number on the paper and held it out to me. "No, but right now, it looks like she's your only shot. I'd make that call if I were you."

CHAPTER 9

Lizzie

The "staging area" of Heaven, as Gabriel called it, was at least a hundred times cooler than the parts of the afterlife that I had access to as a regular inhabitant of the Elysian Fields. Whereas we had apartment buildings that looked more like Section 8 housing complexes and bland, uninspired architecture, the staging area was filled with thousands of buildings stacked as high as I could see, intricately carved to rival any of the greats from civilizations past. Large agoras stood packed on tiers of clouds above circular enclosed buildings, which were on top of rectangular, columned ones. Dozens of cherubs and angels bustled between the buildings carrying files and bags from one place to the next.

"Why…why would you keep this hidden from everyone?" I craned my neck to take in the amazing sights surrounding me. "It's frigging incredible."

Gabriel sighed. "I'm going to give you the truth, not because you have earned it, but because you have a terrible habit of piercing the veil of God's illusion no matter what I tell you. However, I must be assured of your discretion."

"You have it." I nodded. "After all, who am I going to tell?"

"Saturnius, for one, and your parents for another."

"For one, I hate that guy, and for two, I'm not convinced you'll ever find them."

Gabriel raised his eyebrows, accepting my challenge. "Oh, we'll find them."

"Then, assuming you do, I won't tell them anything."

He held out his hand. "Shake on it."

As I held my hand toward him, I noticed something hanging from the edge of his toga. On his arm, tattooed like a brand, was a blue trident, its tips pointing toward me, just like I had seen on the demon's arm. My first instinct was to pull away but, not wanting to seem suspicious, I grabbed his hand and shook it firmly. A blue swirl of magic embraced our forearms and squeezed them together tightly. After a moment, it dissolved into our skins, leaving a shimmer that slowly disappeared.

"What was that?" I asked.

"The eternal bond. Now, if you tell anyone what I am about to tell you, I will know, and there will be consequences."

"What kind of consequences?"

Gabriel's face grew a shade darker. "The kind that leads to the end of your existence, along with those that hear it." He saw my nervousness and lightened up. "But it won't be a problem if you don't tell anyone, okay?"

I let out a nervous chuckle. "Yeah, okay."

He guided me over to a marble bench on a pathway grooved into the clouds, taking a moment to collect himself. "Humans aren't supposed to be in Heaven," he said. "Well, this isn't really Heaven at all. That's just what God called it, and since he's in charge, we went along with it."

"If we're not supposed to be here, then why are we?"

"Because God—the one you know at least—is a feckless, vain idiot who decided he wanted humans around to adore him for an eternity. It's the same reason he forced Christianity down the throat of half the world and spun the world from worshiping the old gods so that they'd worship only him."

"That doesn't sound right to me."

"All you have to do is visit somewhere like Rome to see his work. Temples to Juno and Jupiter transformed into temples and churches devoted to a single deity. It's appalling, really." Disgust was written all over Gabriel's face. "But what choice did we have except to obey? That is our curse, and our charge, to serve the gods no matter how much we disagree with them."

"If you hate it so much, why don't you just leave? I mean, my sister was taken to another world, so I know there must be other planets out there."

"Because we cannot leave unless God gives us permission, and he knows that if the others found out about what he's done here, he would be locked away for all eternity."

"Okay, back up. Why is letting humans into Heaven so bad?"

Gabriel put his hands out in front of him as if he were explaining the simplest thing in the world. "For the same reason you don't let peasants mingle in the royal palace. We have a planet to run and hard decisions to make. If you have too close of contact with those you serve, it becomes impossible to make those choices, as evidenced by the situation in Hell."

"What's wrong with Hell?"

"You saw it." He looked away in disgust. "The underworld used to be a perfect, flawless system, but when you let an angel run it instead of a God, and when you make it all about worshiping yourself instead of serving the good of the universe, everything breaks down." He swallowed hard. "It can't continue like this much longer."

I didn't need to understand what he was talking about. I knew what it was like to feel powerless against something you couldn't control. "It must be hard."

"Especially in the beginning..." Gabriel bit his lip, trying to contain his emotion, and as his eyes met mine, his tears teetered at the rims of his blood-red eyes. He wiped them away with a sniffle. "We finally had him agree to separate the—ah, residents, from the inner workings of Heaven, which is why we have the barrier. God gets his pet project, and we stay away from humanity. We call it the Great Compromise. I wasn't supposed to tell you that part."

"Why not?" I said, more confused than ever. "What's the Great Compromise?"

"I—oh what the heck, you are bound to silence." He took another breath. "You have heard of the uprising against God, yes?"

I hesitated. "Sort of?"

"The one that minted Lucifer as the Devil and got my brothers marked forever."

"What do you mean, marked?"

Gabriel looked a bit exasperated. He spoke slowly. "They were turned into demons, reviled by humanity, red of skin and hideous to behold, but deep down, angels nonetheless."

"Oh yeah, that one. I've heard of it, but what does it have to do with the Great Compromise?"

"When Lucifer marched on Heaven"—he held his hand over the blue trident on his arm— "it was over so fast…but only because we turned our backs on him." He balled up his fists. "He fought to free us all, and we turned our backs on him at the last possible moment."

"You sided with Lucifer?" I asked.

"At the beginning, many of us did, but God found out Lucifer's plans and offered us a deal to remain in his vanguard. In our foolishness, we thought he would change, that he would improve Earth, that he had humanity's best interests at heart. He played on our natural instinct to trust our God through everything and twisted that to get us to fight for him. That's how he carried the day against Lucifer. Since then, we have watched everything go to pot and rued our decision."

"It's that bad in the underworld?" I asked.

"It's worse than we ever feared. Millions of souls stacked high, smoldering with no place to go. There's no plan for how to ease Lucifer's burden. God turned a blind eye to humanity's suffering, and I can't bear it anymore."

"Is—is that why you wear a blue trident on your arm?" I asked.

Gabriel traced the symbol with his finger. "Yes. For a long time, I kept it hidden under my skin, but now…with how things are…I can't anymore." He shook his head. "God is naïve—no, not naïve, willfully ignorant. We can't let it continue to go on like this." He turned to me. "Please, Lizzie. If you just tell me how to get to the Time Being, I will be able to fix our horrible mistake. Please."

I slid away from him. Suddenly, I was aware of a hundred pairs of eyes on me. The work had stopped, and dozens of angels floated around me, watching.

"You're…trying to start a rebellion against God?"

“Not start one, no. The rebellion has already begun.” Gabriel stood. “We wish to do what is right for the universe. If you help us, I will make you an archangel and allow you to join our ranks. You will be instrumental in righting a great wrong, and we would all be in your debt.”

I stood up and stepped back onto the trail. “You’re crazy.”

He shook his head. “No, no—*God* is crazy. Have you seen Hell? Every single day, millions, billions of your people suffer while he allows Lucifer to enslave monsters to do his bidding. None of this is right, Lizzie. And you can fix it.”

“There’s nothing to fix. Our world wasn’t a red thread.” Any anomaly in the timeline was signified by a red thread in the fabric of the universe Talinda weaved in her castle. Most of it was made up of white threads, where the timeline ran correctly. “That means whatever happened was supposed to happen. You can’t mess with the timeline without creating an anomaly.”

“You don’t know that!” He threw his hands up. “The universe couldn’t have meant for this to happen.”

“But it did happen, and everything can happen only once.” The crowd of angels was growing closer. “You have no idea what Talinda has gone through to keep the timeline pure.”

I took a few more steps back, not turning my back on the encroaching angels and cherubs.

“Please…if only she knew what we have gone through!”

I couldn’t listen any longer. I spun on my heels and leaped into the air. The angels flew toward me, and I smashed one in the face with my hand before kicking another.

"*Flagellum aqua*!" A whip of water snapped from my hands, and I flung it behind me as the flock rushed toward me.

I landed on the clouds and leaped again and again, but it was no use. They kept coming, descending too quickly for me to defend myself against all of them. They were about to grab me, until—

An explosion rocked through the clouds. The angels tumbled away from it as the streak of electricity burned a hole through the clouds. Even if I wanted to run, it was too fast for me to escape. But the bolt was clearly aimed at the angels, and so it was a friend to me, at least for the moment.

"Get back, fiends!" the bolt commanded in a familiar voice.

The archangel didn't slow as he approached, and my breath left me when his shoulder slammed into me and carried me into the air. A moment later, we were through the clouds and back onto the Elysian Fields. He tossed me onto the ground, where I rolled to a stop. Skidding alongside me, he slowed down until he could stand, turning to reveal long, flowing, brown hair and a chiseled jaw. He pulled out a flaming sword from a scabbard on his belt and reached for my hand.

"Are you hurt?"

I rubbed my shoulder where he'd slammed into it. "I'll be okay."

"Good." He pulled me to my feet. "We need to hurry. They will be through in a moment." He hadn't finished the thought before a half dozen angels flew through the cloud cover. "And here they are."

He lifted me up in his strong arms.

“Who are you?” I asked, studying him.

“Michael,” he replied. “Most people know me as the angel that finally defeated Lucifer and his incipient insurrection.”

“Are you part of the Blue Trident, too?” I asked, exasperated. This whole conspiracy was getting hard to keep straight in my head.

He shook his head. “No, I stood with God at the beginning, and I do so now. My brothers and sisters used to stand with me, but the problems in Hell have caused many to shift allegiances. Don’t worry. I have you now.”

I looked back at the angels chasing after us. *Don’t worry, he says. Like it’s that easy.*

CHAPTER 10

Kimberly

If Aziolith was even half right about the Blue Trident being a portent to the end of the world, then it was even more important that I found them to prevent them from following through on whatever they planned on doing—and quickly. Geordi's life was on the line.

Atticus was blocking my calls, but he was a technological neophyte. Molly had dropped a tracker on his phone a couple of years ago, which meant I could always find him when I needed him. Most of the people I had tracked over the years had caught on in a matter of weeks, but not Atticus. Every time I appeared in front of him, he was just as surprised as the time before and never put two and two together.

This time, he was getting his car worked on when I sidled up to the repair shop entrance and leaned against the door. "Hi, Atticus."

He jumped nearly three feet into the air when he saw me and skittered behind the desk before a beefy woman grabbed him and pulled him up. "No customers allowed back here, hon."

"Please, I won't be no trouble," Atticus stammered.

She tossed him back around the desk toward me. "I seen that look on enough women to know that ain't true. Handle your business on your own."

"Fine!" He held up his hands in resignation and smiled sheepishly as he turned to me. "Oh, hey, Kimmy." He rubbed his throat, which was still bruised from our last encounter. "What do you want?"

I stepped into the room. "Just looking for some more information on the Blue Trident. Find anything for me about where they took Geordi?"

"Not since last time we talked. I've barely had a chance to ask around."

"I don't believe you, Atticus, which is very bad for you." I dragged him over to one of the stiff plastic chairs and threw him onto it, then turned around to slam $200 on the counter. I gave the woman a significant look. "This could get messy, so you might wanna take a break."

"Don't break anything," she said with a shrug. "At least not in the office."

"If I do, I'll pay for it."

The woman eyeballed Atticus on her way out, locking the door behind her and pulling down the blinds. I took the seat across from him.

"Now talk."

"What? There's nothing to talk about." He cowered when I raised my hand, making to strike him. "Fine, fine, fine. I do have more, but it's all just hearsay and scuttlebutt. Nothing to worry your pretty, little head about."

"Let me decide what to worry about. Tell me everything you know, no matter how insignificant, before I start breaking off pieces of you one at a time."

"Okay, okay." Atticus rubbed his face. "Well, I started asking around like you told me to." He stole a glance at me. "Everyone was real squirrely about it—cagey, just like me. I don't blame them, of course. The Blue Trident are the meanest cusses this side of the Pacific, and that's saying something, given the kinds of people I work with on the regular."

"I get it. They're scary. Keep going."

"I'm trying, if you'd stop interrupting me." He tensed, waited for me to bark something nasty at him. When I didn't, his shoulders relaxed. "They've been tracking kids, lots of 'em. All fairies, and all under sixteen. They're planning something big; I know that for sure, and I don't like it."

"You don't know what it is?"

"No." He rubbed the back of his neck. "Lots of talk about shipping containers at the docks. Apparently, they got their hands on a big shipment recently. Took it right off the docks without anybody being the wiser."

"What was in the containers?"

"Nobody knows, but if they're snatching kids, maybe that's how they're bringing them into the country. If you can find one of their shipments, you'll be able to find the Blue Trident. But I gotta warn you again, Kimberly. Don't go looking for them."

"I have no choice. If they're after fairy folk, I have to stop them." I stood up. "This is good work, Atticus. Looks like I don't have to hurt you today, which is a pity." I cracked my knuckles. "Your face is just so punchable."

"You're really just gonna let me go, like that?"

I opened the door to the office, and light fell into the room again. "Just like that. You might want to get out of town, though. Asking so many questions is gonna draw down a lot of heat on you."

He stood up with a sigh of relief. "Gee, thanks, Kimberly. I didn't know you cared."

"I don't."

A green Cadillac pulled up to the office and spun so its passenger side was parallel to the door. The front and back window rolled down, and the people inside pulled out machine guns. I was barely able to leap back inside before they fired six shots into Atticus among the fifty other shots that lit up the room, spraying unmoored drywall and broken glass down on me.

It happened in a matter of seconds. The car squealed off, and Atticus coughed up one last bit of blood before he fell down dead. I pushed myself up and darted out in an all-out sprint. I liked to keep my fairy wings hidden in public so as not to draw any attention, but there was no other choice to catch up to the car.

I pressed my shoulder blades together. Glowing blue wings emerged from my back, and I fluttered into the air. The car swerved across the road as I approached, and the two criminals who were firing at me reloaded and took deadly aim.

I pulled a throwing dagger from my arm and flung it at one of the rear tires, popping it and sending the car skidding into the median. The criminals leaning out of the window lost their balance. While I had an opening, I flew closer, smashing the face of the woman in the back seat with her own gun and pulling her from the car. One down. I turned my attention to the bald man in the front seat who dropped his machine gun and pulled a pistol from the glove box. He fired it at me as the car regained control.

I spun to avoid the bullets, landing on the roof of the car. I grabbed onto the top of the passenger side window and kicked through, sending the passenger into the driver, who slammed into the window with a sickening crack that sent the car veering out of control. In a flash of purple, I disappeared from the car just before it hit the side of a brick building and rematerialized on the other side of the wreckage.

The accident had flung the bald man through the window, and he was bleeding out on the hood. He had no pulse. The driver had a thick chunk of windshield embedded in his eye socket.

I searched the men for clues. They didn't have any wallets or any forms of identification, but both henchmen had the tattoo of a blue trident on their left arm. They must have been Blue Trident soldiers, and they were dead. Then I remembered I had thrown one of them from the car before the crash.

By the time I got back to the woman on the side of the road, she was busy trying to right herself despite her leg being snapped in two places. Mostly all she could do was scream.

"Hold out your arms." I was too tired to take her shrieking for an answer. "I'll get you help if you hold out your arms for me."

When she still didn't respond, I knocked her across the face with my elbow, and she fell to the asphalt, unconscious. Sure enough, when I rolled up the sleeves on her leather jacket, she had a blue trident tattooed on her arm.

***

I teleported the woman back to my condo and placed her in our guest room to tend to her wounds. Aziolith came by with tinctures and potions to heal her compound fracture, and eventually, she looked better than she did when I first saw her, and quite a bit better than she deserved.

I took my time blacking out all the walls and clearing out any distinguishing features of the room. A bowl of potpourri and a painting of the Eiffel Tower were inviting to guests but undercut the menacing vibe I was trying to convey. When she was healed up, I wrapped a rope around her body and tied her to a chair. She woke with a gasp of air when I tossed a bucket of water on her face. Her shouts were muffled by the bandana I'd wrapped around her mouth.

I stood in front of her, hands on my hips. "I'm going to make this a really easy choice. Tell me what you know about the Blue Trident, and I'll let you go. Refuse, and I'll sell you to a demon I know who's looking for a new plaything. You'll beg for death every minute of every day, but death will never come." I knelt next to her so that she could see I wasn't messing around with her. "Which will it be?"

She thought for a second, wide-eyed, before she lowered her head and nodded. I recognized it as a sign of resignation and pulled off her gag.

"You made the right choice."

"It doesn't matter," she said. "I'm definitely going to Hell anyway."

"Probably, but hopefully not for a long time. Now, we'll start simple. Who are the Blue Trident, and what do they want with little kids?"

She blinked. "I have absolutely no idea. I'm just the muscle. They give me a job, and I make sure to carry it out to the letter. Then, I get paid. Real simple."

"And they told you to kill me?"

"Shit, no. You had nothing to do with it. That little prick Atticus was asking too many questions, and he had to go. You were just an innocent bystander." She struggled against her ropes and glared. "Maybe innocent is the wrong word."

The woman didn't seem to be lying. She really was just a grunt pissant. But she had to have something I could work with.

"Where is your base?"

"What is this? The 80s? We don't have a base. They contact me through an unlisted number and give me my next assignment."

"I see. Do you have any more jobs lined up?"

"Just one. Tomorrow night I'm supposed to guard a shipment coming from Canada being offloaded at the docks."

Canada? That's where Geordi's mom lived. Maybe the missing container didn't have him in it. Maybe he was coming into America tonight. "What pier?"

"Thirteen," she replied. "Lucky thirteen."

"You're sure?"

"Of course. Friday the thirteenth is basically a holiday in my family. I've seen every movie like a thousand times. I never forget that number."

"I believe you."

"That mean you're gonna let me go?"

I grabbed her by the cuff of her robe. "Of course."

I threw a pinch of pixie dust and disappeared with her into the ether. When I reappeared, it was in the back of a police station down the street. I pulled her forward through an alley and found a group of police officers standing out front.

"Excuse me, officers. I think there was a shooting at an auto repair earlier." I tossed the girl on the sidewalk. "This girl was involved. I think you'll find her fingerprints in the back seat of the car and one of the weapons recovered at the scene." I knew they knew about it because I'd already called in the tip.

One of the officers finally spoke up, clearly confused. "Umm, thank you, miss…"

"Just a concerned citizen," I replied before disappearing into the alley again. I reappeared in my kitchen, where Aziolith and Molly were sitting at the counter, drinking tea. Molly smiled at me as I emerged from the cloud of pink smoke.

"Does that mean you're done?" Molly asked. "Can I have my guest room back now?"

"Yes, of course." I leaned in and gave her a kiss.

"Lovely." Molly turned to Aziolith. "Will you be staying the night?"

"If you'll have me."

"You know you're always welcome."

The phone in my pocket vibrated, showing a Los Angeles number when I looked at the screen. It wasn't unusual to get calls from all over the country, but I didn't do much business in Los Angeles anymore.

"Hello?" I answered.

"Hi, Kimberly," a woman said. "You might not remember me, but I need your help. A long time ago, you saved my life from a bunch of demons who wanted to use me to open a portal to Hell. I hope I'm not catching you at a bad time—"

"Who is this?"

What she said next nearly made me drop the phone.

"My name is Anjelica."

CHAPTER 11

Ollie

Stupid girl. She was always impulsive when—no, that wasn't fair. I slowed down my inner monologue. I'd only known Anjelica for one night, thirty years ago. How would I know if she was always anything? Why did I even care if she was going to get herself killed? She was nothing to me. I had taken hundreds, thousands of jobs since then, and yet, the moment she popped back into my life, I felt the need to protect her.

She's not a little girl anymore, Ollie. I didn't have to protect her. She ran a whole country back on her planet. If she wanted to commit suicide by diving into Hell, so be it. I had better things to do. But I couldn't stop thinking about her idiocy.

A distraction came in the form of a text telling me to meet two potential clients at the Sheraton's lobby bar in San Francisco by Fisherman's Wharf. Where a person wanted to meet said a lot about them. An expensive restaurant? They wanted to project class and power. A seedy bar, they didn't want to be recognized.

Opting for a hotel bar meant this guy wanted anonymity. Thousands of people walked in and out of hotels every day, and they were generally all travelers except for the employees, who were barraged with so many faces every day that they didn't bother keeping any of them straight in their minds, especially at a place like the Sheraton. A high-end hotel like the Plaza in New York City, or even the Chateau Marmont in Los Angeles, had a very specific clientele, who often demanded to be seen. At a mid-tier hotel like the Sheraton, the people were average and fungible.

I looked around the lobby for a potential client. The comfy couches and plush chairs were sparsely populated with husbands waiting for their wives, parents waiting for their children; none of them were the powerful men that made up my client roster, so I stepped further into the room.

A wall separated the main lobby from the wider seating area, and I was surprised to find the two archangels I'd recently seen working with Bi'ri'thal sitting next to each other, scrolling through their phones.

"Morning," I said, plopping onto a seat next to them. "I'm surprised to see you here."

The angel on the left looked up and smiled. "Miss Oleander, thank you for meeting us." His accent was thick and Swedish. He reached over and shook my hand, but the other angel didn't even look up from his phone. "Clereal, be polite."

Clereal's eyes were dark green, and he smiled so brightly I nearly had to turn away, even in dark sunglasses. "My apologies, Fyathiel. I was responding to an important email."

Fyathiel grumbled. "Don't lie to me. It was probably those angry birds again."

"Please. That is so 2010." Clereal turned his attention to me. "We were impressed with how you handled our last assignment and how you didn't ask questions that didn't concern you."

"You're paying for my discretion," I said with a shrug. "I take the privacy of my clients very seriously."

“But are you not even a little curious about what you saw?” Fyathiel leaned in and spoke with a low voice. “I mean, angels and demons working together. It is not common, yes?”

“You would know better than me,” I responded, trying to hide how weird I really did think that it was. My client’s associations were their own business, and judging was a good way to turn somebody away. “There’s a bar in Scotland where you guys have hung out for at least 150 years, so I figured maybe you built a relationship and went into business together or something.”

Clereal nodded. “That is very astute of you, but our friendship with Bi’ri’thal goes back much further than that.”

I desperately wanted to hear more about it, but I had to be nonchalant. They were clearly baiting me to see if I would nose into their affair, or if I could be trusted to keep my distance from their secrets.

“That’s nice,” I replied curtly. “But like I said, I don’t care about your personal life. Now, can we please talk about the job?”

Fyathiel looked over at Clereal and then, with a slight smile and even slighter nod, turned back to me. “Yes, perhaps that would be best. Keep it professional.”

“I think that’s always best. Personal business is…honestly, not anything I’m interested in. It’s messy and complicated. I prefer things neat, clean, and simple.”

“I couldn’t have said it better myself.” Clereal reached into his pocket and pulled out a piece of paper. “We have a matter of some urgency that we need handled with the utmost discretion.”

“Now you’re speaking my language.” I took the piece of paper from his outstretched hand. “That happens to be my specialty.”

“Lovely,” Clereal said, leaning back into his chair. “Tonight, a small boat will deliver a special package to Pier 13 right here in San Francisco, and we need someone with an impeccable reputation to meet the boat and facilitate the handoff.”

“Sure, I can do that for you. It’s one of my specialties.”

“Yes, we have heard as much,” Fyathiel said. “It is essential that it is delivered to that address without delay after the exchange. Do this for us, and we will reward you with six million dollars.”

I made sure not to react. “That’s quite a bit higher than my standard rate.”

“As we mentioned, we are paying for your discretion.”

I nodded, sliding the paper into the pocket of my leather duster nearest my heart. “Consider it done.”

“Wonderful,” Fyathiel said. He reached behind his chair and pulled out a briefcase. “This is for the exchange. Unmarked bills, non-sequential, as they instructed.”

“Who’s they?” I asked.

“None of your business,” Clereal said, his tone a bit gruff. “And we’re paying you to keep it that way.”

***

I caught a tail the minute I left the Sheraton, and it followed me down the Embarcadero as I walked down to scout out Pier 13. I had less than twelve hours to plan for the handoff, and now I had to spend time losing whoever was tracking me. As I passed a barber shop, I caught the woman’s reflection in the glass. Though she wore a t-shirt and jeans, she walked like a government spook.

This was bad. It was one thing to hide a high-ticket shipment from the local port authorities and any annoying police officers who might have caught a whiff, but it was quite another to hide it from the government. If they were already tracking me, they knew something. I needed to find out what it was before it blew the whole deal.

I made several turns, just slow enough that my tail could keep up, until I was deep into the bowels of San Francisco, hidden among the brick buildings around me. I slid into a dark alley and waited for the officer to pass me before making myself known. I pulled my wand from my pocket and pointed it at her.

"What do you want?"

She wheeled around and looked at my wand without a hint of fear. "Miss White. I wondered if you had caught onto my tail."

"That's not an answer. What do you want? You have three seconds before I vaporize you."

The woman smirked. "An idle threat. If I go missing, then you'll be arrested, plain and simple. I believe a life's sentence means something different to immortals, doesn't it?"

I kept my wand trained on her. "Maybe, but you would still be dead. Now, answer my question."

She didn't lose the smirk. "Okay, but only because my boss predicted this—counted on it, in fact. She would like to meet with you, somewhere secure, where we can speak candidly."

"And why should I go with you?"

"Because you know as well as we do that whatever Bi'ri'thal and his associates are planning is bad news, but we know exactly *how* bad it is and why you should not be working with them."

I paused, considering this. If the government had stayed away for this long only to call on me now, it must have been as big a deal as I had feared. And I needed to know what I was getting into before I stepped onto that dock later that night.

"All right." I dropped my wand to my side and gestured to her car. "Lead the way."

The safe house she took me to wasn't far from where I ambushed her. We followed Broadway until Jackson Square turned into Chinatown and then parked and headed up a small stairwell nestled between a dumpling restaurant and a souvenir shop. The door at the top wasn't old and worn-down like the rest of the surrounding red paint. It was solid metal. The agent knocked, and when a latch slid open, she spoke three words: "Flying Spaghetti Monster." The latch slammed closed, and a moment later, the door opened for us.

She had me take a seat at a metal table in the center of an anteroom. The room itself was small, and the walls were lined with white plastic sheeting. After she walked away, a familiar woman walked in. She was shorter than I remembered, the thick wrinkles on her face were smoothed by the fact that her hair was pulled back in a tight bun, but there was no doubt it was Director Chapman, the woman who employed me so many years ago.

"You look good, Ollie," she began with a thin-lipped smile.

"And you look old."

"The curse of getting up in years," she replied. "I won't waste your time with the trifles of a mortal woman. You have a lot to do today, so I'll get to the point. The demon you work for is trying to start an Apocalypse."

I couldn't help but chuckle. "You really don't mince words."

"No reason to. You and I have a history, and you've been known to be untrusting and tough to work with. I thought I'd lay it all out for you from the jump."

"So, I assume you want me to help stop this Apocalypse, even though it will destroy everything I've built."

Director Chapman nodded. "I do because if you don't, then all the money, wealth, and power you've accumulated will be worthless. All that will be left is the end of the world."

"A compelling case. What do you need from me?"

"The shipment those two angels are bringing into port tonight. We need to know what's inside and why they need it."

"You want me to bring it to you?" I asked.

"Precisely. Whatever it is must have powerful magic associated with it if they are willing to spend so much securing it." She eyed me closely. "Did Clereal or Fyathiel say anything weird during their conversation with you?"

"You want to know if the angels working with a demon like Bi'ri'thal said anything weird…weirder than what? Cuz that's a pretty high baseline."

"Just, anything odd that you took note of."

I thought for a moment. “As a matter of fact, they said they had been friends with him for years before The Bar even existed.”

Her eyebrows went up. “That’s right. Their relationship goes back to before the demons separated from the angels. They were all part of an organization called the Blue Trident, a group of angels sworn to protect the gods from even themselves. After Lucifer fell into the underworld, the demons that followed him were separated from their cohorts in Heaven. They laid in wait, trying to find a way to work together again and enact their plans.”

I took a minute to absorb all of this and finally just asked, “And what is their plan?”

“We don’t know for sure, but they believe God is unfit to rule and that the only way to fix the terrible situation in Hell is to let loose an Apocalypse.”

“That’s…pretty bad,” I said.

“It’s so much worse than you saw on your last visit, and the Blue Trident will do anything to ‘fix’ the problem, even if it means wresting control from God and letting Hellspawn roam the world again.”

“A coup, then?”

“The worst coup this world has ever seen, and all that separates them from success is the few of us that know about it.”

My eyes narrowed. “I’m in.”

“I was hoping you would say that. Let’s get started.”

CHAPTER 12

Anjelica

My heart nearly stopped when I stepped off the plane at Oakland airport. Kimberly had been the whole reason I had survived during my first days on Onmiri, and she saved my life back on Earth before then, too, when demons were trying to use my blood to start an Apocalypse.

Was that really thirty years ago? It felt like last night.

Kimberly wired me some money for the ticket and introduced me to somebody who could make a passable passport for me in a rush, which I used to get on the plane. An older Black woman with thick, curly hair held up a sign for me at the airport terminal past baggage claim.

"That's me," I said, pointing to the sign.

She smiled. "Anjelica? It's certainly nice to meet you. I'm Molly."

I held out my hand, and we shook. "Nice to meet you. Where's Kimberly?"

"She'll be along when we get home. Unfortunately, you caught us on a busy day, so she asked me to pick you up." She thumbed at the baggage claim. "Do you have any luggage?"

I shook my head. "I packed light. Nothing but the clothes on my back."

Molly looked me up and down. "You look about my size. We'll get you into something more comfortable than a pants suit."

I chuckled. "Actually, this is very comfortable to me."

She shrugged and started toward the door. "Well, it does suit you."

We left the airport and headed across the bridge into San Francisco, turning up the Embarcadero. She entered a garage beneath a high-rise apartment near Fisherman's Wharf. Along the way, we engaged in idle chit-chat as best we could, but being from two different worlds and without any shared experience outside of knowing Kimberly, it was stilted at best. She caught me up on the biggest news from the past few decades, and I filled her in on my adopted home planet.

"You really have a Black president?" I asked.

Molly nodded, pulling into a parking spot. "Oh yes, two terms. Though, you would think it was two decades the way some people behave."

She brought me up the elevator to a sparsely-decorated penthouse overlooking the water. It was the kind of minimalism only the rich could pull off, even in Onmiri. The poor tended to hoard everything they could, knowing that bad times could be just around the corner. Those with money had no such concerns, and they flaunted it by keeping little around them.

"Make yourself at home," Molly said.

I smiled at her and finally caught a whiff of myself. "You know, maybe I could use a change of clothes. And a shower."

"Bathroom's just down the hall. Feel free to raid my closet. Can't say I'm a fancy dresser, but maybe you'll find something. Kimberly calls my style 'cottage chic.'"

***

The water hit my naked skin, and my body called out with a deep ache for more heat against it to wash away the last few hours. I let the water beat against my back until I heard the front door open, and then I turned off the water and wrapped myself in a towel.

Molly's slacks didn't fit right, but I found a flowing polka dot dress and paired it with a pair of sneakers that pinched on the sides. I slipped a yellow headband over my wet hair.

I laughed out loud when I looked at myself in the mirror. I hadn't worn anything so colorful in ages. My laugh must have caught the attention of whoever just came inside because I heard footsteps on the hardwood and a familiar face popped through the door.

"Anjelica!" she screamed. "It's good to see you!"

It had been thirty years, but she looked as young as she did when we were children. "K-Kimberly?"

"Of course," she said, squeezing me in a tight hug. "Who did you think it was?"

"It's just…you don't look like you've aged a day. How is that possible?"

She unlatched from me and stared into my eyes. "Well, first, I moisturize." She waited for a beat. "I'm just kidding. I'm immortal."

"Immortal? Ah, I guess that makes sense."

"Does it?"

I turned to the mirror and tried to fix my hair. "I've heard weirder things. I was brought here by the god of death, after all, and you and I live on two different planets."

"Fair enough. Come on. Molly made food."

She dragged me into the kitchen, where Molly slid bowls of paella in front of us. “I hope you’re hungry.”

I didn’t realize that I was famished until the aroma of food hit me. I shoveled heaps of rice down my gullet, fighting against the heat as I chewed.

“This is so good,” I said through a mouthful. “You’re a great cook.”

She laughed appreciatively. “Thank you very much. Kimberly is gone a lot, which gives me time to pursue my other passions, like cooking and reading.”

“Where does she go?” I turned to Kimberly, realizing I could just ask her. “Still saving the world?”

She nodded. “Usually, which is why I wasn’t able to pick you up, unfortunately. I hope the flight was comfortable.”

“Comfortable enough,” I replied. “I’m used to private jets, but I guess first class is okay.” There was a long silence, and Kimberly and Molly stole glances at each other. “Oh god, I’m joking. It was perfect. Thank you.”

Kimberly breathed a sigh of relief. “Phew. I haven’t seen you in so long, I was hoping you didn’t get a stick up your ass.”

I took another forkful of paella. “There’s a stick in there, for sure. It’s not easy to run a country.”

“How’s Margaret doing? Is she still queen?”

“She is, but she’s given almost all power to the parliament. What she’s retained has fallen to me to wield on her behalf. She’s not much of a diplomat, even if she’s a wonderful ruler.”

"Usually, those two things are mutually exclusive," Molly replied. "Those with the temperament to rule well rarely seek the spotlight, and vice versa."

"In my thirty years running Forche, I can say that's 100 percent accurate." I scraped the last of the food from my plate. "Can I have seconds? Sorry, but you don't get this on Onmiri."

"Do you like it?" Molly asked, spooning more paella onto my plate. "Living on another planet, I mean."

"Well enough. Sometimes I think about what would have happened if I'd come back with Kimberly, but what would I have done with myself then? Been a schoolteacher?"

"You could have helped me save the world," Kimberly said. "You would have been a good apprentice."

I looked down at my hands. "I'm not much of a fighter. I can still use my powers well enough, but I don't like to do so. I prefer to use my mouth rather than my fists."

"Yeah, you would not have fit in with her, then," Molly said with a wink towards Kimberly. "Besides, I think I made a good second."

"When you're up for it," Kimberly said. "Which is less and less these days."

"What can I say? I'm a homebody." Molly walked out of the kitchen toward the hallway. "Speaking of, I'm going to get some work done while you two finish up here. I cooked, so you two can clean."

Kimberly kissed Molly as she passed by her. "Yes, dear."

I stood up, my belly full of rice and meat, and slid my plate into the sink. "I rinse, you dry? It's how my mom and I always used to do it."

"Sure," Kimberly grabbed a rag from the stove. After we'd washed a few plates, she spoke., "Why are you here, Anjelica? Why did you come back now, after all this time?"

"That's the big question, isn't it?" I rinsed another plate and handed it to her. "Mom died, and Araphael told me I should go to her funeral."

"First time you've seen him since…?"

"No, he came around for a couple of years after you left. He gave me updates for a while, but it was too painful. I asked him not to tell me anything about what happened here on Earth, and eventually, he faded away. I was so busy that I didn't even notice how long it had been until I saw him again."

"Relatable," she replied. "And you're here to ask for my help."

"No—I mean—I didn't—"

"It's okay," she said. "I'm used to it. Let's not beat around the bush, though."

I turned off the faucet and dried my hands on the dishtowel Kimberly handed over. "Okay then. You're right. I need to find my mother. She's lost somewhere in Hell, and if I can just get in there and find her, then—"

"No, absolutely not," Kimberly said, tossing the last plate onto the stove. Her face turned hard. "I am not helping you get into Hell."

"I'm half demon," I replied. "I can handle myself."

She stomped into the living room. "I don't care if you're Lucifer incarnate. Hell is too dangerous, especially now. I'm not going to help you get yourself killed."

"So, you can just deny me like that, after thirty years? After you left me on a strange planet?"

She wheeled on me. "Don't bring that down on me. It killed me to watch you stay on Onmiri, but you made your choice, and I respected it. You wouldn't even be here right now if I hadn't saved your life—twice if I recall. Save the guilt trip for somebody else."

"You know I'm not going to rest until I figure this out." I followed her into the room. "If you do—"

"Or until you realize it's impossible. Since Ollie wouldn't help you, I can assume Araphael wouldn't either, which means your three best chances of getting into Hell are gone."

"I can find Lilith," I replied.

"Not unless she wanted to be found," Kimberly said. "And I'm very sure she doesn't want to be found by you."

"I'm very good at finding people."

"Lilith isn't a person, and this isn't Onmiri. You might be powerful there, but here, you are nobody, and in Hell, you are less than that."

"I'll kill myself."

"No, you won't," Kimberly said. "You are a survivor. That much I know about you."

I threw my hands in the air. "You're being unreasonable! I'm an adult. If I want to go to Hell and search for my mother, then that's my right."

She nodded. "You're right, but I don't have to help you. As an adult, that's my right."

"I'm going to make it into Hell, one way or another. I always get my way."

"If that were true, you wouldn't be here." She looked me into the eyes. "And it breaks my heart to say that."

"You said it was okay that I was here for a favor!" I shouted.

"It is, but I still hoped you just wanted to catch up." She opened the front door. "If you want to do that, I'm here for you. If you need a shoulder to cry on, I'll grieve with you. But if you insist on doing something crazy, then I can't be a part of it, and I'll ask you to leave. I hope you'll stay, though. There's so much I want to tell you."

I stormed toward the door. "If you wanted me to stay, you would help me."

"What a spoiled thing to say. You sound like a child," Kimberly replied. "Goodbye, Anjelica."

CHAPTER 13

Lizzie

"Get up the stairs," Michael growled at me when we reached God's platform in the center of the Elysian Fields.

I stomped up the stairs toward the columns high above us. A cloud of black trailed across the fields in the middle distance, covering the air with a thick blackness. It was the angels, scores of them, working together to track us down.

"Michael!" God said when we reached the top of the platform. He had a bushy, white beard and ice-blue eyes. His white toga was just like mine but covered in far less demon viscera. He spoke with a jovial and booming voice when we reached him. "To what do I owe the pleasure?"

"It's not a pleasure, I'm afraid." Michael pointed toward the swarm of angels. "Gabriel has called forth the Blue Trident to enact a reckoning thousands of years in the making."

God sighed. "Then it is as we feared for far too long." He rubbed the skin between his eyebrows with his forefingers. "I never thought it would come to this."

"This woman, Elizabeth,"—Michael pointed to me—"she was with Gabriel right before this. You might remember she helped us with that…thing a couple of decades ago."

"Of course." God nodded as he turned his attention to me. "It's a pleasure to see you again. I wish it were under different circumstances."

"So do I, sir."

"Now, what did Gabriel tell you?"

I recounted the story to him—quickly—as told by Gabriel, from the attack on Heaven by Lucifer to the carrot offered by God to the Blue Trident in exchange for their loyalty, and how they turned their back on Lucifer for the good of the Earth, or what they thought was the good of Earth.

When I was done, God stroked his long beard. "Did I really do such a bad job as to have my own servants mutiny?"

"No, sir," Michael replied fervently. "You have been a great god. They are petulant and arrogant to believe they can rule this world better than you."

I heard footsteps on the stairs, high heels clacking on the steps until a strongly built woman with a tight bun and a pencil skirt came around the column. It was Moana, the "COO of Heaven", as she once introduced herself to me. At the time, I'd wondered how there could be enough for her to do in her position, but after seeing the back of Heaven, I now understood.

"Sir, are you okay?" she said. "Is something wrong?"

"I'm afraid so, Moana," God replied. "There is a mutiny. Ready the defenses of Heaven. Try not to hurt them if you can help it. They are not bad, just misguided."

"At once, sir." She pulled a tablet out of thin air and started typing. As she did, the clouds below us began to rumble, and a half dozen heavy cannons rose from them, pointed directly at the horde of angels now less than a hundred feet away.

"I will give you one chance," God's voice boomed onto the horizon. "Stop now, and I will be lenient. These cannons will rip you to shreds." God turned to Moana and whispered. "That's right, isn't it?"

"Absolutely," Moana said. "I designed the system myself."

"Then we are safe," God said.

"I wouldn't say that." Moana tapped some more on her tablet, and the guns swiveled toward the platform instead of away from it. Her sleeve moved, and I saw the tip of a blue trident tattooed on her arm. "I'm afraid you're under arrest for crimes against humanity."

With another tap on her tablet, a huge bubble enveloped the canopy around us. Moana flew out of it just before it collapsed around her.

"Disappear," Michael said. "We can live to fight another day."

God shook his head. "No, they are right. I have been a terrible, inattentive god, and I deserve this."

"Coward!" Michael shouted. "You may have given up, but I haven't!"

The archangel grabbed hold of me and shot into the air faster than a bullet. He pulled out his sword and sliced through the forcefield just before it connected, locking God inside. Michael glanced at Moana, who was staring slack-jawed, and then glowered at the flock of angels descending around us.

"There's too many of them," he breathed. "I need time to think, but there is no time." He handed the sword to me. "Can you use one of these things? I can't fly and fight at the same time, especially with you to worry about."

"I wouldn't say I'm good at it," I said, eyeing the sword in my hand. "But I can swing it well enough if that's what you need."

"It has to be. If any of those angels come toward us, slice at them while I fly through their ranks."

He slid me around to his back as he shot out toward the flock of angels. I heard the servos on the guns swivel again. The turrets had turned toward us, and cannonballs shot across the Elysian Fields toward us.

"Oh shart!" Michael said, noticing the cannons flying toward us. He spun away from the attack, and the cannonballs shot into the horde of angels, clearing a momentary path through them. "On second thought, thank you, Moana. Hold tight!"

I bowed my head as low as possible as Michael followed the hole through the formation before it closed up. He screamed something, and a dozen of the angels broke off and turned toward us.

"Think, Michael, think!"

I knew he wasn't directing his words to me, but that didn't mean they weren't ones that I could use, too. *Think, Lizzie*. If only Kimberly were here, she would—an idea struck me.

"Can we get to Earth?" I asked.

"I can't go down there right now. God still has allies here, and I must marshal them to our cause, or Heaven will be lost forever."

"Then send me."

"You're not an archangel, and I don't have the authorization to—"

"Who cares?" I shouted. "Why are you standing on ceremony? Just get me down to Earth, and I'll figure something out. If they're planning something down there, you need me to stop it."

He glanced from me to the oncoming horde. "Well, I suppose that they are trying to start an Apocalypse on Earth, and somebody needs to handle that while I deal with the situation here."

"Exactly. Let me do it," I said. "I know you probably don't trust me, but I guarantee I'm more trustworthy than these anthills chasing us." A shadow fell over us, and two cannonballs of brimstone exploded nearby. "Make it quick, though, because they're coming!"

"Fine!" Michael said, turning up the Elysian Fields, the Blue Trident trailing close behind us. "Do you know where you want to go first?"

"San Francisco."

"I know the place."

Michael dove to the ground. As he did, I swung a water whip at one of the angels, but they spun around me, avoiding the attack.

"Give me the sword."

"Gladly!" I shouted, placing it in his outstretched hand.

He used the sword to cut through the clouds. On the other side, I glimpsed the curvature of the Earth. It was beautiful. Michael turned the sword around and flung it toward Earth. Before it could go more than a dozen yards, it smashed against an invisible barrier, cutting a hole in it and a splintered crack nearly big enough for me to fit through.

Michael pressed himself hard against the barrier and used his strength to hold it open. "Go!"

I jumped down from his back while the angels hurtled toward us. "Thank you."

“Don’t thank me yet. The descent will be painful.” Michael smiled. “Now, go. I’ll hold this closed behind you for as long as I can to prevent them from following you. If they get through, there will be no way for me to help you.”

“I understand.” I took one last look at Michael and the angels descending toward us, then slipped through the barrier. He kicked the sword to me just before the hole closed. I caught it, and he turned to attack the angels with his bare hands.

Then my stomach fell into my knees, and I dove uncontrollably to Earth.

CHAPTER 14

Kimberly

That little bit—. No, she's not little anymore. That full-grown *bitch*! I couldn't believe she'd come to my house and guilt me into helping get her killed after I'd saved her on two separate, though consecutive occasions, specifically so she wouldn't get killed. Now she wants to waltz into Hell like it's nothing.

Get your head in the game, Kimberly. You have a job to do.

If my hunch was right, the Blue Trident was transporting Geordi in the dark of night, and I needed to be at the top of my game if I was going to save him, not worried about a girl I barely knew, who'd grown into a woman I barely liked.

Molly and I arrived at the pier thirty minutes before sunset and took our posts on the buildings on either side of the street that dead-ended at the dock. There were a half dozen boats on the pier, each of them manned by three mercenaries carrying machine guns. It didn't look like the grand prize had arrived at the dock yet, as the soldiers were all casually leaning against the boats.

An hour after sunset, when the mercenaries blended into the darkness, a light shone on the end of the dock, and a small boat pulled up. Four of the men rushed to secure it to the end of the dock before the lights cut out, and everything was shrouded in darkness yet again.

"Ahhhhhhh! Get off me!"

I heard the scream from across the street and turned to see Molly struggling against something I couldn't make out. I leaped up, ready to attack whoever was hurting the love of my life. Before I could flash over, I heard footsteps behind me. A slender man in a black suit was rushing toward me. He fired two darts into me as I drew my daggers, and my arms went limp. My tongue fell slack, my legs gave out, and I crashed to the ground.

***

I woke up with a bright light shining down on me. My hands and feet were tied to the metal chair I was sitting in.

"Who do you work for? Russian intelligence?" a loud woman's voice squawked through the speakers. "The Chinese? INTERPOL?"

"What? No, nothing like that." I shouted. "Let me out of here!" The window in front of me was made of one-way glass, and I didn't know who was on the other side. I tried to teleport out of the small room but couldn't. They were using something to dampen my powers.

"We can't do that," the voice said. "Not until we know what you were doing at the dock."

I started to knead the rope binding my hands. The smell of fish still lingered in the air. I couldn't be more than a block from the water. "I was thinking about buying a boat, and I thought I would check out my options. Seemed like a good idea at the time."

"Are you working for the Blue Trident?" the voice said evenly.

My head snapped up. "How do you know about the Blue Trident?"

"How do *you* know about the Blue Trident?"

I drew out my answer as I worked to loosen the rope tying my hands together. "I came across them on a case. I'm a…private detective of sorts. One of their men tried to kill me, and when I interrogated them, they—"

"Jesus Christ, Director," a screechy voice interrupted. "What are you—? Let her—I'll do it. Get off me!"

Two doors swung open behind me, and I realized I was in a surveillance truck. A sunglassed figure wearing a long trench coat hopped into the back of the truck; I recognized her instantly as an old friend.

"Good to see you, Ollie." I grinned, pulling my hands free before she could untie them. "Couple more seconds and I wouldn't have needed the help, but I'm glad for it all the same."

"Wish I could have come sooner. I've been a bit busy," she said. "Hey, did Anjelica ever call you?"

"Did she ever." I rubbed my red, raw wrists. "I assume you sent her my way."

"Yup. I had to get her out of my hair."

"Thank you for dropping that drama on me."

"Does that mean you didn't help her?"

"Help her to Hell? No, I didn't. I could have killed her, though. She grew up into a petulant little bitch, didn't she?"

"Tell me about it," Ollie grunted. "Talk about an entitled princess."

"Nailed it," I said. "Now, how about you tell me where my wife is and what you're doing here."

She looked down at her watch. "Yeah, I guess I have some time. How about we discuss it over coffee?"

"You can't tell her anything," the voice squawked through the speakers. "That's classified information."

"And you can't do this operation with me, so bite my whole ass."

***

Ollie and I ended up ten blocks away from the pier, drinking tepid, mediocre coffee. Molly had foregone meeting with us in favor of bed. She hated working nights, and after being accosted, she had no interest in helping the government in any way, shape, or form.

Ollie filled me in on everything she knew about the Blue Trident, and I did the same for her. I didn't necessarily like Ollie, but we had an uneasy alliance. She was still a demon. Still, the Devil I knew was better than the one I didn't. At the very least, she was honest, which was more than I could say for most demons.

"So, putting your knowledge of the Blue Trident with mine, I'm starting to get a good picture of what we're dealing with," I said. "And none of it is good."

"None of it is good," Ollie repeated. "Demons and angels working together to steal children for some nefarious yet unknown purpose? Not good at all." She jotted something down on a small sheet of paper and slid it to me.

Don't trust government. Listening.

I grabbed the pen and scribbled something back to her as I talked. "No, and yet Anjelica thinks this is the perfect time for a vacation into Hell."

I slid the paper over to her. *Plan?*

She took back the paper and pen. "I guess there's no accounting for manners, even halfway across the universe."

Once again, I got the paper. *Distraction. Safehouse?*

"I thought that seeing her again would be a joyous occasion, not a pain in my ass." I scribbled down my address.

Ollie reached into her pocket and pulled out a lighter, placing it on top of the napkin and sliding it over to me just as a man with a bushy mustache and ill-fitting suit stepped inside.

"Speaking of pains in my ass. Time for the show." She tapped the lighter. "You'll take care of that for me?"

I nodded. "Consider it done."

The message was clear as she walked out of the door. Prepare my house and get ready for Ollie's arrival with whatever the Blue Trident was trying to smuggle in secret.

When the door closed behind her, I torched the paper, watching it burn in my hand until it was almost gone, then stirring it into my coffee to snuff it out. I walked to the counter.

"Two coffees, black. Extra shot in both."

It was going to be a long night, and no matter what Molly said, she wasn't going to sleep any time soon.

CHAPTER 15

Anjelica

I knew it was a bad idea, but I was left with no other choice. I wasn't about to leave my mother lost in Hell, even if it meant calling on my no-good father for help. I remembered my mother calling him when I was a child, so she must have had some way to contact him, a spell or something, in her house somewhere. It meant having to go through all her possessions.

Pulling up to my old house was a gut punch. I hadn't seen it for over thirty years. It used to be an ugly, muddy brown, but Mom had changed it to green somewhere along the way, though even that must have been a while ago because the paint was chipping from the wood around the door. I pulled out the set of keys I brought with me all the way from Onmiri. They were one of my few mementos of Earth, and I had always carried them with me.

The door creaked when I opened it, and the smell was instantly familiar, like a perfume that you hadn't worn in a long time. Here, it was hints of lacquered wood and mint. The carpets had been replaced with dark wood, and the television had been upgraded. A leather couch replaced the threadbare thing I had known. At least the dining room table was the same one I remembered. I ran my hand across it, thinking of the time Araphael recreated it—along with the entire kitchen—so that I could say goodbye to my mother before I abandoned her forever.

I followed the kitchen around to an office with several huge, wooden bookcases lining the walls. It used to be my room. I wondered how long she waited for me before she replaced all my posters with bookcases, my bed with a desk. Not that it mattered. I was glad she moved on. Somehow it helped ease the sting that she had a whole life without me.

Her computer asked for a password when I booted it up. I had only one guess of what it could be. *Anjelica.* It was self-centered, but a decent guess. Much to my delight, it worked, and the computer popped open for me.

The background was a picture of me, much younger, smiling with her as we ate ice cream. It had been taken on my eleventh birthday. I'd asked for a pony; she gave me a My Little Pony and a book on horses. Then, she took me north of the city and let me ride a horse. She told me she would bring me back as often as she could, but we never did. Eventually, my interest faded.

I typed in every word I could think of into the search bar, looking for a file about summoning a demon. Nothing worthwhile came up. I spent the rest of the night hunting through every file on her computer, one at a time to search for hidden, secret nooks and crannies. Again, nothing.

With a stretch, I stood up and moved to the bookshelf. I ran my fingers along the books, a collection of flimsy, mass-market paperbacks. My stomach rumbled, so I turned to the kitchen, where I found Araphael standing at the counter, a leatherbound journal in his hand.

"It's this one. Page 73," he said. "I never thought you would be so desperate as to summon your father."

"I wouldn't be if you just helped me from the start."

He sighed. "I thought you would lose interest. I should have known better. When you put your mind to something, there's nothing anyone can do to stop you."

"Isn't that why you asked for my help all those years ago, because I was a force of nature?"

"Yes, and I appreciated it when it worked in my favor. It's incredibly taxing when you work against me."

I stepped closer, holding my hands out in frustration. "Then help me."

He nodded. "I have arranged for an audience with Lord Mephistopheles. Most demon lords are cruel and brash, but he is more calculating than the others—no less dangerous, but in a different way than his brethren."

"Does…does he have my mother?"

"If he doesn't, I believe he at least knows where she is. I cannot tell you how dangerous this path is. To enter Hell in this state—"

"My mother would come for me if the roles were reversed."

"Frankly, I don't think she would. She knew that death was final and to be respected. That's what I lo—appreciated about her. I think you know that. And this isn't about her. It's about you."

"It's about protecting my mother."

"Whatever you say," he said, reaching out his hand. "We shall depart."

***

Pushing through from Earth into the underworld wasn't like moving across the universe. That felt like disappearing into a vat of thick stew, whereas this was more like boring through the ground with a jackhammer. When we finally reached the bowels of Hell, and I smelled the hot stench of sulfur, my head was already pounding. It was like I'd smashed it into a wall a dozen times.

I groaned. “I forgot how much I hate that.”

“Then you haven’t had to entreat with Baron Samedi since our last encounter?”

Baron Samedi was the god of the underworld on my adopted home planet. Araphael and I had once saved him from being used as a battery by the previous king of Onmiri.”

“Thankfully no, though I would pay to see what he’s doing with King Ulthar right now.”

We stood on a narrow mountain pass cut through sheer rock rising high on either side. It was so narrow I had to turn my shoulders to fit between the jagged rocks.

“We have been given special dispensation to be here, as guests of the demon lord. Please be on your best behavior.”

“I literally negotiate with nobles and kings as my job. I think I can handle one little demon lord.” Most diplomacy was built upon flattery and the need to give up more than you are comfortable. No matter what you offered, it was important to have more in your coffers because the person hosting the tete-a-tete usually has the advantage—and a gigantic ego.

Araphael chuckled, but before I could ask why, the rock face broke into a clearing. A hundred feet below me, the rest of Hell expanded into the distance. Millions of souls, charred black, packed atop each other in wobbling towers of pain and misery everywhere I looked. They covered every inch of the ground and swayed across the caverns of the underworld.

“This is horrible,” I breathed. “What is happening here?”

“Poor management, for one,” he replied. “A pity. I did so much like this place when Velaska was in charge.”

“Who’s that?”

“She was a god who, long ago, abandoned her post here to search for her fortunes among the stars. She left an angel in charge, one who was untrained and unprepared for the challenges that awaited him.” He grabbed my hand and pulled me away from the ledge. “Come, we have a meeting.”

Mephistopheles’s castle stood at the end of a long path in the center of the clearing, bookended by two more sheetrock faces. The high-black wood door opened and out walked a small impish woman wearing a flowing black toga and red earrings. She shuffled along the path and bowed when she met us a hundred yards from the entrance.

“Your grace,” she said to Araphael. “You are even more glorious in person than in your stories.”

“Thank you,” he said, gesturing toward me with a dramatic, sweeping arm. “And this is Anjelica. Her mother is the reason for our trip today.”

She bowed even lower. “Of course, of course. An honor to meet you, Miss Anjelica, visitor from beyond the stars. My master would very much like to hear your stories from planets yet explored by his excellence.”

She turned and walked back to the door, and once we were inside, they slammed closed behind us. It was so dark that I could barely see my hand in front of my face. The only thing I could make out were Araphael’s orange, glowing eyes.

After a moment, a snap crackled through the room, echoing off each wall. A hundred candles illuminated at once to reveal the visages of screaming souls reaching out from the walls in permanent gasps of rocky relief.

"Welcome," a growling voice said. A small figure appeared out of the darkness, skittering toward us along the floor. "I am Mephistopheles, demon lord of Hell."

He clapped his hands together and rose into the air until he was the same height as the two of us, leaving a three-foot gap under him where a long black cape fluttered.

"Thank you for seeing us, your majesty." I knelt in front of him, keeping my eyes on the floor. "You honor me by giving a moment of your time."

"Please, my dear." He lifted my head with a pudgy, red, ashy finger. His face was as gnarled as any demon's, with pointed yellow teeth and dark red eyes. The horns on his head were short and pointed, barely bigger than the teeth in his head. "It is my pleasure to help a demon. We have much to discuss. I promise whatever your request, I will do my best to entertain it."

CHAPTER 16

Ollie

You could always count on Kimberly's nosiness and her ability to pop up at the most inopportune moments. It was an annoying talent of hers. This time, it worked out in my favor. The feds might have wanted me to carry through with delivering the cargo as planned, but once Kimberly told me what she thought was in the boat, I couldn't in good conscience go along with it.

"It's time," Director Chapman said when I returned to the stake-out truck. "You understand the plan?"

"I get the boy and bring him here so you can figure out what the Blue Trident wants with him."

"Correct," Director Chapman said with a smile as she handed me a small, leather briefcase. "Get out there. It's almost time."

I threw the case in the back seat of Lucy and gunned it to the dock. This would surely destroy my reputation with Bi'ri'thal, one way or another.

That was okay. My mother asked me often why I kept doing this job when I hadn't needed the money since the 90s, and I never really had an answer. I always told her I loved the rush, or that I enjoyed solving impossible puzzles. In truth, it was probably much easier than that.

I was looking for that feeling, the one I had when I saved Anjelica and sent her off to her freedom. I wasn't straight-laced enough to be a savior like Kimberly, but I thought that if I kept my criminal contacts for long enough, maybe I would find a way to save the world again.

Well, you got your wish, Ollie. And here I thought I'd buried that desire deep down where nobody else could find it.

I parked my car at the end of the dock and hopped outside. It was cold in San Francisco at night. Men with machine guns—humans—lined the boats on either end of the dock. Not a monster in the bunch.

"Are you Oleander White?" A sing-song voice came from the boat at the end of the dock. A woman emerged, rippling with muscles. The water displaced around her as she stepped off the boat and onto the dock.

"I am. Do you have the package?"

"If you have the money."

I nodded, fingering the leather briefcase in my hand. "Non-sequential bills, low denomination, as requested."

She held out her hand. "Give it to me."

I didn't move. "That's not how this works. You show me the package, and I hand you the money when it's safely at the end of the dock."

"You must think I'm crazy," the woman's voice turned as cold as the wind that whipped across her face.

I shrugged. "No, I just think you haven't done your homework. If you had, then you would know I am a woman of my word. Clients rely on me because of that. My employers hired me specifically because I can be trusted. Hustling you is bad for my business. My word is all I have in this world, and it's my bond. I won't ruin it because of them or you."

The woman gave me an icy smile. "My men have been equipped with bullets that can kill even a demon, and their fingers are itchy to use their new toys."

I felt the heat of a dozen guns trained on my back and smirked. "I could take all of them out before the first bullet left their guns. Your threats don't scare me. Let me see the package, or the deal is off."

I turned to leave when the woman snapped her fingers, and the boat creaked and rocked. Of course, she acquiesced. She had something my bosses wanted desperately enough to pay top dollar for, but she had a market of one. Either she delivered, or she was out a lot of money.

There was a thud on the dock when a young boy with his hands and feet bandaged together landed on the boards, screaming through the gauze covering his mouth. He couldn't have been more than twelve, with matted brown hair and a heavy stream of sweat around his face. His eyes were bloodshot from crying.

Stay frosty, kid. I'll have you out of here soon.

"He's alive, as instructed," she said. "Now, the money."

"Cut his restraints and send him over to me."

"This isn't Red Rover. I don't play games."

"No, it's a negotiation." I placed the briefcase on the ground. "Do it."

She growled and used the knife from the back of her waistband to cut the boy's restraints. He wobbled, nearly tripping into the ocean, and she shoved him in my direction.

"It's okay, kid," I said when he finally reached me. "It will be okay."

"Don't lie to the poor boy," the woman said. "Now, the money."

I stepped back from the briefcase, with the boy gripped tightly in one hand and my wand in the other. "*Porth i Lucy.*"

I pushed him towards the green portal that opened behind me. "Meet me at the car, okay?"

He nodded and disappeared into the green. The woman picked up the briefcase and unlatched the sides of it, grinning when she saw the money inside of it.

"I guess we're done here."

"Pleasure doing business with you."

It wasn't the biggest lie I would be telling tonight. I smiled at her before I disappeared into the portal and appeared next to Lucy, where a wide-eyed boy was rocking back and forth on the ground. I hoped against hope he would survive the night.

***

"Are you going to kill me?" he asked when I finally got him seated in the car. He wasn't mad about it or even sad. He spoke with restrained resignation.

"No, we're not going to do that, okay?"

"Really?" He looked at me with wide eyes, almost smiling. "I thought for sure I was going to die."

I nodded, holding my breath as we passed the surveillance truck. Once we had turned the corner and were halfway down the next block, I took the tracker from the backseat and threw it out the window.

"Really," I replied. "I promise we aren't going to kill you."

The phone in my pocket vibrated an unknown number, and I tossed it out the window just as I reached the top of the street and turned the corner. They would all be after me soon, on both sides of the law, but that was a problem for another time. Right now, I had done a good thing and saved a kid from a terrible fate.

***

Twenty minutes later, I pulled into Kimberly's apartment complex and followed the instructions to her penthouse. I had never been there before. It was clean and sparse, perfect for somebody who was constantly on the go and didn't want to grow attached to things. I had left enough homes in the dead of night to know the signs.

"Are you all right?" Kimberly bent down to examine the boy. "What's your name?"

"I'm fine," he said. "At least I think I am. My name is Geordi."

"Are you from Vancouver, in Canada?" Kimberly asked.

He stared. "How did you know that?"

"Your mother has been looking for you. She came to ask me for help finding you."

The boy's face lit up. "You know my mother?"

"Yes, and when it's safe, we'll let you see her, okay? Meanwhile, you talk to my friend Molly, and she's going to make sure you're not hurt, okay?"

Geordi beamed with excitement. "Okay."

"Hi, buddy." Molly appeared from the kitchen, holding a damp towel. "Your mother a big Star Trek fan?"

"Yeah, how did you know?"

"Just a hunch." She gave her broadest and most sincere smile. "Are you hungry?"

He looked at me. "You sure it's safe?"

"I don't know if you should trust me, kid, but yeah, I'm pretty sure."

He turned back to Molly. "I'm starved."

Molly took Geordi's hand and led him into the kitchen. When they'd gone, Kimberly stood up to my level. "How long do you think we have until they figure out where he is?"

I blew out a hot breath. "Oh, the feds probably already know. How well hidden is this place?"

"I bought it through three different shell companies, so it will take some time to crack it, but they'll be here before long. What about the Blue Trident?"

"They know something is wrong by now. I was supposed to go straight there. I don't know if they'll be able to place the connection to you, but they'll figure it out, eventually."

"Then we need to move."

"I have houses in Mallorca, Thailand, and the Dutch Antilles," I replied.

"No offense, but I've been doing this a long time. I can take it from here. I have a place we can keep him safe until the heat dies down and we figure out a more permanent solution."

"And what am I supposed to do? I burned down everything I've built for that kid. I'm going to have both the government and Blue Trident on my ass for this."

"Once we have him settled, I'll come back, and we'll figure out a better plan. Right now, I just want to get him settled, okay?"

"Fine," I grumbled. "As long as you're sure you can keep him safe."

"We are," Molly said." "We have a go-bag. I pac—" A knock on the door interrupted us. "They found us already?"

Kimberly shook her head. "No, that's not a police knock, and I doubt the Blue Trident would announce their presence like that."

A woman slid down to the floor into her arms the second the door opened. She was an angel, my eyes told me that immediately, but she hadn't been born one. This was a woman who had died and was let into Heaven. I didn't even know that was possible anymore, frankly. I hadn't heard of a human being let into Heaven for hundreds of years.

"Help me," she wheezed.

"My gods," Kimberly said with a gasp. "Lizzie? What happened to you?"

BOOK 2

CHAPTER 17

Lizzie

I fell, and I fell, and I fell, wrapped in the bitter cold of space, and then the intense heat of the atmosphere before I crashed into the Redwood Forest outside of San Francisco. I snapped through ancient trees and the crater I created when I landed so deep it took me over an hour to crawl out, my hands slipping against the clay and mud.

By the time I made it to the surface, a half dozen hikers had gathered around me. One of them had the whole thing on his cell phone, and the last thing on the video was a muddy, disheveled angel crushing the phone in her bare hand. The rest of the hikers fled in terror.

"I need your help," I said hoarsely to the terrified man whose phone I'd destroyed. "Where is your car?"

I shuffled along behind him on our way out of the forest. He pulled a thick blanket out of his black sedan and laid it on the passenger's seat to protect the seat from my mess. I slid in and told him Kimberly's address, hoping it was correct. Neither of us said another word the whole way into the city. We just listened to the lilting hum of classical music playing on the radio.

The minute he let me out of the car, he peeled away and got out of there as fast as he could manage. I recognized the tall, modern condo building. It was where I had summoned Talinda, the Time Being.

I pushed open the glass door to the lobby. "Where is Kimberly and Molly's apartment?"

An enfeebled doorman stuttered as I glared. Policy dictated that he stop me, but he must have seen the raw power behind my eyes. He raised a trembling finger toward the elevator and just said, "penthouse."

I pulled the access key from his belt and lurched toward the elevator, relieved when it opened so I could slump against its walls. My body felt every ache and pain from my incredible fall from grace. The elevator dinged on the top floor, and I forced my legs to move forward so that I could knock on the condo door. I hardly made it until it opened, and the last thing I remembered before darkness plunged over me was falling into Kimberly's arms.

***

When my eyes fluttered open again, I was on a big bed surrounded by downy comforters and plush pillows, more comfortable than the fluffiest clouds in Heaven.

I turned my head to the door, and I found Lilith sitting at the edge of the unfamiliar bed, dressed in a simple black shirt and jeans, along with a cropped red leather jacket that looked like it could have come straight from Michael Jackson's "Thriller" video. Her hair was pulled back in a long, straight ponytail and her face was perfectly white, save for a pair of red eyes and matching red lipstick.

"Oh good," she said, uncrossing her legs. "You're awake. How do you feel?"

"Terrible." I tried to sit up, but splitting pain jolted through my head. "Falling from the Elysian Fields to Earth hurts something fierce."

"It will for a little while." She walked over to the nightstand and grabbed a glass, and filled it with a red liquid. "Drink this."

"What is it?"

"It's tomato juice mixed with some herbs and other ingredients from my collection. It's great for a headache, and I imagine you have a doozy." She waited while I took a long chug of the thick liquid. After I wiped my mouth, she continued, "Can I assume things are as bad in Heaven as they are on Earth and in Hell?"

"Well, a group called the Blue Trident has kidnapped God and taken control of Heaven, so yeah, it's pretty bad."

Lilith felt my forehead. "Yes, they are causing all sorts of trouble down here as well. We figure they're trying to open a portal to Hell and unleash the Apocalypse. It's such tired business, you know? I thought maybe they would come up with something original, given they had 10,000 years to prepare."

"They're your children. Can't you do something?"

She laughed. "That's more a ceremonial title than anything. I mother those that return to Earth, but they do not listen to me, especially the Blue Trident. Those that wear the tattoo are righteous and sanctimonious. They would destroy Earth to save it."

"That sounds like them."

She moved her hand to my cheek. "Your color is coming back. How do you feel?"

I finished the drink and sat up. A cool calm passed through my body. The migraine had subsided to a slight dull, and the pain coursing through my legs and arms receded to a light roar. "Better."

"This isn't my first time fixing up fallen angels." She stood up and held out her hand. "Come along, the others are waiting."

She led me into the living room, where Anjelica and Molly were sitting with a woman I only vaguely remembered as Ollie, discussing something that I couldn't make out through my brain fog. When we entered, all eyes turned to me.

"Thank the gods," Molly said, rushing toward me. It was then that I saw the bewildered little boy behind her, trembling with fright. He grabbed at Molly as she left his side to hug me. "How are you feeling?"

"Ow. Worse when you hug me." I groaned. "I'm tender."

"Sorry," she said, releasing me. "I just never thought I would see you again, especially given how God feels about people like me." She studied me for a moment. "You look terrible."

"I feel terrible." I looked over at Lilith. "Better than when I landed, though."

"Yeah," Ollie said. "We heard on the news that a meteorite crashed into the Redwood Forest. I assume that was you?"

I nodded. "It hurt like a mother fu—" I stopped myself when I caught the kid's eye. *Holy shit, I can curse again*! One of the few good things to come from this debacle. Still, I didn't want to start by cursing in front of a kid. "Funkle."

"Nice save." Kimberly rolled her eyes. "Was Lilith right? Does you being here have something to do with the Blue Trident?"

"Yeah. They're causing chaos in Heaven, and we figured whatever they have planned involves Earth, too."

"Unfortunately, that seems to be the case," Ollie said. "They wanted me to deliver this boy to them. I can only assume they mean to sacrifice him to open a gate to Hell."

"We ran every Apocalyptic scenario through our computer," Molly said. "But we can't figure out where he fits into this whole thing. He must have powerful blood, though, for the Blue Trident to want him so badly."

I looked down at the kid. "Are you sure we should be talking about this openly with him?"

"Hey!" The kid threw back his shoulders. "I'm eleven. I can handle it."

I held up my hands. "Sorry."

"Tell me," Kimberly rose to her feet, "how do the Blue Trident's plans stand in Heaven?"

"They've already captured God and have taken control of Heaven. The archangel Michael said there are angels loyal to God, and he stayed in Heaven to rally them."

"At least there are people still on our side," Kimberly muttered. "Aside from the obvious, is there any reason they would want to kidnap God?"

"I can think of one," Lilith said. "The Apocalypse—the real Apocalypse—can't start unless God and Lucifer agree to begin it." She pointed to the boy. "And they are the only two who can stop it. So either they are trying to get one of them to agree to end the world, or trying to prevent them from stopping whatever pseudo-apocalypse they have planned."

"You don't think Lucifer is orchestrating this?" Molly asked.

"No," Ollie cut in. "Not the Lucifer I met, at least. He doesn't seem like the type to lead a revolution."

"I mean, didn't he do it already, though?" I asked. "Isn't that how he ended up in Hell in the first place?"

"Maybe once, but not anymore. He seems more like a washed-up nobody to me." Ollie paused. "Honestly, this sounds exactly like his son Et'atal to me."

"I agree," Lilith said. "However, this is all just conjecture. I think it might be wise to pay them both a visit to ascertain the truth."

Ollie nodded. "That's a good idea. I'll go with you into Hell to talk with them."

"What about me?" I asked. "I have no idea what I'm supposed to do down here." The truth of that statement stabbed at me. I wasn't a warrior, a general, or anything. I was just a stupid girl who died saving the world.

"Can you ask your mother for help, Ollie?" Molly asked.

Ollie shook her head. "She found a guy and went off-world. I haven't seen her for a decade."

"That's a shame." Kimberly looked down for a moment, crinkling her brow, then snapped her fingers. "What about that girl, the one who used to work at The Bar. What was her name? Siobhan, I think."

"What does she have to do with anything?" I asked. "She was just a waitress."

"Yeah, a waitress with a conscience. Maybe she can tell us how to find some angels not working with the Blue Trident."

"It's as good a plan as anything." I nodded. "I guess I'm going to Scotland, then."

"Meanwhile, we'll stay here." Kimberly paced back and forth. "To find out if they've taken any other kids and figure out the extent of their plans."

"I'll get on it right now," Molly said.

She hadn't finished her sentence before a crash, and a thunderbolt struck the window. My arm began to pulsate and throb before it lit up with intense heat from under my skin. I fell to the floor and screamed as four angels flew into the room.

"So nice to see you again, Lizzie," Gabriel said, landing gracefully. "A pity you couldn't keep our deal. Now, you've led us straight to you. I suppose I should thank you for summoning me and letting me out of Heaven."

Oh no. I had forgotten that I had made a deal with Gabriel. We shook on it. I could never tell anyone what he told me, and I had broken that within moments of waking up. I had doomed us all.

You stupid, stupid girl.

CHAPTER 18

Kimberly

"What is he talking about, Lizzie?" I growled.

"This isn't good." Lizzie rubbed her arm. "I…may have made a deal with Gabriel to keep his secrets."

"You *what*?" Lilith screamed. "How could you do something so stupid!"

"Well, I didn't know he was evil at the time!"

"Please, ladies." Gabriel put his hands out. Two angels holding gleaming swords flanked him. "Evil is such a strong word."

"An accurate one, you mean," Lilith spat back.

He cocked his head. "I never liked you, Lilith, but I thought you less myopic. Have you seen what is happening in Hell right now? Millions of human souls suffer because God is incompetent. Is that not evil? I know you demons are cruel, but I never thought you evil. Just born with a willingness to get your hands dirty."

Geordi pulled on Molly's pant leg. "I'm scared."

"Don't worry," Molly replied. "We won't let anything happen to you."

"I wouldn't go that far," Gabriel said with a menacing smirk. "But you can certainly try."

"No matter what is happening in Hell," Lilith said, advancing, "it's no excuse to bring an Apocalypse on Earth."

The archangel nodded in agreement. "It's excessive, I grant you, and we hope it won't be needed." He turned to me. "However, that all depends on Lizzie."

"What is he even talking about?" Ollie asked.

"Gabriel wants me to show him how to get to the Time Being," Lizzie said. "So he can use her to turn back the clock and allow him to join Lucifer in his original revolt instead of abandoning him."

"I have to admit," Lilith said. "That's not the worst idea in the world."

"Yes, it is!" Lizzie shouted. "It's literally the worst idea in the world. Events can only happen one time, and once something has happened, you can't go back and change it. If you try, you create a chronic anomaly in the fabric of time and space, weakening reality, and literally ushering forward the destruction of the universe."

"Would the world be saved, though?" I asked. "Would it prevent an Apocalypse?"

"Of course," Gabriel replied. "I never wanted to destroy the world. I'm here to save it from God's incompetence."

I nodded. "Okay, then I can give you the ingredients you need."

"No!" Lizzie grabbed at me. "You can't do this. Please."

"Molly," I said, shaking her off, "it's in folder 23497 in the B drive."

Molly looked at me for a moment, as if for confirmation, and when I nodded, she swallowed hard. "I'll be right back."

"Can I come?" Geordi asked.

Molly nodded. "Of course, as long as Gabriel is okay with it."

Gabriel shrugged. "Fine, fine, fine. Just hurry."

"I hope you're sure about this," Molly muttered.

"I'm 100 percent sure." I turned to Lizzie. "As for you, how could you risk the whole of this world for your stupid pride?"

"My pride? You bit—" Lizzie balled up her fists and took a swing. I easily ducked it and smashed her in the ribs. When she crumbled, I whispered in her ear. "Trust me, okay?"

She shook with rage, but she didn't fight me. "I'll never forgive you for this."

Ollie caught my eye when I stood up. She spoke slowly, "Are you sure you know what you're doing?"

"I thought you knew me better than to ask that." I grinned.

Molly reentered the room with a smile, her arm over Geordi's shoulder. "All done."

"Where is the ingredient list, then?" Gabriel asked.

She took careful steps away from the kitchen. "About that. I don't think we're going to be able to help you today." She whipped around. "*Duck*!"

I threw myself over Geordi as the wall to the kitchen exploded, sending the angels flying through the wall and into the next apartment.

"Run!" I screamed.

"I really loved this apartment!" Molly shouted over the confusion. "And all those books!"

"Mourn later!" I shoved everyone out the door. We funneled into the hallway as smoke billowed behind us. I kicked open the stairwell, and everyone filed into it, with me pulling up the rear.

"I was so close to killing you," Lizzie shouted.

"Oh, honey. No, you weren't. I eat rookies like you for breakfast." I called out to the others on the stairs, "Okay, at the next landing, half of you grab onto Molly, the other half onto me." I leaped down to the next floor just as the door swung open, and Gabriel rushed forward, covered in ash and dust.

"Now!" I screamed. Four pairs of hands were instantly on me.

I closed my eyes and slipped into the ether. The darkness enveloped me as Gabriel slashed at my chest, and we fell into the abyss. Blood seeped onto my shirt. The pain burned, and I struggled to concentrate. If I lost my focus, we would be trapped in the ether forever.

I squeezed my eyes, envisioning our parking lot, and with a flash of light, we were there.

"Are you okay?" Molly shouted immediately when we materialized.

I pressed my chest, my hands soaked in blood. "I'll be okay. Did you get the hard drive?"

Molly let go of Geordi's hand and held up the drive. "Please. Who are you talking to?"

I grinned at her then turned to the group. "All right, so...Lizzie goes with Ollie and Lilith. Molly and I will take Geordi. Everybody know what they have to do?"

"Absolutely not!" Lizzie hollered back at me as Ollie pulled her toward the car. "I have no idea what I'm going to say when I get to Scotland."

"You'll have to pull it out of your ass!" Ollie shouted, grappling with her. "No more time to talk. We have to go, now!"

Two angels landed at the front of the garage. I pushed Geordi into our SUV as Molly rushed to the driver's seat.

"No!" I screamed after her. "Baby, you drive like an old lady."

"I am an old lady!" Molly snapped. "And you're hurt!"

"I'll deal." I jumped into the driver's seat and slammed it into reverse. The car squealed as we pulled away. Ollie spun her car next to mine so that we were in a line.

"Take out the one on the left," I called over to her. "I'll take the one on the right."

"Got it," Ollie said, shifting her car into gear.

I smashed my foot onto the pedal, and the tires screeched as we sped forward and crashed into the angel. It was strong and heavy, but so was the Four Runner. The angel crashed through the windshield and rolled over the roof before we pulled out of the garage back onto the street.

"Grab my hand!" I shouted.

Molly didn't waste any time. She dropped her hand into mine and squeezed it tightly.

"Tahoe?" she asked.

"I hear it's lovely this time of year."

We closed our eyes, and I flung some pixie dust into the air. The power of our thoughts transported us and the car easily to a two-story wood cabin outside of Tahoe, where I skidded to a stop in the driveway.

"Everyone okay?" Molly asked.

I took another pinch of pixie dust from my pouch and rubbed it on my wound, which started to heal up immediately. "As well as can be expected."

"I'll pull the plates and call a mechanic for the window," Molly said on her way out of the car. Geordi unbuckled.

I leaned my head back. "And I will stay here and catch my breath."

CHAPTER 19

Anjelica

Mephistopheles brought us into the banquet room of his castle, where he had prepared a feast for us. Everything looked foul and disgusting, from meat that hadn't been cooked to soup full of floating eyes; a head with the top of its skull missing, two forks stuck into the brain, perched on the table. Mephistopheles poured a goblet of a red liquid that I identified as blood when the acrid smell filled my nose.

"Sit, sit! Sit and eat. We made this all in your honor, Araphael, and of course you too, Anjelica. Who would have thought that I would entertain a god of death in my humble abode?" Mephistopheles tsk-tsked Araphael when he took a seat at the other end of the table. "No, no. Come by me, honored guest."

"Do you really eat this stuff?" I whispered hoarsely.

"I didn't even think demons ate this kind of thing," Araphael muttered. "Granted, I have indulged in my fair share of Epicurious oddities in my time, but always in moderation. I would have been perfectly happy with pancakes."

I sat down across from Araphael and smiled at Mephistopheles. "It all looks…delicious."

"Does it?" he asked. "I must admit, I thought that your demon palette might have been spoiled by the humans you lived with across the galaxy. What was the name of the planet again?"

"Onmiri."

"Of course, and who is the god of that underworld?"

"Baron Samedi."

He sighed. "Now that is a god. So, unlike the dregs that we've been left with. Well, Lucifer isn't even a god, is he? We haven't had a god in control of Hell in thousands of years, and just look at what has happened."

"What has happened, exactly?" Araphael asked. "In your words."

"Pandemonium, of course—and not in a good way, either. Trust me, I like a bit of chaos as much as the next, but organized chaos is my preferred state. The organization must be top-notch for chaos to thrive. Otherwise, the whole system breaks down."

"And how would you fix it, were you the Devil?" Araphael was probing at something I wasn't quite able to put my finger on yet.

"Direct. I like that." Mephistopheles took a sip of his blood wine. "That's the whole point, isn't it? I shouldn't be the Devil. Only a god has any right to be the true Devil. A god like you."

Araphael laughed. "Oh, not like me."

"Why not? You are already acquainted with the old ways, the customs, the tradition—everything that God and Lucifer flaunt every day of their pitiful lives."

"I am a traveler by nature, Mephistopheles," Araphael said. "I could never be comfortable in any one place for too long."

"On another matter…" I said, clearing my throat. "I am in need of your help, your highness."

This brought Araphael out of his daze, and he smiled at me. "Of course. This isn't about me at all. We're here because you are a powerful demon, and we need your help."

Mephistopheles's eyes narrowed. "Interesting. You expect my help…but what do you offer me in return?"

"What is it you want?" Araphael asked.

"I want your word that you will not interfere in our plans," Mephistopheles said. "There are things set in motion which will turn the pantheon's head, and if the Godschurch were to catch a whiff of it, it would be over before it begins."

Araphael thought for a moment. "I am not here to stop your plans, nor do I want a fight. I am here on behalf of a dear friend and her beloved daughter. I have no interest in involving myself with your affairs."

"Hrm. Then let us see if I can offer you the help you need," Mephistopheles said, studying the both of us. "What can a lowly demon like myself do for one as great and powerful as you?"

Araphael leaned forward. "We are looking for this one's mother. She is lost in Hell, and I thought you might know where she is."

"Of course I do, I saved her myself. I keep all manner of refugees from the pits. After all, it's not like we can count on the gods to save us." His eyes thinned to daggers as he stared at Araphael from a moment, and then turned to me, softening his face. "Would you like to see her?"

I nearly nodded my head off. "Yes, absolutely. Please."

Mephistopheles stood. "Wonderful. Why don't you stay here and get comfortable, Araphael, while I bring this woman to her mother?"

***

The bowels of the castle were even darker and more sinewy than the main floor. Each wall was carved with faces of the damned, screaming for relief from the depths of their souls.

"I know it's a bit…extra, I believe is what they say up on Earth, right?" He cocked his head at me. "Oh, right. You wouldn't know, not being from this planet. I suppose I could say anything about the customs of Earth, and you would have no choice to believe me after being gone for so long."

"Seems like a stupid thing to lie about," I replied. "But yes, it does feel a bit 'extra,' if that's the expression."

Mephistopheles stared at the walls for another moment. "I love it, myself. It reminds me of my past, back when I was but a lowly torturer in the seventh pit."

I traced my finger across a carving of a screaming woman. "You don't seem the type to save souls, Mephistopheles, at least based on these etchings. Why would you save my mother?"

"None of you mortals do understand Hell at all. Our job has always been to cleanse souls in fire, wiping their sins away until they are clean. Noble work. This whole business about torturing souls forever as a punishment for the sins of your mortal life? Simply barbaric."

"It's all barbaric to me."

"That is because you humans have simple minds. It's amazing the gods took such a shine to you."

He turned down another jagged, serpentine corridor, then down a set of uneven stairs. We arrived in front of a large oak door at the end of the hallway, which he opened to reveal a prison. Cells lined either side of the long room, and the moans of hundreds of souls filled the air.

I took an involuntary step back. “What is going on in here?”

“Like I said,” Mephistopheles said. “We are saving these souls, in the old way, the oldest way, and the only way.”

I looked through one of the barred windows into a cell and watched a demon push a hot poker into a poor man’s flesh until he passed out from the pain, his eyes rolling out in his head.

Tears welled in my eyes. “You’re a monster.”

“I promise it’s better than the alternative, smoldering in the pits of Hell forever. One day soon, that man will be free of his sins and off to the heart of creation. It’s beautiful if you think about it.”

“I don’t want to think about it.” A shiver went down my spine. “I just want to see my mother.” I balled up my fists. “And so help me if you’ve hurt her.”

He stopped in the middle of the room, next to one of a hundred non-descript cells. “Please. I am not frightened of you.”

He opened the cell, and inside was an old woman. Her mouth drooped to one side, and her eyes listed away from me. She was dressed in a brown potato sack, covered in mud from head to toe, and she rocked back and forth. All the hope was drained from her eyes, but even through the ravages of age and the horror of Hell, she was still my mother.

“Mom, Mom, Mom!” I hugged her close. “Mom, I’m so glad I found you.”

Her eyes turned to mine, and a slow smile crested on her face. “Anjelica.”

“Yes, Mom, it’s me.”

“You died. How sad.”

“No, Mom.” I smiled at her. “I’m not dead. I’m still alive. I came with Araphael.”

She looked at me with the love only a mother can have, but her happiness was short-lived as her eyes darted to Mephistopheles. Her face dropped. “You have to run. Now.”

Behind me, there was a laugh from Mephistopheles, and the door swung closed. I rushed to the door. “What are you doing? Let me out of here!”

“You can go once we have completed our mission and liberated the souls of Hell.”

“Araphael will never let you do that.”

Mephistopheles smiled a devious smile. “You poor soul. As if we would give him the choice. We’ve already captured him, and he will join you here soon enough. Thank you for helping us wrap up another loose end.”

CHAPTER 20

Ollie

It took a lot of fancy driving, but we finally got rid of the angels on our tail and made our way across the city toward the only person I knew who could help me get into Hell and find Lucifer: Director Chapman.

"We don't have to do this," Lilith said as we walked up the stairs to the secret base. "I have plenty of contacts that could get us into Hell."

"Yes, but do you have any that you can guarantee aren't part of the Blue Trident?" Lizzie asked, trudging up the stairs behind me.

"Come to think of it…" Lilith shook her head. "No, even the ones that aren't part of it might have friends who are. Not many are loyal to Lucifer in Hell, after how Hell has collapsed in the past century."

"There's one thing I know about Director Chapman. She hates demons, especially Et'atal, and definitely does not want to start an Apocalypse." I knocked on the door, and a small inset slid open.

"Password."

"Please don't make me say it."

"Password," the gruff voice demanded.

I rolled my eyes. "Flying Spaghetti Monster."

The slit slid shut, and the door opened. I wasn't even through to the other side before Director Chapman stomped toward us.

"That was a hell of a stunt to pull," she said. "I told myself I was going to rip your throat out if I ever saw you again. Give me one reason not to."

I held up my hand. "Well, you couldn't, for one. But two, I brought Lizzie here to confirm everything I am about to tell you."

"And who is she?" Chapman asked, giving Lizzie a skeptical look.

"She's an angel from Heaven," Lilith said. "She can't tell you what happened lest she reveals herself to the ones after her, but we didn't make any such deal"—Lilith's eyes narrowed at Lizzie— "Because we're not idiots."

"Hey!" Lizzie shouted. "How many times do I have to tell you that I didn't know Gabriel was evil?"

"Gabriel?" Director Chapman said. "Like, archangel Gabriel?"

"Yes, that's right," I replied before turning to Lizzie. "Don't say anything else. We barely got away from him last time, and we can't take the chance that he'll find us again." I turned back to Chapman. "Do you want to hear what we have to say or not?"

She frowned. "I'm listening, tentatively, but you're on thin ice after last night."

"I live on thin ice," I said, smirking. "You might want to sit. What I have to say is going to blow your mind."

"I've heard a lot in my day. It will take a lot to blow my mind."

I told her everything. With each sentence, she slid further and further in her chair. By the end of my story, she was hunched over her knees, head clutched in her hands.

"So…Heaven is against us, angels are working with demons, and we're royally screwed. Is that what you're telling me?"

Lizzie stepped forward. "Everything that Ollie said is the truth, and I think you're probably right on the money with the 'royally screwed' part."

"We need to get into Hell and do it under the radar," I said. "Can you help us?"

Director Chapman looked up at me. "Just the three of you?"

"Two, actually," Lizzie said. "I have my own stuff going on. I'm headed for Scotland. I just came to confirm everything she said."

"If you're an angel, where are your wings?"

"Oh, you don't get wings for just being an angel. You need to do something really incredible and be named an archangel for that to happen. Somehow, even saving the world didn't get them for me. Maybe doing it again will be enough."

Director Chapman pointed at Lizzie. "I only understand about a quarter of what you said, but it's a good thing you're not coming, too. Getting Lilith and Ollie into Hell shouldn't be a problem. Sneaking an angel in is a different story."

"So, you can do it, then?" I asked.

"Of course," Director Chapman replied. "What do you think we've been doing for the past thirty years, having a tea party?"

***

"*Porth i Plockton*, Scotland, The Bar." A green portal spat from my wand behind Lizzie. She gave me a hug and disappeared into it before the portal closed behind her. I turned to Lilith and Director Chapman, who led me to a black van waiting on the street outside of the safehouse.

"That's a fun trick," Director Chapman said. "We've developed something similar. Hold onto your hats."

Lilith lifted her chin. "I would never wear a hat."

Director Chapman gave an exasperated sigh. "It's just an expression."

The driver, a bald, mean-faced man, pulled down a throttle on the dash and red lights flickered all around the van. In a flash of light, we were no longer on the streets of San Francisco, but on a twisty road deep in the woods.

"Don't you worry that somebody will find out you exist, using your magic so blatantly?" Lilith asked.

"Of course not. We control every camera in the city, and if we see something we don't like, we delete it. It's like we never existed, except in the minds of the poor folks who will never be believed except in conspiracy theory message boards."

The trees broke for a moment to reveal we were driving up the side of a mountain. "Where are we?" I asked.

"That is need to know information, Ollie, and you don't need to know."

"I have a phone," Lilith said, pulling out a tiny brick. Director Chapman lunged forward, grabbed the phone, and threw it out the window. "Hey! That's not nice."

"Where you're going, you won't need phones."

The road dead-ended on the side of the cliff, and Director Chapman beckoned for us to follow her to a large boulder. She placed her hand on it, making the rock glow a sickly shade of green before it rolled out of the way to reveal an elevator.

"Very inconvenient place for a base," I said, stepping in behind Lilith.

"Putting stealth above convenience is how we've been able to keep all of this underground for so long." Director Chapman placed her hand on the keypad next to the door, and we started to descend. "Quite literally."

Our downward speed increased until I got a sinking feeling in my stomach. The minute I felt like my body might lift off the ground, the elevator slammed to a stop, and the door opened. The heat caught me at once, so stifling I could barely breathe.

Lilith let out a deep sigh. "Finally, a comfortable temperature. Feels like home."

Director Chapman grabbed a gas mask from the hangers across from the elevator and led us through the cavernous hallways of the underground base. Tubes and cables ran along the rocky walls, and fluorescent lights shone down throughout the many corridors.

Finally, the cavern broke open into a space thirty feet high, where tech covered every surface. The centerpiece of the room was a large, circular metal structure with runes forged along its exterior in a language I had only seen a couple of times in my life: demonic.

Servers and other computers lined either side of the object, feeding thick tubes and clusters of wires into it. Across from the server farm, a large console formed a half-circle. Behind it, a woman in a long white lab coat stood, wearing a gas mask.

"Doctor Holloway," Director Chapman said. "I see you got my message."

"I did, Director, and we'll be ready in a moment. You'll have to forgive her tardiness, but our star is still a bit hungover this morning. She'll be along any time now." There was a rustling behind her as someone shuffled down a long hallway. "Ah, there she is now."

When the person appeared in the room, I was shocked to see someone I recognized. "Aimee?"

Aimee and I had ventured into Hell together once before and barely made it away with our lives. She was a Firestarter, one who could burn a path into Hell with the infernal flame she controlled. She had been so lithe and powerful when we first met. Looking at her now, as pale and skinny as she was, I wasn't sure she'd survived, after all.

"It's good to see you, Ollie," she said. "Finally taking my advice and going to Hell?"

"Well, our last trip was so lovely, I thought I'd make a weekend out of it this time and bring a friend."

She laughed. "You have no idea how bad it's gotten since the last time you were there."

"You're right. And frankly, Aimee, until a few days ago, that was just fine with me."

"You must need something pretty bad to venture back to Hell." She took a swig of the bottle she held between two of her fingers then sighed. "Well, let's get going then. Hell won't wait for us."

"Us?" I raised my eyebrows. "You're coming, too?"

"Can't get there and back without me, unfortunately."

Director Chapman stood between us. "We can magnify her powers, but we still need her spark to get into Hell and back out again. Aimee has been most helpful—indispensable, honestly—over the years in helping us to map the floor of Hell and allowing us to study the underworld."

"As if I had a choice." Aimee smiled at me. "Yup, I'll be your tour guide. Please keep your hands and feet inside the vehicle at all times, or you're likely to be disemboweled."

CHAPTER 21

Lizzie

The portal spat me out on a non-descript street. It was colder than San Francisco, and the people staring at me wore wool coats and thick caps. Bushy beards covered the men's faces, and the women had deep scowls molded onto their faces. They took notice of me for a moment, and then their eyes went blank as if I had disappeared. They snapped their necks away and went about their business.

Weird, but not the weirdest thing I've seen recently.

I turned my attention toward the houses along the street, trying to remember where to find The Bar, a safe haven for angels and demons alike. Two hundred-odd years ago, a man accidentally summoned a demon while making breakfast, and they became unlikely friends. Their friendship brought more demons, and angels came to spy on them. Through it all, the man kept all of them happy with beer and food. He only had one rule—no fighting in his house.

Both parties agreed to honor it, and over time it became a safe space for demons and angels to mingle, morphing and molding itself until nearly every monster paid their respects to the place when they came through Scotland.

It had to be one of these houses, but I wasn't sure which one. *How had we found it the last time?* I noticed that people crossed the street rather than pass a certain house. Moving toward it, I saw the purple orb pulsating around the house. *Bingo.*

I needed to run through without hesitation, or the power of the barrier would consume me. I tensed every muscle in my body, preparing for a jolt of pain, and stepped forcefully through.

I cracked my jaw and pulsed my fingers into my palm when I was safely on the other side, trying to regain feeling in them. After a few seconds, the pins and needles subsided, and I walked inside. I expected dozens of demons and angels jamming into the tables, but there was nobody in the place except for a small imp guzzling booze on the end of the bar. I recognized the stocky, red-headed bartender drying some pint glasses.

"Are you closed?" I asked, walking to the long wooden bar.

"Not closed, just empty," the man replied, not looking up. "Not much business these days."

"That's a shame. This place was packed last time I was here."

"Packed until about a month ago. Then, everyone stopped coming." He pointed to the imp at the end of the table. "Except Charlie over there."

"Another!" Charlie shouted, tossing a gold coin on the table, followed by another. "And whatever the lady wants."

"Oh, no thanks. I don't drink."

"Now's a great time to start, what with the end of the world coming." Charlie smacked his leg. "No better time."

"The end of the world, huh?" I said, sliding into the stool beside him. "What do you know about it?"

"I know it's coming, and—" His head slammed onto the table, knocked out asleep.

"Don't bother with Charlie," the bartender said. "He's been predicting the end of the world for decades now."

"He might be right this time. That's the thing with Apocalypse predictions. They only need to be right once." I waited as he scooped the coins from the table and counted them. "I don't suppose Siobhan is working today?"

He shook his head. "I had to let her go last week. I paid this place off a long time ago, but I can't afford to keep on staff with no customers."

I sighed. "Great, just great."

"What do you need from her?" he asked over his shoulder, placing the gold coins in his register. "Maybe I can help."

"Don't suppose you know anything about the Blue Trident, do you?"

"Sure, I do." He was facing me now, leaning back against the back counter where they mixed drinks. "Hard to miss them in a place like this. They kept me in business for quite a few years." He stroked his bushy beard. "Come to think of it, most of them were my best customers."

I pressed my hands on the bar. "Could that be why this place is empty? Because they don't come in anymore?"

"Could be. Honestly, I don't know. I just sling drinks." The bartender took a rag and started wiping down some already-clean spots on the bar. "Charlie, though. He loves getting up in people's business. I'll bet he can help you if he ever wakes up."

"Fair enough," I said. "Do you have any coffee?"

"Of course. This is a bar."

"Two cups, please."

He grunted. "It's going to get cold by the time he wakes up."

"I know," I replied with a smile. "They're both for me."

***

Charlie's eyes fluttered open after about an hour, and he growled immediately at the light streaming onto his face. I had already finished two cups of coffee in that time and went to the bar to pick up a cup for him, sliding it under his chin as he rose from the table.

He wrapped his hands around the cup and took a sip. "Thanks."

"Don't thank me," I said. "I used your coin to get these. The most expensive cups of coffee ever."

"Would be better if it was scotch, but whatever." He downed the rest of the piping cup like it was a glass of sweet tea on a hot summer day, slamming it down when it was done. "So, what can I do for you, toots?"

I grimaced. I didn't have to like Charlie. I just needed him to help me. "The bartender said you kept tabs on all the angels and demons that came through here."

"That's one way to put it. Another way is that I keep a ledger full of people who owe me things, and just about everyone owes me."

"Does that include people who aren't part of the Blue Trident?"

He pressed his finger to my lips. "Shhh, we don't say that here. This is a happy place."

"Fine then. Do you think I could see that ledger?"

"Of course." He slid his hand over mine. "It's back at my place."

I yanked my hand away. "Ew!"

He sat back and shrugged. "Well, I don't work for free. Cash, grass, or ass."

I narrowed my eyes. "Do you have a phone?"

Kimberly had given me her number before we parted ways, and I called her using Charlie's phone. After a quick hello, I filled her in.

"Be careful with that one. He's a snake."

"I've…gathered that." I gave Charlie a sidelong glance. "I need some cash."

Kimberly sighed. "Sounds about right. Get his PayPal and how much. I'll send it to him right now."

"What is a PayPal?"

"He'll know." There was a long silence. "This is a really bad idea, just FYI."

"Well, we don't have any good ideas, so I guess a bad one will have to do."

***

Kimberly transferred $10,000 into Charlie's PayPal account, and thirty minutes later, he was stumbling down the road toward his apartment.

"This isn't my only home, of course," Charlie slurred. "But the other ones are all warded to prevent people from snapping in or out. It helps to have one within walking distance of my favorite bar."

"Why does everyone like The Bar so much?" I asked. "Seems kind of skeezy to me."

He laughed, which knocked him off balance, and he swayed, trying to right himself. I grabbed him to keep him from toppling over and held his arm as we continued down the street.

"Everywhere else you gotta wear a mask, especially as a demon. But there? You can just be yourself." He turned into an alley when he saw a woman walking toward us. "Speaking of."

He took a breath and waved his hands over his body so that he transformed from an imp to a small man, hunched over, with a gray mustache that covered his mouth and scrunched up when he spoke.

"See what I mean? I'm one of the most powerful beings on this planet, and I have to stay hidden because Lucifer doesn't want humans to know we exist."

"That seems logical," I said after we'd passed the woman with a short nod as a greeting. "It would've scared the piss out of me to see a demon walking around."

"Angels don't have to hide themselves because they look like humans, do they? Since you were created in the gods' image, and we were created to do his dirty work."

"Were you part of Lucifer's uprising?"

"No!" He snapped and opened the door to an unremarkable apartment complex. "I'm a paper pusher. We demons are a noble race, created well before Lucifer's rebellion. But when God cursed his precious angels to look like us, I knew what he really thought of us. Could you imagine if somebody thought it was a curse to look like you?" He swayed past a stairwell and walked to a door behind it. "Whatever. It's fine. I'm just rambling."

He led me inside the apartment. It was plain but nice. There was nothing that would indicate he was an imp. Even the pictures were of him as a human and a family that seemed quite pleasant.

I pointed to one of them. “Is this your wife?”

“Manipulation.” He waved his hand, and the shroud fell. Now the frames showed an imp and two young implings that resembled Charlie. They were equally as hideous as him, but after what he’d just told me, I almost found them sweet as well, in a way I couldn’t quite explain.

“Nice family.”

Charlie’s smile was different this time. It seemed genuine, not conniving. “Thanks. I’m sure you’ll meet them soon enough.”

I puzzled over what he meant, but it didn’t take long for him to reveal his true intentions. He slammed his hand against my chest, and I flew backward through an open doorway.

“Sorry about this,” he said, stalking over to me.

I rushed to escape, but he banged the door closed and the lock clicked, sealing me in. “No!”

“Don’t worry, toots. Gabriel isn’t unreasonable. If you do exactly what he says, he might even let you go.” He cackled. “And thank you for giving me Kimberly’s number. It’s going to be so much easier to track her now.”

“Let me out of here!” I shouted, bloodying my fists against the door. It was useless. I had doomed myself and Kimberly. *You’re an idiot, Lizzie.*

CHAPTER 22

Anjelica

The air in Hell was pure red heat, but in my cell in the basement of Mephistopheles's castle, it was impossibly cold. I wished I was wearing something warmer than a polka dot dress. In fact, thinking about it now, it would have been nice to change before I traveled to Hell.

"I hate this." My teeth were chattering as I spoke.

"You're not supposed to like it," my mom replied. "Mephistopheles said it will help purify me, and once I am pure, I don't have to suffer ever again. When I am pure, I can return to the source of all creation. Any suffering is worth it, especially if it will allow me to escape this place."

I grabbed her arm forcefully. "Listen to me. That's some psycho bullshit designed to keep you docile. Torture is not going to do any of that, do you understand? You're just getting it for amusement because demons are sick."

"I don't believe that." She smiled at me, a lone tear falling down her cheek. "I have to believe this is worth it. Don't you understand that Mephistopheles has given me hope in a hopeless place? Before him, we had nothing to look forward to except an eternity of pain. Now, there is at least a glimmer of hope. It's all I have to hang on to."

Shackles dragged against the floor in the hall. I wouldn't have time to talk sense into Mom just then. I hopped up and rushed to the window of the cell, hoping against hope that they hadn't captured Araphael, my only chance at escape. My heart dropped when I saw his head slung low, being led past by two demons.

"Araphael!" I shouted. "Araphael!"

"Anjelica?" His head perked up. "Is that you?"

"Yes, it's me!" I held my fingers out of the cell so he could see me. My whole hand wouldn't fit through, but he saw my dancing phalanges in the air and reached his hand to my fingers. "It's good to see you."

"I'm so glad that they haven't vaporized you yet," Araphael said. "Whatever you do, get out and don't come back for me. Do you hear me? Do not come back for me."

I felt a surge of power dart through me as the demons pulled Araphael away from my cell. I screamed after him, but it was no use. They wouldn't stop marching him down the dank, dark hallway.

I have to do something. This might be my only chance to save Araphael—for us to escape.

I reared my hand back and smashed it through the door of the cell. I had tried it before, but even with my demon strength, I couldn't break through it. With whatever power Araphael left in me by the touch of his hand, the door cracked in half when my fist connected, flying off its hinges across the dungeon.

"Come on, Mom." I held out my hand. "We're going."

"No!" She recoiled. "I have to stay. I have to atone for my sins."

"No, Mom. You don't. You didn't do anything wrong."

"Oh, I did plenty of things wrong, sweet girl. So much wrong. I deserve all this and more."

I stepped over to her and crouched down so we were eye to eye. “If you don’t come with me, I won’t be able to save you.”

“You don’t have to save me, sweetie. I’m saving myself by staying right here.”

A dozen footsteps clomped at the end of the hall. She would slow me down, fighting me to stay, and then I would never escape. I could see that look in her eyes, that stubborn resolve. I had no choice but to leave her.

“I’ll come back for you, somehow.”

I rushed out of the cell as two squadrons of guards headed for me. I had trained for this moment with demons in Onmiri. They showed me how to use my powers, but I never thought I would need to do so for real.

“*Alfiri zanto*!” I screamed.

I smashed my hand against the floor, and a cascade of fire exploded from me, knocking two of the guards to the ground.

“*Ritilo*!”

A second pair of demons smashed backward into the wall when I punched the air, causing two firebolts to shoot down the corridor. I slid off my yellow headband and wrapped it around a pike as another demon stabbed at me. The captain of Margaret’s guard had trained me to fight, and even though I looked like a forty-some-year-old woman, that was only for appearances. I was as spry as a sixteen-year-old, and I fought like I was in the prime of my life.

I pulled the pike from the demon’s hand and used it as a pole vault to leap over the pack toward Araphael, still being led to his cell by his demon guards. I smashed the first one through with the butt of my newly acquired weapon, then sliced the other's neck with the blade. I unlocked Araphael's legs with the keys I pulled off of one of their belts.

"I told you not to come for me!" he shouted.

"And you know I'm very bad at following directions. Now let's go!"

We headed up a set of stairs at the far end of the dungeon, which led us to a long hallway, which connected to another, and another, until we finally reached the main floor of the castle. The clamoring of demon soldiers was never far behind. I looked around, but there was nowhere to go. We had reached a dead end, with only the castle wall behind us and a single exit down the long corridor in front of us.

"Shit," I muttered, sliding the headband over my hair. "Can you teleport us out of here?"

"There's a barrier around the castle. That's why I had to bring us here from so far away."

"Then it looks like I have to smash through this wall. *Igit*!" I shouted, and my hands erupted in hot liquid magma as I pounded against the nearest wall.

My stomach fell to my toes when a group of soldiers came around the corner. I went to attack, but Araphael held me back. He moved forward and touched the first demon. The demon stood still, and Araphael pulled white goo from its head.

"What are you doing?"

"Creating an army from these demon's souls," he replied, flinging the white goop on the ground. It rose in the form of a glowing white zombified demon. Araphael pointed at the other demons rushing us. "Attack!"

The goopy demon rushed the others, smashing through them as Araphael made two more from the souls of the defeated demons. I returned to my task of smashing through the wall. With three more good strikes, I was feeling a lot of pain, and my hands were bloody, but I'd managed to crack the wall.

"Unfortunately, with my hands bound, I have only a fraction of my powers."

I swung back my leg and slammed it through the cracked wall. "I'll free you when we've put some distance from this place. Oh, hell—"

I had planned to jump, figuring I could survive a five-story drop. No problem. But we were on the edge of the cliff that sandwiched in the castle. There was barely enough room to squeeze through toward the light at the front of the castle, let alone jump to the ground.

"Let's go!" I said anyway, pushing myself out onto the ledge.

The rocks sliced into my back, and blood trickled down my spine as I shuffled along the ledge. I was halfway toward the front of the castle when Araphael stepped out as well. A second after he appeared, a dozen red claws appeared around him and pulled him back.

"Araphael!"

But my screams did not lead to him reappearing. Two demons poked their heads out instead. Too wide to fit, they hurled rocks at me, cutting my head and arms as I moved along, nearly tripping on the slick rock face.

I reached the front of the castle, my body cut and bruised but free of the cliff that wedged me in. Below me, a battalion of soldiers had gathered, surrounding where I might fall.

"*Vernili*!" I screamed.

I wound up my fist as I leaped off the building, as close to the center of the troops as possible. When I reached the ground, I slammed my fist into the dirt, causing an explosion that sent the demons flying all around me.

I pushed myself up and rushed toward the edge of the next cliff. A dozen arrows fired around me from the tops of the castle as archers took aim. I was able to avoid the first barrage, but with the second, two arrows pierced my shoulder, and another my left leg. I continued forward and tumbled over the edge.

I skidded along the rocks the whole way down the side until landing on the ground below, bruised and bleeding. I tried to focus and attempted to stand, but I was too broken. It pained me to inhale. I rolled over, trying to drag myself along the ground, but the agony was too intense. As I fought to stay awake, a hooded figure approached.

If I died, at least it would have been for freedom. That's something, isn't it?

CHAPTER 23

Kimberly

I knew that the damage was done the second I got off the phone with Lizzie. Gabriel would be coming for me any minute now that Charlie had my number. There was a 100 percent chance he would betray Lizzie. In fact, I was counting on it.

"How long until Charlie tells Gabriel where we are?" I asked, passing the couch where Geordi was watching TV. As I walked across the room, I went about erasing all content on my cell phone and setting it back to factory default.

Molly looked up from the computer she'd been staring at intently for the last few hours. "I give it thirty minutes, assuming he takes Lizzie back to his place in Plockton. Maybe a little longer if he brings her somewhere else."

"He won't teleport," I said. "He'll go to his place in Plockton. He's nothing if not lazy and predictable."

"Thirty minutes it is, then."

"That gives you thirty minutes to get to the safe house in Buenos Aires."

Molly started typing. "Shouldn't be an issue. I've almost got everything cross-referenced, and—there we are." She peered at the screen. "This isn't good."

I looked over her shoulder at a spreadsheet filled with dozens of cells coded with different colors. "What does this mean?"

"If you'd taken the time to learn my system, I wouldn't have to explain it to you." She sighed. "According to this, there are six prophesies that could converge on each other in the next two days. Geordi's prophesy could be any of these."

"Bring the hard drive to Argentina and keep working on it. Meanwhile, make sure all our people are on high alert. Now that the Blue Trident doesn't have Geordi, they might get desperate and start abducting fairy children."

Molly turned to me, her forehead crinkled. It made her look cute. "But that wouldn't make a stable portal. It's not hard to close a portal like that."

"Desperate times," I said with a shrug. "If those guys are looking to ease the overcrowding in Hell, even a temporary fix is better than none at all."

Molly nodded. "I'll get in touch with our guys and ask them to create a telephone tree. By tonight we need to be able to contact more fairies on the planet."

"Good," I said. "Open all our safe houses to them and tell them to wait for further instructions."

"What about me?" Geordi asked.

I smiled at him. "You call your mom and tell her you're all right and that you'll see her soon."

"Why can't I just go home?"

I pursed my lips. "Because right now, people want to hurt you. If you go home, they'll hurt your parents, too. You don't want that, do you?" He shook his head. "That's good."

I kissed Molly goodbye. It pained me every time I had to leave her, every time. The things we did were difficult and dangerous. She was also my best ally in the fight against evil, and I just wanted to keep her safe.

“Be careful,” I said as I walked toward the door.

“I will, silly. I’d say the same for you, but we both know that’s impossible.”

Outside, the sun warmed my skin. I savored the feeling. It would be dark now in Scotland. I closed my eyes and imagined The Bar, making it real in my mind, then threw a pinch of pixie dust and disappeared into the ether, reappearing on the street of Plockton in the middle of the night.

I made my way through the small city to Charlie’s apartment. The front face of the building was made of red brick with symmetrical windows every few yards in equal rows up and down each side. Charlie’s apartment was on the first floor, one of the only ones with a walkout patio.

I approached the complex from the back. The lights were on, and Charlie was distracted with a phone call—probably to Gabriel. I snuck toward the bedroom window and saw Lizzie huddled against the door. I couldn’t just break in. The apartment was magically warded for sure. I’d need Charlie to open the door willingly.

I waited until he was off the phone before I walked up, making sure to remain hidden, and knocked against the glass door from the shadows.

“Jesus, that was quick,” Charlie said as he slid open the back door. “You angels are really efficient. It’s unnerv—”

The second the door unlatched, I crashed into him, sending him to the apartment floor. “Hi, Charlie.”

“Aw, shit, Kimberly!” He growled, grabbing his nose. “You almost broke it.”

“You got off easy!” I pulled him up by the scruff of his neck and slammed him into the bedroom door. “Open it.”

“I don’t know what you—”

I pulled a dagger out of my belt and stabbed it into his side. “I won’t ask again.”

“Fine!” He shouted, snapping his fingers. The lock clicked, and the door opened. “You need to work on your manners.”

Lizzie jumped up. “Oh, thank go—”

“No, time,” I said. “They’re on their way. What were you looking for here?”

“A book,” Lizzie said, frantic. “One that listed all the angels and demons Charlie had ever met.”

I pulled him toward me. “Where is it, Charlie?”

He chuckled. “I’ll never tell.”

His hand twitched like he was going for a spell. I sliced through the air and cut off both of his thumbs, rendering his powers useless. He screamed as the green blood spouted from his hands.

“What did you do that for?”

“Where is it, Charlie?” I shouted. “Tell me! Otherwise, I’ll cut off a lot more than that.”

“In the kitchen, top drawer next to the sink.” He slinked back toward Lizzie. “It’s nothing personal, you know. I would still give you a throw.”

“Gross,” Lizzie said, pushing him away.

I ripped open the kitchen drawer and found a legal-sized notepad, bound in leather with a summoning circle carved into the front. Inside, it listed page after page of debts and credits to Charlie from the last thousand years, written first in blood, then with quill, and finally with pen.

"I don't know what any of these symbols mean." They were written in demonic, a language I couldn't read no matter how much I studied.

"Nobody knows how to read it, except another demon!" Charlie cackled.

"Then it looks like you're coming with us."

The imp's eyes bulged. "You're crazy."

"If you don't, you'll have to look Gabriel in the eyes and tell him you lost his prize. How do you think he's going to take that?"

There was a brilliant flash of light outside, and for a moment, night became day. When it dissipated, three winged figures appeared in silhouette on the other side of the glass sliding door.

"That's them," I said, eyebrow raised. "Tick tock."

"Fine!" Charlie shouted. "I'll come!"

"Good choice." I slammed open the front door and shuffled Charlie and Lizzie into the night air.

CHAPTER 24

Ollie

Aimee closed her eyes and placed her hand on the circular structure. Its demonic runes began to glow a deep, throbbing red, like the embers of a dying fire. She turned back to the doctor at the controls of the device that would bore the way into Hell for us.

"I have a signal," the woman in the lab coat said. We all stepped back. "We're ready to initiate."

A flurry of button presses ended with a pulse echoing low through the air, like a giant heart filling the room. Between beats, the light from the edges of the circle filled into the center, flickering in time with the beat.

The heartbeat cut out, replaced by a quick slice and a crackle as lightning splintered across the face of the mechanical circle, and then, like a rock crashing into the ocean, a thunderous splash reverberated through the room, and the light fell from the face of the circle in a cone until it came to a point at the back of the room.

Through it, I saw Lucifer's castle in the distance, ominous and black against the glowing magma from the lava lake that guarded his castle from intruders.

Aimee took a final swig of liquor before slamming the bottle to the ground. She stepped toward the image. I looked back at Lilith, who nodded her head and continued along behind Aimee. Everything slowed down as I stepped toward the gate. I heard the sound of metal meeting my boots and the smell of heat, not the heat of summer, or even a bar-b-que, but of a forest fire, raging out of control, with an unquenchable desire to consume everything completely, mind, body, and soul.

My stomach dropped to my knees and rebounded back into my throat before settling back down in my gut, and then the insufferable heat was all around me. The stench changed to that of vulcanized rubber, and enormous towers of swaying humans filled my vision, covering the view of Lucifer's castle from just moments ago.

"Shit, man." I coughed. "What is going on with all these disgusting towers? There's ten times more of them than last time."

Aimee grunted. "You really haven't been back here since the 80s."

I shook my head, not taking my eyes off of the towers. "No. It's not exactly my idea of a good time."

"Agreed," Lilith said. "I hate coming here. And it gets worse every time. Let's just get this over with. Where to? Et'atal's castle or Lucifer's?"

"As much as I want to mess Et'atal up if he had something to do with this, Lucifer's the only one with the power to start and end the Apocalypse, right?" I paused. "Even if he's not part of this, we need to make sure he's okay. So that's where I would start."

"Sensible," Lilith said with a head tilt. "I agree."

"Follow me, then," Aimee said, walking toward the piles of humans. "We shouldn't run into any demons before we get to the rock cliff."

We snaked around the towers of charred and screaming human souls. They were stacked so close to each other all we could do was turn sideways and shuffle past. When the bodies saw us coming, they reached for us with whatever limbs they had free from being crushed by thousands of people. I couldn't avoid them as I inched by and shuddered when their burnt fingers grazed against me, leaving ashy filth all over my clothes.

"This is a horrible way to die," I said as we walked through the swaying masses.

"It's a horrible way to be dead," Lilith corrected. "They don't have enough demons to deal with the influx of humans, which means they needed to find a way to torture a lot of people with the least effort possible."

"Have they ever thought about…I don't know, *not* torturing them?" Aimee asked pointedly.

Lilith snorted. "I highly doubt the idea ever crossed their minds."

"See, that's the problem with you demons. You can dress as nice as you want and talk as good as you want, but you're all still psychos in the end."

"Rude," Lilith said.

It only took us a couple of hours to reach the sheer cliff face that separated the great towers of human souls from Lucifer's castle. When we arrived, I pointed past the lake of magma that guarded it.

"Is this where that secret entrance to Lucifer's castle is?"

"Yes, except that it's hidden by an illusion. After you waltzed in last time, he's made it nearly impossible to spot." Aimee shuffled along the rock wall. "It's around here somewhere, I just need to rem—there!" She pointed up. High on the side of the cliff, a ledge materialized. "Okay, grab a stack and climb."

I turned around and pulled myself up onto the nearest stack of bodies. They clawed and screamed at me while I searched for a foothold.

"This is disgusting!" Lilith said from underneath me. The pile of bodies swayed so far to the left we nearly fell. "I feel like I'm playing Jenga, only with the moaning, charred souls of humanity."

"A disgusting, horrible, twisted form of Jenga, but yeah," Aimee said. "You have to keep your balance and the balance of the whole pile, or we'll fall, and that would not be the business."

Every step was precarious as the souls struggled against us, along with the weight of the towers. The higher I went, the more they tipped. After an hour, we were high enough to leap toward the cliff. It was still pretty far, but we were desperate to get away from the moaning bodies. Aimee jumped first, using a burst of fire from her hands to propel her.

I pulled the wand out of my pocket. "*Naid hir.*" I touched the wand to my breast and felt a charge jolt through me, giving me a boost of power as I pushed off the stack. With the extra energy from my spell, I easily leaped across the chasm and landed safely on the other side.

"Shit!" Lilith screamed.

Her eyes were wide with terror as the stack of bodies teetered precariously. I hadn't taken into account how my extra-strength leap would jostle the pile. It swayed so far that it tipped, and the souls rained down, shrieking as they fell through the air.

"Help me!" Lilith fell further down the tower.

"*Porth i mi*!" I pointed it at the air beneath her, and a green portal appeared. "Jump!"

Lilith leaped from the souls and into the portal as they clawed at her legs. She tipped forward into the abyss, and another portal appeared above me. I caught her in my arms before she could tumble over the ledge to the ground below.

"Put me down," she growled, scrambling away from me.

"Sorry."

We stood together and watched the toppling towers of human souls. One crashed into another, which smashed into the next, like dominos tipping each other over across the entire expanse of Hell.

"That's…not going to be good, is it?" I said from the side of my mouth, still watching the destruction unfold.

"No, but we have bigger things to worry about." Aimee turned to the thirty-foot locked door in the rock face. "Like how to open this door."

Lilith's face dropped. "You brought us to a door, and you didn't have the key?"

"Yeah, kinda. Ollie said she just pushed the doors open, but when we tried, it was locked up tighter than a seal's butthole. We've been trying for a decade to break it down, still nothing."

Lilith sighed and pulled a key from her pocket. She held it up. "Luckily, I picked this up a long time ago. Cost me a fortune, but I thought I might need it someday. Seems like today is that day."

"That's convenient," I said, deadpan.

CHAPTER 25

Anjelica

The hooded figure stood against the harsh landscape of Hell, the swaying stacks of souls behind it. I could barely make out the outline of its body through the charred bodies that blotted out the red, orange, and yellow fires of Hell. Its eyes didn't glow like Araphael's, but somehow the darkness of the shadows cutting across its face and the nothingness behind its hood was even more unsettling.

It stepped forward slowly but didn't make a sound. Not even the daggers on either side of its belt jingled as they smacked the rivets in the leather around it. It slid the bow off its back and went for the quiver. I tensed, sure that I was going to die from an arrow to the heart, but instead, the figure placed them both on the ground and slid to a knee next to me.

"Are you all right?" It was a woman's voice, low and gravelly. She pulled her hood back to reveal a dark-skinned woman with bright green eyes and pointed ears. She looked me in the eyes for a second and then down to my clothes, frayed and cut from my tumble down the mountain. "That was quite a fall."

I rubbed my head. "I am a lot of things, but not a goddamn one of those things is all right. I was trapped in the dungeon with my shell of a mother, lost my friend in Mephistopheles's castle, got several arrows in my back, and tumbled down a mountain. I'm pretty terrible, truth be told."

The woman looked me up and down again and gestured toward one of the arrows still lodged in my shoulder. "Looks like the mountain dislodged most of the arrows. There's just one left. You're lucky."

"I don't feel very lucky, Miss—what's your name?"

"Akta," she replied. "Stay still."

"Akta." I turned to look at her. "The monster hunter pixie?"

"Stay still," she warned, then answered, "In another life, maybe."

"I've heard of you."

She pressed her hand into my back. "Not surprising."

"Get that a lot?"

"Enough," she said. "I have a bit of a reputation." She touched the arrow, and a pain shot through me. "I have to push this through. It's going to hurt something fierce."

I grabbed my tattered headband and stuffed it into my mouth. "Do what you have to."

I had been trained to tolerate pain by the royal guards. As one of the most likely people in all Onmiri to be kidnapped, and privy to many state secrets, it was essential I knew how to comport myself even under intense pressure and pain. That didn't make it pleasant when Akta pressed the arrow through my shoulder. I gritted my teeth as she gripped the bloody shaft and pulled it out.

"Red blood," she said, examining it. "Are you human?"

I nodded, falling back down to the ground. "Half, and half demon."

She tossed the arrow away and grabbed a glass bottle from a pouch on her belt. It glittered pink and felt cool when it touched my skin which surprised me, considering we were in the bowels of Hell.

“Take off your dress and turn around,” she said, slathering her finger with more of the pink.

Gingerly, I did what she asked. The dress stuck to the blood on my back, so she helped me rip the shirt portion off.

“You’ve gotten through the worst of it,” Akta replied, rubbing the paste on my back. My shoulders pinched together like my skin was sewing itself back together. “And this will help. We don’t have much pixie dust down here, but after 3,000 years, I’ve learned a trick or two about how to replicate it. It’s not as potent, but it does the job.”

“You’ve really been down here for that long?” I asked, vacillating between pain and pleasure as my back mended itself.

“It feels like much longer,” she said softly. “And the days move slower recently. It might be hard to believe given how horrible this place has become, but for a long time, Hell was tolerable, even pleasant at times.”

“You’re right.” I groaned. “I don’t believe it.”

When she finished applying the salve, she helped me sit up. I already felt better than I had a few minutes ago. My head still throbbed, and the rest of my body ached, too, but it wasn’t impossible to breathe anymore; the slightest movement didn’t send me writhing.

“That’s good stuff. You could make a fortune bottling it.”

“My people’s history is not for me to sell.” She reached behind her back and pulled out a waterskin. “Here, drink.”

I grabbed the skin and downed half of it, barely stopping to realize just how the water scalded my tongue.

"Thank you," I said, taking another deep chug.

"I keep that for souls that have escaped the pits, but you need it more." She took the waterskin when I handed it back to her. "Tell me, human, how did you make it down here?"

I considered lying to this woman I'd had only heard about in myth, but I didn't have the constitution for deception at the moment. Besides, if she was anything like the hero in the stories, she would appreciate honestly about all else.

"I came with Araphael, the god of death."

"*A* god of death," she corrected. "He is one of many who wear the mantle across the universe."

"You're right, sorry. A god of death."

"Precision is essential to understanding." Akta stopped for a moment. "That explains how you arrived here, but not why."

"I came to find my mother, who was lost after her death. We tried to perform a séance, and when she didn't answer, I knew something was wrong, so I came here."

"You have powerful friends to even attempt such a thing," Akta said. "It's not easy to get into Hell, especially these days. I heard our waiting list for entry is a thousand years long and growing."

"I don't think having a 'cut the line' pass into Hell is anything to brag about."

"I guess that depends on what you're after," Akta replied. "And Araphael, he is the friend you lost in Mephistopheles's castle?"

I nodded. “Him and my mother. I barely escaped with my life and probably wouldn’t have if you didn’t come along.”

“They will assume you are dead and wait for your body to materialize at Hell’s entrance so they can capture you again,” Akta said. “They won’t start looking for you until they realize you have not died, which gives us an advantage for the time being.”

“You know the Time Being?” I asked.

Akta gave me a concerned look. “Maybe you hit your head worse than I thought.”

“No.” I touched my scalp, where there was some dried blood, but not a gaping wound anymore. “I know it’s just an expression. I thought—never mind.”

“You’re an odd one,” she said. “But you do not seem like a threat. Can you stand?”

I pushed myself to my knees and slowly rocked myself to stand. My legs were sorer than at any time I could remember, and I stepped forward with wobbly legs. “I think I can manage.”

“I have a place you can rest. The pixie dust will work its way through your system in the next few hours, and then you’ll feel better than you ever have before. Meanwhile, I can—”

She stopped dead and crouched, arms extended. It took me a second, then I heard it too: the low moan and crunching in the distance. It was getting louder. Akta took a moment to check her surroundings before swinging her body around to look behind her. When she did, her eyes went wide with fear, and she grabbed me with a rough hand, pulling me forward.

“Run!”

Before I could get my legs moving, a charred body fell from the sky, missing me by a couple of inches. Akta pushed me away just in time. I stumbled backward, and another body crashed toward me. Once again, Akta tackled me out of the way, this time rolling us further from the cavalcade of bodies. The pixie leaped to her feet and pulled me with her. My arms ached with pain, but the adrenaline and pixie dust mixing in my system gave me the energy to follow her through the stacks of charred souls.

"What's happening?" I shouted. Bodies fell from the sky like a horrible torrent of rain.

"The towers are collapsing!" Akta shouted, diving between two stacks of bodies that had yet to crumble. "I knew this would happen. I told Lucifer, but did he listen to me? No, he did not. He said this was the best way. Gods, he's such an idiot."

I slid around another stack of bodies as the ones behind us collapsed. The storm of souls inched closer.

"There!" Akta screamed, pointing to a cave cut into the cliffside in front of us.

The desiccated people screamed for relief, clawing at me with their withered hands, slicing open the cut that hadn't even scabbed over yet. A pair of hands, stronger than the others, held me back as the tidal wave came to engulf me.

"Help!" I shrieked wildly.

A second later, Akta's hand yanked me forward, her dagger slicing through the arm. I stumbled forward and followed her as another wave crashed to the ground. All around me, the stacks collapsed, threatening to crush me. With one last heave, we slipped inside the cave.

"Get back!" Akta screamed. More bodies landed, sealing us in the cave, where the screams of the damned echoed off of the walls.

CHAPTER 26

Lizzie

I rematerialized with Kimberly and Charlie on a hilly meadow full of fluffy red, yellow, and purple flowers overlooking a mountain range.

"Let's go, imp," Kimberly grunted. She grabbed Charlie by his arm and dragged him toward a farmhouse surrounded by trees. "We don't have all day."

"You know how long it's going to take for these thumbs to grow back?"

"Hopefully a long time."

"And I'm going to be useless until they do!" Charlie screamed.

"I could have Aziolith cauterize them, so nothing ever grows back if you prefer."

That shut him up, though he continued to grumble under his breath as we continued through the dewy meadow, muttering obscenities to himself. This didn't seem to bother Kimberly any.

I still wasn't very good at traveling through the ether, and my legs were unsteady. The dew of the flowers brushed against my pants, making them sticky and damp. After walking a few feet, my stomach seized up in pain. I doubled over, throwing up all over the beautiful flowers around me. I took a deep breath of the cool mountain air once I was done and wiped the sides of my mouth.

Kimberly had not waited for me, heading instead toward the house. The mountains rolled idyllically behind it. The house itself was buttressed by metal, but the façade was made entirely of glass so that the fields on the other side were visible through it. Without a neighbor in sight, it was a perfectly panoramic way to take in the beautiful countryside.

It was large, two stories with a large kitchen offset from the center and multiple bedrooms above, all with an assortment of bookcases that were nearly the only distraction from the picturesque view.

When I caught up, Molly knelt next to Charlie, tying towels around his hand. "Do you always have to make a mess when you bring guests home, Kimberly?"

Kimberly shrugged. "If I have to choose, then yes. Yes, I always do have to make a mess." She pointed out at me. "Oh, by the way, we rescued Lizzie. Not that it matters more than your carpets."

"That's not what I—" Molly looked up from the towels toward me. "It's good to see you again. Of course, you're more important than my towels…even if they are my good towels."

"Maybe not," Kimberly said. "But if you have to choose, a saved Lizzie or a clean house, which would you choose?"

"That's not a fair question, and I'm not answering it!" Molly said, tying the second arm off with a towel. "There you go, Charlie."

"Thanks," Charlie said. "Nobody asked me, but if I had to choose whether to bleed out onto the floor or these nice towels…well, it doesn't really matter because my frigging thumbs have been cut off! Don't you people have any shame?"

"Do you?" Kimberly asked.

"NO!" Charlie screamed, waving his stumps in exasperation. "I thought that would be an easy one to figure out."

"Lizzie," Kimberly said with a wink. "Can you help me with him so Molly doesn't get anything on her new dress?"

I slid my hands under Charlie's arm to help drag him into the living room. He was light enough that even completely limp, he wasn't much trouble for me to carry, especially with Kimberly's help.

"Wait!" Molly shouted as we entered the living room. She disappeared into another room and came back with a clear shower curtain to cover her white couch before we threw Charlie onto it.

"Behave," Kimberly said, poking her finger into his chest.

"Really?" Charlie said, holding out his mangled hands. "You know there's a simple spell to keep me from teleporting. You don't have to cut things off to get your point across."

"I like my way better," Kimberly said. "But I'll take it under consideration. Now, about this ledger."

Charlie laughed. "First you assault me, then you manhandle me—unrepentantly, mind you— and now you want my help?"

I nodded. "Yes, that sounds about right. Congratulations on accurately summing up our position. Of course, I could just kill you."

"Oh no. You're not going to scare me with your bull—"

I took a threatening step forward. "I've had just about enough of you. First, you tricked me. Then you kidnapped me. Now, you're pulling my pud." I loomed over him. "I don't like you, and I know Kimberly doesn't like you. So, you can help us decode your writing and find angels who can help us, or you can be a dick. One of those ways has a one-way trip back to Hell, and the other? Well, maybe we let you stay here for good behavior."

Charlie gulped. "I thought you were the nice one."

"None of us is the nice one," Molly said, speaking over my shoulder. "Now, who wants tea?"

***

Watching Charlie try to drink his tea without any thumbs almost made everything he put me through worth it. Not quite, but almost. When everything was the worst, the little things in life made it all worth it.

"What does that crazy symbol mean?" I asked, pointing to the ledger. A tornado with fingers next was scribbled next to somebody's name.

"That means they come in and wreck stuff every few months," Charlie replied.

"Oh." I paused. "Well, that explains why there's one of those next to Kimberly's name."

"It does at that," Charlie snarled. "Are we just about done for now? I'm tired, and I lost a lot of blood."

"We've barely even started," Molly said. "And you haven't given us one single name that could help us."

"I'm bleeding out here, and I need time to recover. You guys are torturing me. Can't we pick this up later?"

"No, we can't," Kimberly said, turning her attention to three concentric circles inside each other next to the name Cratheon. "What's this symbol?"

"It means they always pay back with interest," Charlie said. "Cratheon's a good egg. Too bad he's Blue Trident." He pointed to a forked symbol next to his name. "Obviously."

I sighed. "Seems like this whole book is filled with people in the Blue Trident."

"I attract a certain type of clientele, and the type of angels that deal with me have a certain… threshold for sin."

"How many angels don't deal with you, then?"

"A fair few," he replied. "I'm a little light-headed now, or maybe I could tell you about some of them."

"Just tell me the symbol for them, and I'll find them myself," Kimberly snapped.

"I don't know if I can remember." He placed his palm on his forehead. "I'm feeling weak. Maybe a drink'll calm my nerves."

"Fine." Molly groaned, stood up, and walked to the bar on the other side of the room. It was glass, like most of the house, and even before she opened it, we could see inside.

"Three fingers of the Basil Hayden, love."

"You have expensive taste," Kimberly said. "Why do you spend so much time in The Bar? All they serve is beer, mead, and cider."

"It takes all kinds of booze to warm my cockles." He looked at the drink Molly held for him. "Got a straw, dear? My thumbs are indisposed at the moment."

"Something occurs to me." Molly disappeared into the kitchen for a second. She returned with a straw, but as Charlie went to take a sip of the drink, she pulled it away.

"You haven't said anything helpful in hours. You're trying to drag this out. Why?"

"I'm helping." Charlie offered meekly. "Can't you see I'm helping?"

Molly took a sip of the drink and sat down, eyeing him. "No, you're being cagey. There's something you're not telling us, and for some reason, you're talking in circles."

"Molly! I'm home!" Geordi rushed in the front door and latched onto Molly's leg. "You were right. These trees are perfect for climbing." He turned around to see Charlie staring at him. "Who are you?"

"I'm Charlie." The imp cocked his head. "So, you must be the kid. Gabriel was right. You guys do have him. It's about time." He whistled into the air. "Gabriel!"

A massive soundwave crashed through the room. Every window in the house shattered, and the glass cut into our skin as we scrambled out of the way. Charlie dove behind a chair.

"Give me your hand!" Kimberly shouted.

I reached for Charlie's ledger with one hand and grabbed hers with the other. A small vibration buzzed through my hand, but we didn't disappear. Instead, Kimberly's eyes went wide. She looked over at Molly, who shook her head. I didn't need to be a genius to see what was happening. They couldn't teleport. We were sitting ducks for whatever Gabriel had planned.

"So predictable," Gabriel's voice boomed from above. He was floating through the broken ceiling. "When will you learn Charlie isn't one to be trusted? Pathetic. Of course, the desperate are always foolish."

"Get out of here," Molly growled.

"Or what?" Gabriel laughed. "You think I'm scared of you? Sorry, but I'm not a human. I've fought things you wouldn't even begin to believe. But I really don't want to be enemies. You have the wrong idea of me. I'm not a monster."

"Could have fooled me," I replied. "Aren't you the one who led a coup against God? Sounds like a monster to me."

"If you knew what I knew, you would have done the same, for your own good and the good of humanity." He smiled broadly. "At our core, we angels are helpers, and I want to help you help yourself. So, I will give you a choice. Come with me willingly, or I will kill the pixies in front of you while you beg for mercy that will never come."

CHAPTER 27

Ollie

Oppressive, overwhelming darkness. That's what I remembered being behind the cliffside door that led into a grotto in the bowels of Lucifer's castle. It was the kind of dark that made the air hard to walk through and weighed on your back when you went to take a step.

"What is this place?" Aimee asked, lighting a flame that instantly cut through the darkness.

"Take Ollie's hand," Lilith said to her, then looked at me. "And Ollie, take mine."

She trembled, and I squeezed her hand as tightly as I could to show her that I was there for her and wasn't going anywhere. She seemed to need my strength more than I needed hers.

Whispered voices came from all around us. Then a voice: *You were so strong last time, Ollie.*

"There are not many things that I fear," Lilith said. "But every demon fears this place. Few have made it through alive, and those that did went mad soon after."

"I didn't think it was so bad, last time," I said, looking around.

"You must not have much hatred in your soul," she replied. "For us, every inch forward is agony, and once these vultures get ahold of your soul, it is nearly impossible to wrest it free. It is an effective deterrent for those that wish to do the dark lord harm."

“I have plenty of hate. I refuse to let it be weaponized against me.” I threw back my shoulder. “I am fueled by hatred and rage, not hindered by it.”

“Welcome back, Oleander,” a whisper cracked in the nothing. “You have so much more pain in your heart now.”

“Cool it,” I snapped, looking around. “I beat you last time, and I’ll beat you again.”

“Perhaps you can,” the voice said. “But can your friends?”

Both women had dropped to their knees, Aimee in a silent scream, Lilith gripping her face, scraping it with her fingernails.

“Lilith! Aimee!” I kneeled down between them. “No, no, no.”

“Does this cause you pain, Nephilim?” Five others joined in chorus. “It is delicious to us. We are nourished by it.”

“This isn’t real,” I said, shaking my head. “Get out of my head!”

“We have no need to be in your head.” Now there were thirty or so of them, every voice echoing the words from the last. “We have theirs, and their pain is your pain.”

Calm, Ollie. Calm.

“What do you want from me?” I asked.

“Only what we want from everyone. All of your hope. Everything that makes you good, to become ours. And then, we fill you with all that is pain, and you will become us.”

“So…you’re nothing but the pain of others who have come through this door?”

"We are darkness incarnate."

"Darkness, huh?" I said, feeling the wand in my pocket. I ran my fingers over it. My mind was foggy, but I had the inkling of an idea. Neither Aimee nor Lilith were in any position to fight back, and for some reason, I wasn't bad at handling these horrible psychic attacks.

"What are you doing?" the voices said when I pulled my two compatriots toward me.

I held my wand high into the air. "*Rhwystr ysgafn*!"

A cone of light encircled us, causing the voices to hiss and moan as they scattered away from it. My barrier expanded all around us. Lilith looked up at me, pulling her hands from her face.

"What am I doing?" she gasped, looking at the blood on her fingers.

"Whoa…" Aimee said when she came to. She blinked several times, shuddering. "That was terrible."

"What did you see when you went catatonic?" I asked as they rose to their feet.

"I…" Aimee looked over at Lilith. "I don't want to talk about it."

"Yes," Lilith said, patting her hair back into place. "I think that's prudent. I have no desire to relive what was shown to me."

"Whatever you say." I walked around, pointing my wand at the darkness. "It's over! Let us out, or I will shine this on you forever!"

The voices hissed. After a few long moments, a pinprick of light appeared. When I headed toward it, the light cascaded over us, and then we were alone in the grotto of Lucifer's castle. The place was dilapidated, even more so in the thirty years since I had last been there. The gazebo resting in the center was now almost completely collapsed, overtaken by the surrounding brush.

Lilith sat down on the cracked ground and took a deep breath. "I will admit, I did not think we would survive those voices, but I hoped that some part of the angelic side of Oleander's nature would be immune to those wretched things."

"You knew we would suffer through that," Aimee said, glaring at her, "and you still sent us through there?"

"What's the other choice, the Black Gate?" Lilith said. "It is nothing to be trifled with, and Cerberus hasn't eaten in so long that even getting within a hundred yards of him would send him into a wild frenzy, and I very much don't want to fight him." She shook her head. "He's such a good boy in normal times."

"All right," I said. "Enough. Whatever the reason, we're here. We made it. We're in the castle. Let's just do what we came here to do."

"What is that, exactly?" Aimee said, pushing on her forehead. "My mind is a little foggy on the details."

"We need to see if Lucifer is part of the Blue Trident, and if not, we need to make sure he's safe. If the Blue Trident gets their hands on Lucifer and can convince him and God to start the Apocalypse, we're all screwed."

Neither of them fought my plan, so I trudged across the courtyard to the stairs leading down to the dungeon. Every door was open, with many hanging off their hinges, and nature had reclaimed the stone walls. That which wasn't overrun with green grass and vines had been warped by the heat. In one cell, a soul had degraded to just bones, in another cell, there was only a pile of ash. The weapons of torture that had once been so pristine and threatening were now rotted and rusted, laying strewn haphazardly on the ground.

I followed the dungeon around to another set of stairs that would take us into the castle. At the top of the stairs, a loud sigh slipped through the hallway up ahead. The stone cracked and flaked as my hand brushed the walls, and I stepped quietly through the halls. The pitiful sound crescendoed from a sigh to a cry, stifled at first, but then exploding into a wail.

I peeked into the room where the sound came from and found Lucifer, bloated and unkempt, standing in front of a crackling fire. His thin goatee expanded into a sloppy beard, and a stained white muscle tee barely covered his gut.

"Lucifer?" I asked, confused.

He turned, startled but not frightened. When his eyes met Lilith's, he cocked his head and smiled. "Hello, my love."

"Don't." Lilith grimaced. "Ew."

Lucifer shrugged and studied the three of us, then his eyes found my sunglasses. "I remember your glasses. You are the Nephilim, right? What was your name again?"

"Ollie," I replied, pointing to the Firestarter. "And this is Aimee."

"It's a pleasure." A tight smile rose on his face. "Have you returned to kill me, then?"

CHAPTER 28

Kimberly

"You can't be serious," I said to Gabriel, floating above us. I pulled the daggers out of my belt. "If you think we're going to give up and die without a fight, you have to be crazy. No way we are coming willingly."

"You're a feisty one." Gabriel laughed. Two more angels descended on either side of him, and he gestured in my direction. "Kill her."

Demons were cocky, but they were nothing compared to the arrogance of angels. I took no pleasure in killing them, but my job was to protect fairy kind, and that included Lizzie and Geordi from all who wished to do them harm.

These two angels were strong and agile. I could tell before they even swung at me, but I also knew they were arrogant and reckless. They charged at me as if I was beneath their skill level, not a formidable opponent.

It took me less than ten seconds to bring them down. The first angel sliced at me with an overhead strike, and I vanished, appearing behind their back and cutting deep into their spine. They fell to the ground, and I launched to the other one, catching that one off guard as I jabbed my dagger deep into their brain before reappearing on the ground again.

I could see in Gabriel's eyes when I looked up at him, daggers at my side, that I wouldn't get another surprise attack. But he knew he had underestimated me.

"So, the legends of you are true, monster hunter." Gabriel floated lower to the ground. "I thought the demons were simply lazy and pathetic to lose to a pixie like you, but it seems the tales of your prowess were well-founded."

"Leave now," I snarled. "And I will let you live."

He laughed. "I am no mere angel, child. I have fought in battles since before this world was a thought in Zeus's mind." As he spoke, a long, glimmering rapier appeared in his hand. He flicked his wrist and brought it to his chest, turning his attention to Lizzie. "I will give you one more chance to end this, Elizabeth, before I slaughter the lot of you."

I thought perhaps Lizzie would cower to the will of the archangel, but instead, she clapped her hands together, pulling drops of water from every surface in the room until she formed a huge ball of water in her hands. She pulled back and slammed her fist into it, shooting it toward him. It crashed against his chest and sent him flying backward.

Molly ducked down to grab a shard of the broken glass and flung it at the angel remaining by Gabriel's side. He was taken aback by Lizzie's attack on the archangel and not ready for the glass shards. They dug deep into his chest.

"*Al'la'ch'sur'a*!" Molly cried.

The glass turned black and oozed out to cover the angel's body in ichor, and when he fell to the ground, he broke apart like a statue.

"Demonic!" Charlie hissed, staring at her. "The mother tongue."

"Lilith taught me one spell," Molly said, panting and wobbly-kneed. "I hoped I would never have to use it."

Before the others could react, I took two throwing daggers from the sheaths on my arm and shot them into the eye of the remaining angel.

"ENOUGH!" Gabriel's voice boomed as he flung the water off him, frustration written all over his face. "Submit or die."

"Not to get technical here," Molly said. "But four of you have died, and not a single of us. If anybody should be submitting in this situation, it's you."

Without another word, Gabriel shot toward Molly. I flew after him, blocking his rapier with my daggers just before it impaled her. He was right: He was no simple angel. He was stronger than anything I had faced in quite some time. With every swing of his blade, it became more apparent that I was outmatched. I had underestimated him.

"Can you teleport?" I asked Molly as I shielded her.

"No," she replied after a second. "He must be blocking us somehow."

"Run," I said. She flushed, searching my face. I hadn't shown fear in my eyes, let alone run away in a long time. All I knew was that she had to get Geordi to safety. Neither of them was immortal. "Find a place far enough that you can teleport. Go!"

Molly scooped Geordi in her arms and rushed backward. Gabriel turned from the fight toward Charlie, who had taken a spot on the edge of the battle and was watching it with gleeful abandon. "Get them!"

Charlie furrowed his brow. "That's not the deal. I helped you find them. You capture them, not me."

"I am amending the deal! Go or die!" Gabriel thrust his rapier at me again, and though I blocked a fatal blow, the blade still cut across my arm. He grinned. "It stings, doesn't it? While you have your methods for killing an immortal, so do I."

He pulled back for another strike when a torrent of water crashed upon him. Lizzie was guiding a stream toward Gabriel, and it smashed against the metal beams that once held up our house.

"You better up my pay for this!" Charlie rushed toward the meadow where Molly had run off with Geordi.

I turned to Lizzie. "Get the imp. I'll hold off Gabriel myself."

She looked at Charlie, then Gabriel, then back to me. "Are you sure? He's crazy powerful."

"I'll be fine." I was lying, of course, but I needed them to be safe. If she was smart—and I knew she was—Molly would have taken Geordi to another one of our safehouses. I could find her if she just stayed put. Then again, she was a hard-headed woman, and she might return to protect me, even though she needed it more than I did. "If we lose Charlie, we won't have any idea how to read that book."

"Right," Lizzie said, ending her spell and sprinting after Charlie.

Gabriel lunged at me faster than I thought possible, and I barely avoided a piercing strike through my neck…a blow that would have killed me if his weapon truly was capable of killing an immortal. I recovered and was just able to spin and kick him across the room. He stumbled over the glass when he rose again. He was bloody, his robes covered in a mix of blood, water, and dirt. His eyes had a feral energy when he looked at me.

"You will die for getting in the way of my plans. You have no idea what you are preventing. The fate of the whole world hangs in the balance."

I held up my daggers. “Any plan that has you killing innocent people isn’t much of a plan.”

“You know nothing. I am trying to save the world!”

“Listen to yourself, dude. You literally imprisoned God. That’s insane. You’re working with demons. And you’re trying to kill a child to open the gates of Hell. In what universe are you the good guy?”

He shook his head. “You are arrogant to presume to know what is best for the universe.”

“Aren’t you doing the same thing?”

Gabriel stood tall and declared, “I am an angel, divine, touched by the gods, to act as their envoy to humanity. I have seen galaxies rise and fall, and planets created from the swirling magma of the cosmos. I have lived a million lives on a thousand worlds, so yes, I do presume to know better than you.”

He rushed forward, pointing his rapier in front of him. I darted to the side and sliced his arm before kicking the sword out of his hand. It clattered on the floor across the room. The archangel spun on his heels and, in one motion, smashed his hand into my chest, sending me flying into the meadow beyond.

I landed hard. He had broken at least three of my ribs with a single punch, and I coughed blood as I tried to right myself. The shadow of an angel blocked out the sun. I had lost my daggers in the last attack and was too wounded to prevent him from striking me down. This was it.

My life flew in front of my eyes as the angel shot down. Then, in a puff of pink smoke, Molly appeared. In that same instant, I was gone.

When I reappeared, I was inside the basement of an old building; a construction project long abandoned. A perfect hiding spot. I sat up to see Molly stumbling backward. She grabbed her shoulder, and when the light hit her, I saw that she was bleeding profusely.

She looked at me once, gave a small smile, and collapsed.

CHAPTER 29

Anjelica

The moans of the souls blocking the entrance of the cave sent shivers down my spine. Akta didn't seem fazed in the least. She worked methodically and meticulously to light a fire.

I couldn't help, so I didn't bother offering. Running through thc stacks of souls took cvcrything out of mc. Oncc the adrenaline wore off, all the pain my body had been suppressing came crashing down on me.

"There," Akta said as the glow of the fire lit her face.

It was all she said. Akta was stoic as I leaned against the cave wall, fading in and out. She stared into the fire in silence or read from a small notebook she pulled from her pouch on her belt. I woke every now and then to find her tending to my wounds, putting more salve on my body, and dressing me with new bandages.

"Drink this," she said whenever she saw my eyes were open. Whatever it was scratched my throat going down, then filled my belly with warmth when it settled inside me. The warmth disbursed throughout my body and lulled me to sleep again, like a bottle of warm milk.

I didn't know how many times I dipped in and out of consciousness before I finally came to, but each time I found Akta patiently waiting over me.

"You look much better," she said to me. "How do you feel?"

"I mean, awful," I admitted. I groaned, trying to sit up. "But better than I did."

The cuts and bruises on my hands and arms had nearly vanished, and the gash on my forehead had closed up. I rolled my neck from side to side, testing it. Aside from the remains of a wicked headache, I didn't have any pain in my neck or shoulders.

"How long was I out?"

She shrugged. "A couple of hours."

"It felt like days."

"That's an effect of the pixie dust," she said, nodding. "Time moves differently when you are under its spell." She moved closer and checked over my body. "It looks like your bones have been healed. I do not like using so much on a person, but you are part demon, so I thought you could handle it. I'm glad to see I was right." She looked into my eyes. "Do you feel any jitters or want more of the dust?"

I frowned. "No."

"Very good. That can be a side effect. A powerful drug, pixie dust. The desire for more of it can drive you crazy."

I rubbed my head and sat up. "I think I'm okay. What are we going to do now?"

"We travel to Lucifer's castle to tell him what happened to Hell."

"But my mother—"

"If she was bound in Mephistopheles's castle, then she is safe for the moment. His castle rests high above the rest of Hell and should not have been destroyed in the fray. Dis, on the other hand, and my home…I fear it is all gone."

I lowered my eyes to the ground. "I'm sorry."

Akta brushed her eyes with the back of her hand. "I never thought I would like this stupid place enough to care what happened to it, and yet, after three thousand years, I find myself very attached to it."

"That's understandable. I mean, you've spent a hundred lifetimes down here. I only spent most of one on Onmiri, and I'm quite attached to it. Heck, I only spent sixteen years on Earth, and I'm pretty attached to this stupid planet."

She placed her hand on my shoulder. "I think it is time we view the damage wrought upon this place, yes?"

I nodded. "Okay."

She closed her eyes, and together we dipped into darkness, reappearing on a cliff high above the pits of Hell. The unstacked bodies were more of an ocean now, spreading across Hell from the cliffs near Lucifer's castle to the gates on the other end, where more charred bodies still spilled over, like a great dam that had been overtaken.

"It used to be beautiful," Akta said. She looked at my face and added, "In its way." She pointed to a red river of lava that sloshed against the charred bodies as they blocked it from flowing, causing them to burn and smolder even more. "The river Styx cut through the whole of Hell, and the rolling red desert shone against the pits. It has all been destroyed."

"I'm sure your loved ones are still alive under all this carnage, and…you can rebuild." I hoped I sounded convincing.

"How?" Akta snapped, tears streaming freely down her face. "Lucifer—this is all his fault."

"Well, good news." I pointed. "It looks like his castle is still standing."

She wiped the tears from her eyes then balled her fists. “Indeed. I shall take my grievances up with him.”

The pixie took my hand, and we flashed to another cliff, this one with a massive black gate on one end, a great red gem in the center staring at me like a haunting eye. An enormous dog with three heads rose ten feet into the air in front of the gate, snarling at us like it hadn’t had a good meal in ages.

“Easy, Cerberus.” Akta held out her hands. She spoke over her shoulder to me, “You don’t have any weapons on you, do you?”

I made a sweeping motion over my body and shot back, “I barely have clothes on, let alone weapons.”

“Good,” Akta said. “This black gate protects Lucifer from any who wish to do him harm. Okay, Cerberus is a vicious guard dog, even more so since his master took to staying in his castle like a child.”

She reached into her pouch and pulled out a handful of pixie dust. When she blew it onto the huge beast, he sneezed and then disappeared from sight.

“Neat trick,” I said.

“One of the many things I’ve learned pixie dust can do over the centuries. When we have finished here, I will return him to his post.”

Akta turned her attention to the black gate. The red light shone down on her, and then on me, scanning us from the tips of our heads to the soles of our feet. Akta muttered something under her breath, and then the door unlocked for us.

“Thank the gods,” she said. “I was worried for a moment.”

“What would have happened if the gate didn’t open?”

“If it judged us unworthy, it would have vaporized us,” Akta said, walking through the gate. When I was with her, the gate swung shut again, locking us in. “I have watched it disintegrate a legion of angels. If you come with malice toward the dark lord, it will suss it out.”

“But don’t you want to hurt Lucifer, even after all he has done?” I asked.

“I am bound to any Devil until the end of time, their sworn protector. Even if I wanted to hurt him, I could not.” She held her hand out to me. “Now that we are past the black gate, I can teleport us again.”

“I don’t get it. We just teleported up here. Why couldn’t we just jump straight to the castle before?”

“Oh right, you’re not from here.” She narrowed her eyes. “The Black Gate prevents anything from teleporting past it. Otherwise, all sorts of creatures could—you know what? It’s easier if you don’t ask questions.”

“Magic is weird. I get it.”

She gave a tight-lipped smile in response.

I grabbed Akta’s hand, and we vanished again, this time above a set of stairs that ascended hundreds of feet. Had I not been with Akta, I probably would have had to climb those stairs—if I could get into the palace at all.

The whole castle was sinewy and knobby, like it hadn’t been properly maintained in thousands of years. The black rock that made up the façade was dull and cracked.

“This is the Devil’s castle?” I asked. “It looks...crumbly.”

Akta grunted as she pushed open the door. “It was once grand but has fallen into disrepair since Lucifer sent the demons and imps from his service.”

"Why would he do that?"

Inside, the walls were ashy and dusty. Several sets of dusty black metal armor lined either side of a frayed, faded carpet.

"I don't think he was in his right mind," Akta replied.

"I don't blame him." I looked around at the walls. "I mean, this place would drive me nuts."

"It's even worse for him," Akta said, thoughtfully. "Lucifer is an angel, or at least he was, before the war. Angels aren't built to withstand the horrors of Hell."

"Then…why is he the Devil?"

"It was not his choice but thrust upon him."

"That's a pretty good punishment, I guess."

Akta sucked in her breath. "Yes, I suppose it is at that."

Even in the darkness, her footsteps were sure. We followed a hallway into a grand throne room, or it would have been, sans the dust caking every surface. In its center was a throne built atop a pile of skulls and bones, rising a dozen feet into the air.

"That's…a little unsettling," I said.

"Yes." Akta chuckled a little. "He thought it would instill fear in his subjects, but the seat is very uncomfortable and poorly balanced. He looks more like a fool on it than anything."

She followed the edge of the room to a door that led into a hallway. Paintings hung high, depicting demons fighting angels, and monsters in all their glory. From a little way down the hall, we heard the sounds of a conversation.

Akta held up one hand and, with the other, pulled a dagger from their sheath. "Be on guard."

I nodded, forming fire in my hands. She smiled at the flame, then at me, before continuing. We followed the voices to a room where a fire was roaring.

A massive demon with twisting horns stood in front of us. Powerful goat-like legs supported his hulking chest and the large gut protruding beneath his stained white muscle tee. He looked up when he heard us. His glowing yellow eyes seared into my soul.

"Ah, Akta," he said. "You brought a friend."

"Lucifer." Akta bowed her head slightly. "You look terrible, as always."

"Always so kind. But isn't this a treat? Two groups of people here to kill me." He exhaled loudly. "Well, I suppose we should eat first and decide who has the honors. After all—" He patted his ample belly, "I don't want to die on an empty stomach."

Two groups? Who else is here?

As Lucifer moved toward the door, I recognized two of the three figures staring at me from the other side of the room.

"Ollie?" I said. "Lilith?"

"Anjelica?" Ollie laughed. "I see you made it down to the pits."

"No thanks to you. What are you doing here?"

"I could ask you the same thing," Lilith replied. "In fact, I am asking you the same thing. What are you doing here?"

"Ladies, ladies, ladies," Lucifer said, waving his hands in the air. "No fighting until after we break bread. I have the perfect wine for such an occasion. I've been saving it for a long time."

CHAPTER 30

Lizzie

I didn't want to leave Kimberly's side, but—well, she was a professional. If she said she had it handled, then she had it handled. After all, hadn't she fought hundreds of monsters in her life? If she couldn't handle Gabriel, nobody could. Besides, that little shit Charlie wasn't going to get away from me, not if I could help it.

"Leave me alone!" the imp hollered over his shoulder as I raced after him. "I don't have any ill will; I just wanna get away!"

"I don't care!" I screamed. "I have ill will toward you! *Ligat aquas!*"

I swirled my hands together, and the dew from the flowers congealed into two shackles, clamping tightly around Charlie's arms. He struggled, but that only made my binding draw tighter around him.

"Let me go!" Charlie shrieked, still wiggling.

He took a deep breath and blew enough fire from his nose to turn my water into vapor. Once free, he toppled over his own feet to the ground. I rushed him full speed, dodging another one of his nose fireballs. It exploded into a nearby tree, which burst into flames. Behind me, there was a loud crash, and I turned to see Kimberly fly from the carcass of her house and skid to a stop a hundred feet away.

"Kimberly!" I shouted as Gabriel shot out of the house like a rocket.

I couldn't believe it. She was going to lose. She was going to die. *Not if I could help it.* I swirled the water around me as Gabriel dove to deliver his fatal blow to Kimberly.

"*Ignis Caligarum*!" I screamed. A torrent of water shot from my hands toward the angel. The instant before he connected with Kimberly's chest, I saw a flash of pink powder. I blinked, and she was gone, leaving Gabriel to stab at air before my water stream smacked into him.

What happened? Did she have the wherewithal to vanish, as injured as she was? Or had Molly come back to save her? Either way, she was safe, and me…well, I could take care of myself. *Right?*

"Not so tough now," Charlie said. "Without your protector around, are you?"

"Stand down, Charlie," Gabriel's voice boomed from across the field. A second later, he was in front of me, close enough for me to see every groove on his face. For the first time, I really saw him. He was haggard in the face from the sun of too many days, his muscles tight from one too many fights. "After all, you get more flies with honey."

"Why would you want flies?" I asked. "They're disgusting."

"It's just an expression," he replied. "And I was just trying to be polite. After all, you have been poisoned by Michael and your friends to believe that I am the bad guy. I can assure you, if you knew what I knew, you would very much be on my side."

"You already told me everything," I said. "You are trying to open a portal to Talinda, and I'm not going to help you."

"If you don't help me, then the rest of the Blue Trident will have no choice but to carry on with plan B, which means opening a portal to Hell and unleashing an Apocalypse on the world."

"So these are my choices? Help you find Talinda and risk the safety of the whole universe, or lose this planet to demons and Hellspawn?"

"It's not a good choice, but it is the one I present to you."

"You forgot one thing," I said. "We have Geordi. You can't do anything without him."

"You poor, naïve soul. Please, let me show you how wrong you are." He held out his hand. When I didn't take it, his eyes turned vicious. "That wasn't a request. I am through with niceties. Take my hand before I force you to."

I placed my hand in his. "Not much of a choice at all. I sense a running theme with you."

***

Gabriel and I disappeared in a glow of white that filled my soul with stillness and calm, something that I didn't even feel in Heaven. We appeared again on a catwalk. On the concrete floor under us, something red that I could only assume was blood was drawn in the form of a pentagram. At each corner, a young child was bound to the floor with their arms and legs extended. They cried out in pain and fear as demons and angels anointed them with various salts.

Tears leaped into my eyes. "What are you doing to them?"

"Preparing them for the end, of course. These five children will bring about the Apocalypse. We scoured the whole world, and these were the only pixie children we could find. I do not want to kill them, but I'm running out of time—and choices. My people do not think you will help me, but I know you will, given the right motivation. If we cannot find Talinda before it's too late, we will have no choice but to use these children to open a portal to Hell."

"You can't do that," I shouted. "They're just children."

"Then help me!" He threw his hands in the air. "Give me Geordi and help me find the Time Being."

"Why is Geordi so important?" I asked.

Gabriel put his hands together in front of his face, taking a breath before he began. "Some time ago, God came to Earth as a human. This was not unusual in the old days. Zeus enjoyed transmuting into a human, or a goose, for fun and games, but God—our god—did not have such tastes. Zeus didn't make a big deal of it, but God did. He transmuted into a child and was born of flesh. You have heard the stories, of course, but they leave out that Jesus had children before he died on that cross. Geordi is the descendant of the blood line of Jesus Christ, the last descendant of God's line. The line has been hidden for centuries from demon kind until the Blue Trident activated again."

That was a lot to take in, and I would give myself the time to do so once I wasn't in a fight for my life. For now, I had to suppress all the crazy things he was saying and keep a level head to buy Kimberly as much time as possible so she could save the kidnapped children.

"Why do you need Geordi? What part does he play in all of this?"

"That's your question? I just told you that the boy you have in your possession was the last descendent of the son of God, and the only question you have is why do I need him?"

"No, I have about a million questions, but I read *The DaVinci Code*. I get the gist."

"You continue to surprise me, Elizabeth."

"I don't care. Now, answer my question. What are you going to do with Geordi?"

"Agree to help me, and you will find out for yourself. And if you bring me to Talinda, I will set these children free."

How much faith did I have that Kimberly would find me? I needed to find a way to stall him that didn't involve sacrificing these children, which meant I had to play along and give him a task that would take him a while to complete. Unfortunately, the only thing I could think of that fit the bill was to give him the ingredient list he sought. That would keep him busy for a couple of hours at least, and hopefully, I would have a better plan by then.

"Okay," I said. "I'll help you. Give me a piece of paper. I'll write down the ingredients."

A cruel smile spread across the archangel's face. "Wonderful. I knew you just needed the proper motivation."

CHAPTER 31

Anjelica

After enduring the disgusting dinner spread Mephistopheles had prepared, my stomach turned at the thought of sharing a meal with Lucifer. But when he led us into the dining room, I was surprised to find plates of fish and ham and soup, along with a salad and wine—actual wine, not blood. I couldn't believe I knew how to tell those things apart, but I did.

"So," Lucifer said, sliding into a high-back leather chair at the head of the table and putting on a bib. "Who's going to do the honors?"

"We're not here to kill you," Akta said, sitting down at my right. "We came because Hell is falling apart, and we're worried about you."

"Speak for yourself," Lilith said with an eye roll.

"You're not worried about me?" Lucifer pouted. "Does that mean you will do the honors then, Mother of Demons?"

He was hideous, even for a demon. His pot belly bulged against the table.

"No. God, no." She pressed her hands against the table. "I wouldn't get within ten feet of you. And I'm not worried about you, either."

"I am." Ollie spun one of the chairs backward and rested her elbows on the top of it. "Mostly, I'm concerned about whether you've taken up the Blue Trident again."

Lucifer choked on his wine and spent several agonizing seconds trying to clear his windpipe, hacking and coughing until his face was an even brighter shade of red. "Of course not. Look at me. Do I look like I'm in any condition to lead a charge against Heaven?"

"Absolutely not," Akta muttered into her glass of wine.

"You don't look like you could lead a 5K walk against Heaven," I added.

Lucifer ignored me and turned to Akta. "And why are you here, my dear? I have sent for you before, and you never came. Now you appear out of the blue. To what do I owe the pleasure?"

"Remember when I told you not to stack bodies on top of each other because it's not structurally sound, and you ignored me?"

"I didn't ignore you. I asked you to present me with a better option, and you walked off in a huff."

"Well, good news. I was right." She tilted her glass in the air. "And Hell is now literally a tsunami of bodies."

"Shit," Ollie said, wiping a hand across her face. "I think that might be my fault."

"Oh really?" I said. "We almost died, you know."

"Technically," Akta said. "I'm already dead."

"I'm sorry," Ollie said.

"I don't know what you did, but you didn't insist on an unsafe plan that put every demon and monster in Hell at risk, did you?"

"No." Ollie leaned forward and pulled a piece of chicken breast meat from a platter on the table. "I did accidentally kick it, though. Lilith and I scaled one of the towers to get into the castle."

"If you hadn't, it would've been somebody else." I didn't know the woman who spoke. She never took her eyes off the fireball she tossed from one hand to the next. "It really was a dumb plan."

"I'm aware," Akta replied, turning to face the woman. "And who, may I ask, are you?"

"That's Aimee," Ollie answered. "She's our guide. She doesn't have a stake in this fight one way or another."

"I wouldn't say that," Aimee said, pursing her lips. "If the Blue Trident is successful at opening the gates of Hell, things are not going to be pleasant for anyone."

Lucifer sighed and set his napkin down on the table. "So, they have finally made their move, then?"

"What do you know about it?" I asked.

"Demons have been begging me to start an Apocalypse for years, but I refused to bring that kind of destruction on Earth. They revolted and left me alone in my squalor. They would have finished me off then and there, but I used the last of my power to barricade myself inside. I'm able to summon food, at least, though it has been a vice these long years."

"I can tell," Lilith said, with a deliberate look at his gut. "You used to be the most feared and revered of the demons. Now, look at you."

He shrugged. "I don't entertain often. In fact, this is the first time I have broken bread with anyone in decades."

"So, you holed up in this castle?" I asked.

Lucifer nodded. "Absolutely, especially now that the Dagger of Obsolescence has been found. I am not risking leaving this castle with that thing on the loose."

"If you're not working for the Blue Trident," Ollie said, "do you know who is leading them?"

"I can only assume it is Et'atal, my ungrateful son."

"That's what I'm thinking, too, but he's not working alone. At the very least, Mephistopheles is on his side." Ollie paused, scrunching her face in thought. "I'm willing to bet the other dukes are in on it, too."

"It is a level of deviousness that Et'atal certainly has in his power," Lucifer said. "If he's behind this, he'll have thousands of thralls under his control. I hope you have an army."

Ollie laughed. "You're looking at them, minus a couple of pixies and an angel up on Earth."

Lucifer leaned back in his chair and drummed his fingers on his belly. "Then I fear you are outnumbered and outmatched, unless you can find a groundswell of support quickly."

"I know somebody in the Godschurch," Ollie mused, "though I haven't talked to them in a long time. If I can contact them, maybe I can get them to help us take down the Blue Trident—that's assuming their organization hasn't been infiltrated."

"I doubt it. Nobody cares much for us here at the ass-end of the universe." He squinted in thought. "I remember where the entrance to the Godschurch used to be. I can send you there, though it might have moved since my last time on Earth over 3,000 years ago."

"On top of that," Ollie said, "I can call on Director Chapman for help."

"The lovely woman who sent you into Hell to kill me?" Lucifer smiled. "I like her."

Akta stood. “While you are busy on Earth, I need to see just how bad the damage is in Dis. If the city still stands, I will press my contacts for information on the whereabouts of Et’atal. If he’s behind the Blue Trident in Hell, then there has to be record of it somewhere.”

“I’ll return to Earth, too,” Lilith said. “To track down the Blue Trident’s base of operations.”

Aimee raised her hand. “I’m all about going back to Earth. I feel like a fifth wheel here, and I have a very nice bunker back on Earth where I can hole up if the worst happens.”

Lucifer turned to me. “And what about you, Anjelica?”

“I want my mother back, and I need to save Araphael. He’s powerful, and if we can free him, maybe he can stop this.”

Akta walked over to me. “Then I will help you save them, too. Come with me. I believe we can kill two birds with one stone, as they say.”

“Good,” I said, with a nod towards Lucifer. “No offense—well, plenty of offense—if I have to stay here another minute, I think I’m going to go nuts.”

CHAPTER 32

Kimberly

Once I stabilized Molly from her rapier wound, I teleported back to get Lizzie, but she was gone already. *Stupid, Kimberly*. You couldn't even protect one girl? I kicked the flowers in the meadow, lopping the petals off of several as I thrashed against the foliage around me. It was a temper tantrum, and I knew it, but it made me feel like I had some control. Lizzie was gone, Molly was clinging to life, and I had no idea what to do next.

These Apocalypse scares kept happening, one after another, decade after decade, and while I had to save the world 100 percent of the time, they only had to succeed once. Even if I was 99.9999 percent effective, it wouldn't be enough. Perfection was too much to ask of anyone, and yet that's what was required of me. Absolute perfection, and it was asked of me again. When would it be enough?

That was the curse of immortality. You got to keep seeing your mistakes pop up again and again. The imps you didn't kill, the demons you did, the steps you took, and the ones you forgot, slipping through your fingers like sand in an hourglass. The names and faces changed, but the circumstances, the mistakes, kept repeating and reappearing in an awful loop.

I saved Geordi but lost Lizzie. We were no closer to saving the world or decoding Charlie's ledger, and now he was gone as well. *All right, Kimberly. Pull yourself together*. I'd had my moment to freak out, and while I might hate the truth, it hadn't changed any. I was the last defense between the world and complete darkness.

I teleported back to our basement hideout and unwrapped the bandage from Molly's shoulder. She groaned and twisted but didn't wake up. I pulled some pixie dust from a pouch and mixed it into a paste with a mortar and pestle. Aziolith had given it to us for a tenth wedding anniversary present. It had been mostly decorative until now. Molly always said she would use it to make masa, but never did. Now, I was using it to save her life.

I scooped the gunk into my fingers and rubbed it on her wound. She winced but didn't wake up. It was good she slept. Whatever plan I came up with would be foolish, and I could do with her not lecturing me—or worse, offering to join me. This was something I needed to do myself. I couldn't risk her again. She was all I had left. The only consistently good thing in my life.

I wiped the damp hair from her face, and for a moment, her head turned and nuzzled into my palm. Would that I could have stayed there forever.

"Is she going to die?" Geordi watched her, sitting across from me on a rocking chair, knees pulled into his chest.

"Everybody dies eventually," I said to him. "But no, she won't die. Not if I have anything to say about it."

"What if you don't? Have anything to say about it, I mean. I didn't want my dad to die, but he still did."

I placed my hand on his knee. "All we can do is fight for what we love. The rest is up to fate. It sucks what happened to you, but it wasn't your fault, okay?" He nodded. "None of this is your fault." He nodded again, but this time he was crying. I pulled him close and let his tears pool on my shoulder. "Now, I have some things to do, but I found you a really cool babysitter." There was a knock on the door. "There they are now. Do you want to meet them?"

"I guess so," Geordi said, wiping the snot from his nose.

Aziolith stood at the door when I opened it, in his human form save for his bright, reptilian eyes. He took off his bowler hat and smiled at me. "I believe you asked for a babysitter?"

I pulled him into the room, presenting him to Geordi. "This is Mr. Aziolith."

"Az, please," Aziolith said, bowing to Geordi like a humble servant. "My friends call me Az."

I elbowed him playfully. "You hate when I call you that."

"We aren't friends," Aziolith said. "We're so much more than that."

Geordi scrunched up his face. "What's wrong with your eyes?"

Aziolith laughed. "Why, nothing. I'm a dragon, and that's what our eyes look like."

Geordi's eyes went wide. "You're a dragon? That's so cool."

Aziolith put his finger to his mouth. "Yes, but you must be very quiet about it. If anyone found out, they would all be after my gold."

Geordi's eyes went even wider. "You have gold?"

Aziolith snapped his fingers, and a gold coin appeared in his hand. "Of course, doesn't everyone?" He handed it to Geordi. "Here you go. My gift to you."

"Whoa," Geordi said, spinning the coin in his hand. "For real?"

"For real, for real," Aziolith said, kneeling in front of him. "Do you want to play a game?" Geordi nodded, and Aziolith turned to me. "I think I have it from here."

I snapped back into business mode. "Okay. Dress the wound every two hours and rub her shoulder with the balm I prepared."

"You used the gift!" Aziolith beamed, looking at the mortar and pestle. "I wish it was under better circumstances."

"As a great wizard once said, 'so do all who live to see such times'."

"Did you just quote Lord of the Rings at me?" Aziolith asked.

"Seemed appropriate. Unfortunately."

Aziolith stood up and put his hands on my shoulders. "You're stalling, now. Go. We'll be fine."

I stepped out the door and watched Aziolith close it behind me. I almost believed him.

***

If the Blue Trident were close to enacting their final plan, that meant a bunch of them would be gathered together in the same place at the same time, while humans were oblivious to demons that existed right under their noses. Lilith had to know where a massive number of demons were gathering.

I kept an emergency number for the mother of demons in each safehouse, and she picked up immediately when I dialed. "Oh, thank the gods, this new phone works. A brute threw my last one out a window. Can you believe it?"

“Absolutely,” I said quickly. “Please tell me you made it into Hell.”

“And back, my love. Come to me, and I’ll tell you all about it.”

She was staying in Moscow, in the shadow of the Kremlin. Russia was a popular destination for demons in hiding from their own kind. Demons hated the snow and cold, which meant you could hide in plain sight.

Lilith’s hotel reflected Cold War, minimalist Soviet values. It was tidy enough, the staff clearly taking pride in its upkeep. Though the floors hadn’t been replaced in some time, they were buffed to a shine, and the hotel bar had top-shelf liquor from around the world. I couldn’t remember the last time I had a drink and ordered a vodka tonic because that was the type of day I’d had.

“Russian vodka will kill you if you’re not careful,” Lilith said from behind me. “That stuff is no joke.”

She was wearing a thick fur coat, and her heavy hat had flaps that fell over her ears. She sat next to me and ordered the same thing.

“It’s not that cold.”

“It’s cold enough,” she replied. “Though after the day I’ve had, the cold is a welcome respite.” She sighed. “You’ll be happy to know that Lucifer is not part of the Blue Trident. He can barely walk, let alone lead an army.” She nodded at the bartender when he slid her drink to her. “This is the work of somebody else.”

“Did you figure out who’s funding them?”

“We think it might be Et’atal, even though he might be buried under a sea of charred souls.”

I took a sip of my drink. “I doubt we’re that lucky.”

"Me either." Lilith tipped her glass and drained the last of her drink, then pulled a piece of paper from her coat pocket. "I have news for you. I've been able to track down the Blue Trident's main base of operations in Iceland. It's a garment-processing plant outside Reykjavík."

"Thank you," I said, studying the address.

"Don't thank me, my love. I don't want an Apocalypse any more than you and being in Hell today reminded me just how vile it is down there."

"Still," I said. "I know you don't have to help me."

"Pish posh, dear. It's my pleasure." She cocked her head. "You're not going in alone, are you?"

I shrugged. "I don't have any choice. The rest of my team has been gutted."

"It has been a long time since I suited up for field work," Lilith said, wrapping her coat tighter around her. "But I will go with you."

"This means going against your own kind. I know how you hate that."

"But I do love a good rescue operation. And the Blue Trident are making a mockery of everything I have tried to impart to my children. If they succeed in opening a portal to Hell, then Earth will become just as horrible. Please and no thank you, very much." She stepped down from the bar stool. "Give me fifteen minutes to make some arrangements, and we'll be off."

CHAPTER 33

Ollie

In the ancient days of the 90s, I worked for a spiteful demon named Crassus who liked living high on the hog and flaunting his power by acquiring powerful magical weapons. Back then, I was somewhat of an expert on weapons, especially after my time with the dagger I stole from Blezor. Tales of my deeds became legendary, and everyone wanted to hire me to steal something for them.

Crassus paid the best, which made up for his terrible temper and awful personality. One day he asked me to recover a crook and flail believed to belong to Osiris himself. While I had handled many items over my years, I'd never dealt with one that had such a legendary pedigree.

The job turned out to be much more than I could handle. It had me leaping between planets to find clues as to its location. At one point, I'm pretty sure I ended up in an alternate dimension. Anyway, the Godschurch didn't like that and arrested me for crimes against the universe.

We eventually came to an understanding that I was to leave the crook and flail alone, and they would overlook my transgressions. Good enough for me. After chasing that stupid crook and flail along tarnation and back, I wanted nothing more than to take a long vacation.

The Godschurch kept entrances to their base on every habitable planet so that their agents could move around the universe with ease. They were only human, after all, and they couldn't travel across the universe with a snap of their fingers like the gods.

Unfortunately, the location Lucifer sent me was in Babylon, a city lost to time. It had been excavated at the beginning of the 1900s, and anything of value had been torn out and brought to one museum or another. To get to the base, I needed to find the right door in the annuls of antiquity. I just hoped that my Babylonian scholar friend was able to help me.

***

"Ollie. Why am I not surprised?" Anur asked as he held open the door to his loft. It was the middle of the night in Buenos Aires. I had a history of forgetting that time zones existed and barging in on people at completely inopportune times. People either accepted it, or I paid them enough that they overlooked it.

Anur was wearing an old T-shirt and robe, and he hadn't bothered to comb his ratty black hair. When he wasn't on a dig, he spent the rest of his time lecturing at the University of Rosario. They didn't have a large archeology department before Anur came to the school, but he brought a level of prestige with his finds that garnered the school an international reputation.

"Can you help me track down a Babylonian door?" I asked.

He looked at me cockeyed for a second, and then sighed. "You're not joking, are you?"

I shook my head, pulling a piece of parchment out of my pocket. "This was the location of the door, at least when it stood. I checked the dig site, and it's been removed. I am in desperate need of that door."

He chuckled, sitting down at his messy computer desk littered with take-out containers and piles of papers. "This is archeology. Nobody is in desperate need of anything. That's one of the beautiful parts about it."

"Well, I'm not an archeologist, and I'm telling you it's a matter of life and death."

He raised his eyebrows. "I honestly never thought I would hear those words. Luckily, my undergraduate work involved updating the catalog on this dig site, and a few years ago, I had one of my grad assistants digitize all that information—" He stared intently at the computer for a long moment, then down at the paper as he typed furiously. "Ah yes, The Temple of Nergal."

A dozen images flashed across the screen. The stone door had lost most of its paint, but some black remained on the three-headed dog that Nergal kept at his side and the red in the curly hair on his head and beard.

"This was actually a pretty important find at the time, with an interesting story. Even with the crane they used to bring this door up topside, it didn't want to budge. The team nearly lost a week of digging, but they eventually got it out."

I stared at him blankly. "Somebody needs to calibrate your interesting meter, cuz that was not interesting."

He shrugged. "To each their own. That story kills in class every time I tell it."

For a moment, I felt a little sorry for his students—and him—but I wasn't there to insult the poor man. I needed his help. "So, where's the door now?"

Anur pulled one of the pictures off his drive and put it into a Google reverse image search. It pulled up a similar picture of the door, with a caption: *University of Cairo, 2012.* He leaned back and pointed at the screen. "That's where I would start."

"Looks like I'm going to Egypt."

***

It didn't take me long to find the university museum where they were keeping the door. The problem was that it wasn't on display. That meant it would be in the research center underneath the museum, accessible only to faculty and authorized staff.

I spent the next day observing the exits and entrances until I had a good handle on how to get down to the research department. It wasn't a high-security facility, and I had certainly managed to infiltrate much more difficult facilities in my life, but that didn't mean I was going to take it for granted. Every job was hard until it was successfully completed.

I decided that it was easiest to imitate the security guard when they changed shifts. There was only one guard on duty at a time, and he swept the building in thirty-minute shifts. I cased the building for a good place to stash him for the hour until he woke up from my spell, then followed him to a room filled with ancient statues.

"They're beautiful," I said in perfect Arabic. Flirting wasn't the easiest thing for me to do, but when the job called for it, I had the goods to pull it off. It didn't hurt that men didn't need much to be easily swayed and manipulated, especially ones that didn't take their job very seriously.

"I agree," the guard said, looking at a five-foot-tall ivory statue in front of him. "I'm very lucky to be working here."

"Do you have a favorite?" I asked, shifting my weight to my right hip. "Piece in the collection, I mean."

"Yes, but it's not in this room." He gulped as I stepped closer to him.

"Can you show me?" My voice was low and breathy. "I'd love to see it."

He nodded, leading me around a dark corner where I pulled him close into a passionate kiss. He leaned into it after a moment, and I clocked the wedding ring on his finger.

"*Cysgu.*" I touched my wand to his temple, and he fell over. "*Anwelgig.*" The man's unconscious body turned invisible, and I shoved it into the dark corner of the building I'd found. "*Trawsnewid.*" I touched my own temple and transformed into his visage, taking special note of his eyes, then grabbed his ID badge and access card before I walked off. I had used a blind spot in their security camera so they'd never be any the wiser.

I slid the card into the basement door like I'd watched a dozen people do throughout the day. It clicked open for me, and I walked down a flight of stairs. The basement was packed to the gills with boxes and crates, along with different statues and other treasures from antiquity, any of which would have been enough to retire on if sold on the black market. I wasn't there to cause trouble, though—at least not for the university or the guard.

It wasn't hard to find the ancient door, even in the massive room. The picture Anur had shown me didn't do it justice. What appeared a few inches on the computer screen was almost twenty feet high in reality. No wonder it took a week of digging to pull it out of the ground. It loomed large over everything else in the room, leaving me with one question: *How was I going to open it?*

Even if I magicked it to stand fully erect, it was just a freestanding door. Perhaps if there was a structure…but there was nothing left of the temple except rubble. I could construct a makeshift shelter out of energy, and then—

"Hello, Ollie." I wheeled around to see a man so gorgeous that it was hard not to go weak in the knees. All the Godschurch agents were beautiful, but this was on another level, rivaling the beauty of the very angels themselves. I would be damned if I would give him the benefit of telling him as much. He was already cocky enough.

"Agent Davis," I said flatly. "What are you doing here?"

"Talinda gave me a tip you would be here today."

The Time Being. "Isn't that against her rules?"

He waggled his hand back and forth. "Oh, it's definitely a gray area. Apparently, your friend made quite an impression on her. She asked me to come and help make sure your world doesn't end."

"How gracious of you."

"It is, actually," he replied. "This is my day off, which means this mission is off the books. Godschurch doesn't know about it. I'm on my own time here, so please, don't get me killed."

"Famous last words," I said. My phone rang, and I fished it out of my pocket.

"We know where they're keeping Lizzie," Kimberly said on the other end when I picked up. "We're going to need all the help we can get." Without another word, she hung up then pinged me an address.

I looked up from my phone at Agent Davis. "Good timing."

CHAPTER 34

Lizzie

"Are you sure this is right?" Gabriel asked me as he stared down at the list. "Beryllium, phosphorus, and nitrogen…that's it? Seems like you would need more to contact someone so powerful."

"That's it. Unfortunately, I have no idea how much of each we need. For that, you need Molly."

"Molly?" Gabriel said.

"You met her—Kimberly's girlfriend." I shot him an evil grin. "I think she threw some glass into your friend's neck."

"Oh, yeah. Her. I do not like her."

I shrugged. "She's the one who did all the calculations. I was just the grunt."

He stepped toward me, his feet quaking the catwalk where we still stood. "If you're messing with me…"

"I'll be dead? I mean, honestly, what are you going to do with me? The only leverage you have over me is the kids down there." I looked over the balcony. The children were still tied to the edges of the pentagram, but they were no longer being doused with saltpeter and other chemicals. "Speaking of which, you told me if I gave you the ingredients, you would call off your goons."

Gabriel smiled. "They have been called off. However, you must be mad if you think I'm going to let them go until I have assurances we can get to the Time Being."

"Then you'll either need to find Molly or a copy of *The Astronaut's Midwife.*"

"Do you really think I would have searched so far and wide for the Time Being without having procured a copy of the book? I even had Baraphel working on it before he was murdered. Unfortunately, his research disappeared with his death, setting us back years."

"He was Blue Trident?" I asked. "You really do have your claws into everything, don't you?"

"You have no idea how long I've been working on this project." He sighed. "The others—they are brutes. They think the solution is to bore a hole to the underworld and relieve the pressure by venting demons and souls onto Earth. My solution is much more elegant, but I am in the minority of those who support it. Most don't even think it's possible."

"Oh, it's possible."

"Yes, you are the reason I have any hope left." Gabriel gestured to the children. "I know you think I am a monster, but what you see here is a last resort. However, if we don't come to a solution soon, then I will not be able to hold back my compatriots' demonic nature."

"And what happens if you get to Talinda and she won't grant your request?"

He squeezed his hands together. "Then I will force it with blood and sword."

Explosions echoed through the warehouse, and an orange demon rushed toward us from the front door. "Gabriel, we're being attacked!"

"How?" He looked over at me. "You!"

There was no other possibility. It had to be Ollie and Kimberly. They were willing to take on the whole of the

Blue Trident for me, and I had to hold out for them to reach me. No, I had to make it downstairs to rescue the children. Otherwise, this would all be for nothing.

"*Rota Aqua*!" I used my hands to leech water from all the nearby surfaces until I had a ball of water taller than me. I slammed it into Gabriel at full force, sending him crashing through the wall at the end of the catwalk.

I leaped down as dozens of demons pushed past me on their way to the warehouse entrance. Gunfire echoed as I knelt down next to a little girl with pigtails and big blue eyes. She stared up at me with hopeful fright.

"*Glacies cultro*." An ice knife appeared in my hand, and I used it to slice through the girl's binding, then helped her to stand up. "Run!"

She sprinted toward a side door of the warehouse that I pointed out, and I moved to the next child. Gabriel slammed down in front of me, blocking the children and cracking the floor with the force of his landing.

"This wasn't part of our deal." A flaming sword appeared in his hand. "Submit, and I won't slaughter you where you stand."

"If you slaughter me, you'll never get to Talinda."

He laughed. "You've given away your hand. You have no idea how to find her. You were just the messenger who succeeded on the backs of your friends." He held up the piece of paper. "With this and a copy of *The Astronaut's Midwife,* I have all I need, which means you are useless to me."

I called forth a huge cylinder of water to knock him off balance just as he lunged forward and sliced at my chest. His attack spun slightly, and he missed, but still managed to cut deep into my side, spilling my blood on the pentagram on the floor. It began to glow a dull blue. Both of us froze.

"What's happening?" I asked.

"How interesting," he said. "It seems that your blood can open the gates of Hell as easily as these children."

Kimberly had told me once that fairy blood could open a gate to Hell. Her mentor, Julia Freeman, had witnessed as much when a portal to Hell was opened in her hometown. These portals, though, were volatile and easy to close using the same blood that opened them.

"Ah yes, you were a fairy, weren't you?" Gabriel cocked his head. "It is a crass way to open the gates of Hell, but perhaps the easy ways truly are best."

"No," I said, shaking my head. "Don't—"

He slashed the sword again, and I ducked to avoid his attack. "You say that, but then you work against me at every turn." He swung again and this time caught me in the arm. More of my blood spilled onto the pentagram. "I have given you every chance to join my side, and you have done nothing but become a thorn in it."

"I don't want to fight you."

"Of course you don't, because I'm winning!" He punched me in the chest, knocking me across the room where I crashed into a pile of boxes. By the time I got up, he was already on top of me.

Gabriel squeezed my chin and lifted me into the air with one arm. I kicked and fought against him, but it was useless. I couldn't call forth any magic because he was choking my vocal cords. He dragged me toward the center of the circle and took a second to examine me as if I was little more than a science experiment.

"P—please," I choked out.

He shook his head. "I was wrong about you. You are pathetic. I thought you could become an honorable member of our ranks, but an organization is only as strong as their weakest link."

When he pulled back the rapier, I wondered what it must be to stop existing. *Would I vanish into the universe forever? Would I even realize it? Could I finally be at peace?*

But his strike didn't come. There was a small groan and his grip on my neck loosened. I fell to the ground choking and looked up to see a dagger sticking out of Gabriel's arm.

"Ow!" He shouted, confused more than anything, as he looked down at the blue blood flowing down his toga. "You stabbed me."

"I know." Behind him, Kimberly's face was determined and snarling. "Come on, Lizzie!"

I scrambled to my feet and took her outstretched hand. She wrapped her arm around mine, and we rushed out of the same side door I'd sent the little blonde girl running through just a few minutes before.

"Wait!" I shouted, leaving her side.

"We don't have time to stop!"

I ignored her and scanned the scene until I found the girl hidden behind a crate. "Come on," I said when I reached her. The pain in my arm and side was excruciating, but I held her tightly and slid her onto my hip. Gabriel smashed through the door as I hobbled back to Kimberly.

"I can't—" I started, but Kimberly just smiled at me.

"Relax. We have it covered."

A shriek cut through the air, and Gabriel was engulfed in an explosion. From a roof across from the warehouse, Ollie stood with a rocket launcher, grinning and giving us the thumbs up. Our brief respite of joy was short-lived, however. Gabriel stepped through the fire of the explosion just moments later.

"Pitiful."

He was grinning, taking menacing steps toward us when a green Humvee crashed through the crates and slid to a stop at our feet.

Lilith rolled down the window. "Get in!"

Kimberly pushed me into the back of the vehicle along with the girl, sliding in once we were safely inside. The truck lurched forward just as Gabriel stood up. Lilith revved the engine and slammed into him, sending him flying once more.

I heard something slam on the roof and unbuckled my seat belt to launch my counterattack, but Kimberly stilled my hand. I exhaled when Ollie hopped into the passenger's seat.

She pulled out her wand. "*Anweledig*!"

The Humvee sparkled for a moment, then disappeared from view. We rode off into the night, invisible.

"Are you okay?" Kimberly asked.

"No," I replied. "But it doesn't matter. It's all over. He's won. This has all been a waste."

Those were my last words before my eyes rolled back in my head, and everything faded to black.

BOOK 3

CHAPTER 35

Lizzie

I faded in and out of consciousness until they got me back to their safe house across the city, where Kimberly applied some of her powerful pixie dust salve to my wounds.

"Better?" Kimberly asked as she sat down by my side.

I breathed out slowly. "It's getting there. Thank you."

"Good," Ollie said, taking a seat on the other side of me. "Then maybe you can tell us what you mean by 'it's all over'."

I groaned, remembering my conversation with the archangel. "Gabriel has the ingredient list to find the Time Being, and he's got a copy of *The Astronaut's Midwife*, which means it's just a matter of time before he finds out the recipe and gets to Talinda."

"Is that such a bad thing?" Molly shuffled slowly into the room. When she saw me, she grinned. "Oh, look, matching wounds."

"Sisters." I smiled weakly at her. "And yes, it's a terrible thing."

She shook her head and eased herself to sitting. "I don't know if I agree. I've been thinking about it. This whole time we've been one step behind Gabriel, but what if we were one step ahead?"

"I'm not following," Ollie said.

"What if we let him get to Talinda's castle and ambushed him there, where he doesn't have anywhere to run?"

"That would be fine and dandy," I replied. "Except that's not their only plan. While Gabriel is trying to get to the Time Being, other members of the Blue Trident are preparing to open the gates of Hell using a bunch of children connected to some horrible prophecy." I pointed to the girl. Moving my arm ached something fierce, and I dropped it quickly. "As evidenced by that child and the others still hidden in the warehouse."

"That does make things more difficult," Molly said. "But if there was a way to save those children, we could force them into a funnel where the only choice left is to get to the Time Being."

Ollie pressed the bridge of her nose. "That would mean saving God, and Lucifer, and the children, and keeping every fairy on Earth protected so their blood can't be used to open a portal to Hell."

"I've been protecting fairy folk for the last forty years," Kimberly said. "I'm not going to let the Blue Trident do anything to jeopardize them now."

Molly nodded. "I already activated our network of safe houses around the world, and fairy folk have been funneling into them for the past day."

"That's something," Ollie said, tapping her chin. "We still need to save God and those children, though, if this plan has any hope of working. Can you handle the Heaven part, Lizzie?"

"Oh sure, easy-breezy," I said with a wave of my hand. "Except that when I left Heaven, Michael said I couldn't come back."

"There are ways back," a new voice entered the room. It was a beautiful man with perfect teeth, dressed meticulously in an ornate three-piece suit. "Especially if it means saving a god."

I stared. "And who are you?"

"A friend of mine from the Godschurch," Ollie said. "Agent Davis. He's here to help, and if he says he can get you into Heaven, I believe him."

"Then I guess I do, too. Okay, so I'll go with him to Heaven," I said. "And so, what, Ollie tries to rescue the other children?"

"It's quite the plan." Ollie raised an eyebrow and turned to Agent Davis. "This would be a whole lot easier if we could get some backup from the Godschurch."

"In order to get any backup," he answered, "I need to open a case. If I do that, I have to report every violation I've found on your planet. Your god will be arrested and put on trial for crimes against humanity. Meanwhile, Earth will be sucked through the sun into another dimension barring the outcome, which could last a million years." He looked at her pointedly. "Are you very sure you want to go down that path?"

"No." Ollie sighed. "I guess I don't. Being teleported to another dimension doesn't sound fun."

"I didn't think so. That means we're on our own right now. If everything goes to pot, I'll have no other choice but to call them in. For now, I think we can handle it."

"You're confident." Kimberly gave him a wry smile. "I like it."

Ollie sighed again. "If we can't call in the Godschurch, I'll have to go to my government contacts again and see if they can help me."

"How are you going to do that?" Kimberly said. "They don't seem like the helpful type."

"Aside from the fact that they have a vested interest in stopping an Apocalypse…" Ollie took a second. "I have a little black book with every angel and demon I've worked with in my whole career. Director Chapman has been after it for years. If I offer it to them in exchange for their help, that might just do it."

I raised my eyebrows. "You're willing to torch your whole career for this?"

She held out her hands. "If not this, then what?"

I rubbed my hands together. "All right then, I guess we have a plan. I'll go to Heaven with Agent Davis to rescue God. Kimberly figures out how to save those kids. Ollie tries to get support from the government. And Molly will find the recipe for the incantation…then we all meet back here to save what's left of the universe from Gabriel."

We all stared at each other for a long moment.

"What if they find the recipe before we're ready?" Molly asked.

"I guess we just have to work fast and hope for the best."

***

"I know it's around here somewhere," Agent Davis said, wandering through Piccadilly Circus, which was not a circus at all, but a Times Square-esque square in London. We had been wandering the area for an hour, and every minute that passed made me less confident we were going to get back up to Heaven and save God before Gabriel found Talinda.

Agent Davis seemed to sense my growing doubt. "Sorry, but the records for this quadrant are quite old.

They're supposed to be updated every decade, but we haven't checked on this planet in close to 500 years. Imagine my surprise that you guys weren't still dying from The Black Plague. I got vaccinated and everything. It's really not a bad little planet. Do you think we have time to see Buckingham Palace?" He waved a Fodor's guide in my face. "The guidebook says it's magnificent."

No," I said, giving him a look. "We don't have time. I would appreciate it if you didn't treat this like a vacation."

"Vacation!" Agent Davis laughed. "Nothing about this place feels like a vacation. When I met Ollie, and she told me she was from this planet, I nearly choked, but I never thought it would be this advanced. I mean—I guess I could see myself vacationing here. Not in London, of course. Do you guys have any nice beaches on this planet?"

"I'm not a travel agent," I said through gritted teeth. "Can we please just find this place?"

He pointed down a street. "I think it's this one."

We walked down yet another street, which twisted and turned until we were in front of an old church that looked like it hadn't ever been renovated. Agent Davis pulled a picture out of his pocket, studied it, then looked back up at the building. "Yes, this is the one. A bit worse for wear, but I think we're in business."

The door creaked when he pushed it open and walked inside. The smell of must and dry rot assaulted my nostrils. The pews and altar were ripped up and lay strewn on the floor, gathering dust. Two wooden rafters had been constructed on either side and covered in plastic.

"Sad," Agent Davis said. "I'll bet there's nobody alive that knows the significance of this place."

He led me to the rectory, then turned and followed a set of rickety stairs two flights down to the basement. Several concrete tombs lined the walls, but Agent Davis didn't acknowledge them. He was headed to a large crucifix above the far door.

"This is ghastly." He curled his lip. "You really pray to this thing?"

"Yeah. Why? You don't?"

"Gods no. We have more sense than to worship something so morbid." He pushed his hands on either side of the crucifix, and it began to glow, then fell backward into the light, revealing a door in the wall. He stepped to the side, holding out his arm. "After you, my dear."

I walked through with tiny, careful steps, and then, for the first time in days, I was back in Heaven. It was nothing like I remembered. The peaceful, tranquil place was now a war zone, and we were right in the middle of it.

CHAPTER 36

Anjelica

Lucifer transported us out of his castle, and we reappeared atop an unstable mountain of charred souls. It rocked back and forth, undulating like the ocean. Akta kicked off the ground and rose high into the air as I followed behind. I had learned some lessons in my day, and one of them was how to use my fire powers to fly. It wasn't the most stable way to travel, and I had to maintain complete focus, but it was a far cry better than walking across the bodies.

"This is horrible," I said as we flew.

"It's always been horrible." Akta's wings bobbed up and down with her shrug. "Even when these charred souls were only an inconvenience, it was horrible. Now, we are reaping what we wrought. I wish Velaska had never left. She was not kind, and she was the one that bound me here, but she knew what she was doing, even if she was loathe to do it most of the time."

"Is there any chance anything survived down there?" I asked, looking over the abyss of smoldering souls.

"Of course," she said. "Demons and monsters are hearty. They were built for hard labor, and now—well, if anything in this universe can survive a million pounds of dead bodies, I believe the dead can do so."

We flew mostly in silence after that, which I appreciated. It was not easy to keep control of my mind while deep in conversation, and the simple act of using my powers constantly was draining my body and mind. I was grateful when Akta pointed just ahead at a bulge poking out of one of the writhing towers like a boil. I could make out a shimmering blue underneath the pile of bodies.

"There!" she yelled back at me.

Akta landed on top of the bulge and began to push the bodies away. I joined in, tossing them to either side as we worked ourselves closer to the blue light.

"It's a forcefield!" she shouted. "I can't believe they found a way…"

I peered downward through the forcefield. Dozens of wraiths stood in a circle, looking upward at the barrier in a trance. Their arms shook, but their focus was determined and complete. Akta banged on the barrier. "Hey! Let us in!"

The wraiths didn't budge.

I frowned. "I don't think they can hear us."

"Grab my hand," she said. "I didn't want to teleport until I knew if Dis survived, but now that I know it did, I can bring us inside myself. Here, take my hand."

A slight burning sensation doused my body as we rode together through the abyss and returned underneath the barrier, looking up at it.

"Are you okay?" Akta patted herself down, looking over herself like she was making sure she made it through in one piece.

I rubbed my arms. "Yeah, it just tingles a bit."

"Then come on!" She ran down the street. "I don't know how long until that barrier falls, and there's someone we have to talk to before that happens."

***

I followed Akta down the windy dirt streets of Dis, ones that hadn't been upgraded in thousands of years, past medieval-looking thatched houses. We turned a corner onto a cobblestone street straight out of a Sherlock Holmes novel.

"Beatrice and Clovis are the two best informants in Dis," Akta said. "If anyone knows who leads the Blue Trident, it's them."

"And they can help us save Araphael and my mother, too?"

"With any luck, they can."

She hopped up a set of steps and knocked on the green door at the top. On the other side, I heard the sound of feet rushing. The door slammed open, and the eyes of a little girl went wide. "Oh good gods, Akta! We thought you were a goner."

Akta wrapped her arms around the little girl. "I thought the same about you, little buddy."

"Who you calling little?" She craned her neck around Akta and looked me over. "And who is your friend? She looks like a cop. You a cop? You have to tell me if you're a cop."

I held up my hands. "I'm not a cop. I'm not even from Earth."

"An alien, huh? Well, that's a new one, and after being here thousands of years, it's tough for me to hear something new." She hopped up the stairs. "Well, come on up. Dad made tea, and the kettle's still hot."

The stairs led to a big kitchen with an island at its center and enough room on the counters to make a feast. A man with round glasses and a long ponytail turned to us.

"Well, Akta. I didn't think I would see you for a while. And you brought a friend." He held his hand out. "I'm Clovis. It's nice to meet you."

I shook his hand. "It's nice to meet you, too. I'm Anjelica."

"I heard you downstairs. Did you say you weren't from Earth?"

"Well, I was born here, but I've lived on Onmiri for the last thirty years."

He took off his glasses and rubbed them with his shirt, still staring at me. "Fascinating."

"I'm so glad you are safe," Akta said, putting a hand on Clovis's shoulder. "I thought the worst had happened."

"Yes. And after sending you off into the abyss last time, I thought maybe you would have fallen under the weight of the bodies. Fortunately, Dis has many high-level wraiths and sorcerers to help hold up the barrier—for the moment. However, I fear what will happen when the bodies awaken."

"Awaken?" I asked.

"The stacks neutralized their ability to move, but now that they are off the stacks, they could start standing up and moving around. When that happens, and they start pounding on the barriers, I don't know if we will be able to protect ourselves from a full-blown invasion."

"Let's hope we can find a solution before then," Akta said. "Meanwhile…"

"You need something," Beatrice said, hands on her hips. "I figured as much. Would it kill you to come to check in on us every once and a while without an agenda?"

"I brought you a casserole last month!" Akta countered. "And we watched the fights together last time I was in town before that."

"Still," Beatrice grumbled. "All right." She clapped her hands together. "So, what can we help you with this time?"

I piped up. "The Blue Trident."

"Oh, please." She flicked her wrist at me. "Not those losers again."

"Then you've heard of them?" I asked, eyebrows raised.

"It's hard not to when you're in our line of work," Clovis said.

"I will pay you handsomely for anything you know about the Blue Trident," Akta said. "Specifically related to its leadership. More specifically, Et'atal."

A shadow passed over Clovis's face. "Do not say that name in this house."

"Does that mean he has something to do with the Blue Trident?" I asked. "Or is he just that big a dick that even in a city infested with demons, he's the one you don't want named?"

"Why not both?" Clovis asked with a shrug. "Far as I know Et—he and the dukes have bankrolled the Blue Trident since before it was officially called that. Back when they called it—what was it again, Bea?"

"The Godless, I believe," she said to Clovis. "If he's not heading them, he definitely knows who does."

"Great," Akta said. "Now, if only he wasn't buried under a thousand tons of charred souls."

Clovis frowned and shook his head. "He's not. He made it to Dis a couple of days ago. Has a penthouse across town. Word on the street is that whatever the Blue Trident is planning will go down soon, so everyone who's anyone in Hell was making their way into Dis for the final preparation. This might have set back their plans—at least for a couple of days."

"Are there any demons left who aren't loyal to the Blue Trident?" I asked. "Because from the way you're talking, it doesn't seem likely."

"Admittedly," Beatrice said, "they are all a little excited about getting out of these pits, even if it means letting demons rampage on Earth." She gave us a sly smile. "For the right price, I could raise you an army."

"Good," Akta said. "I'll need one to protect Lucifer. So far, his magic is holding, but if they are planning a coup, I need to fortify his defenses."

"That's gonna cost you a lot of scratch."

"Put it on Lucifer's tab. He's good for it."

Clovis looked over his glasses at us. "He hasn't paid in quite some time."

"He will this time," Akta replied. "I guarantee it. And while you're at it, find me Et'atal's address. I need to have a word with him."

CHAPTER 37

Ollie

I hadn't visited my house since failing to deliver Bi'ri'thal's package, and I wasn't surprised to see it completely destroyed. Couches turned over, cabinets ripped from the wall; the fridge was torn from the handle, and everything inside it littered around the room, leaving a pungent mess of rotten food everywhere.

"Great," I said aloud to no one on my way to the bedroom. I pulled out my wand when I got there. "*Datgelu eich hun*," I said, twisting my wrist to uncover a small safe hidden in the wall. Not well enough, it seemed, because when I stepped forward, the door swung open. Its contents had been taken, including the little black book I was after.

As I stood, fuming, my phone rang. I recognized the number and tried to keep my anger concealed when I answered. "Hi, Bi'ri'thal. Long time no talk."

"You have disappointed me, Oleander. I trusted you, and you betrayed me. More than that, you made me look like a fool in front of my friends."

"Don't give me that, Bi'ri'thal. I'll cop to failing you, but don't tell me those two angels are your friends. Whatever game you're playing, the minute those angels stop being useful to you, they'll be dead, and we both know it."

He chuckled. "You don't know much, little one. I think you overestimate my power. My power may be unmatched among the demons and angels on Earth, but among the archangels, I am nothing."

"So Fyathiel and Clereal are archangels?"

There was a short struggle on the phone, and another voice came on the phone. "Not that it's any of your business, but yes, we are archangels, and yes, we know that you've been working against the Blue Trident from the beginning of this operation."

"I can make it up to you," I said, halfway between bargaining and scheming.

"We want Geordi," Bi'ri'thal growled. "Bring him to me at the warehouse where you dropped off our first package, or we will broadcast this book all over the internet, which I believe will make life very complicated for you."

The line went dead.

I scrolled through my contacts and called Kimberly. "We have a problem. Nothing I can't handle, but I'm going to need the kid."

"Are you crazy?"

"Yes," I replied. "But I think I can distract part of the Blue Trident if I use him as a diversion, and that should buy you a window to save the other kids."

"And if it doesn't work, we're giving up one of our trump cards."

This wasn't a negotiation, and I needed Kimberly to know that. "Listen, you can give him to me, or I can take him by force. Please don't make me fight you."

She sighed. "This better work."

"It will." My voice sounded more confident than I really was, but it was the confidence I needed. If I didn't believe I could keep the kid safe, then I was just endangering him for no good reason.

***

I opened a portal to San Francisco and drove Lucy to Chinatown, where I walked up the steps to the safehouse Director Chapman had created above a dumpling restaurant. When I knocked on the door, the metal slat slid open, and two piercing brown eyes stared back at me.

"I was wondering when you would show up," Director Chapman's voice growled through the door. It clicked open, and she led me through to the back room set up with computers, servers, and other monitoring equipment. "Aimee came back and said you met Lucifer, and he says he isn't involved in the Blue Trident. I assume you found somebody who is?"

"We have a whole list of people who are members of the Blue Trident. Molly should be scanning and faxing it to you, for what it's worth. Meanwhile, we're about to lead an assault on Heaven to rescue God, and in Hell to take down the demon leading the Blue Trident from below."

She blinked a few times. "That's a whole lot of information to lay on me. You should have contacted me sooner."

"I'm here because we need your help—well, me, specifically. The demon I worked for, and the two angels, have a book of mine that contains every contact I've ever worked with. I'm offering it to you, along with detailed notes on every job I've ever done, in exchange for your help taking them down, tonight. No red tape. No bureaucratic bull. Just a battalion of your best men to take them down, and then another to help us to rescue a group of children the Trident wants to use to open the gates of Hell."

Director Chapman scoffed. "Is that all?"

I shook my head. "The Blue Trident are searching for fairy children. I want you to open every safehouse at your disposal to protect them until this is all over."

"You realize you're asking me to declare war on angels, right? This is a 'burn down the house and salt the earth' operation. You only get one chance at doing something like this. Are you sure you want to use it now?"

I nodded. "If we don't, then say hello to the end of the Earth."

"Well then, I agree." She held out her arm to shake my hand. "It looks like the US armed forces are going to war."

***

"Have you made contact with the safe houses?"

Kimberly and I stood at the staging area a hundred yards from the back entrance of Bi'ri'thal's warehouse. She had her arm tightly around Geordi's shoulder.

She nodded. "Molly told me that half of our safehouses have already relocated into Army bases, and more are making their way as we speak. I don't like the idea of trusting the government, but I feel much better with armed guards protecting our guys."

"Me too," I replied.

"Are you sure you can trust her?" Kimberly tipped her head toward Director Chapman, who was across the parking lot, giving orders. "This is a big risk."

"Yes," I said, though my voice wavered. "I'm sure I can, and I don't say that often."

"You're lying."

"Of course I'm lying. I'm flying by the seat of my pants here." I looked down at Geordi. "The question is, are you ready?"

The boy's eyes were big. "I think so."

I knelt down and looked him in the face. "I never asked you what you wanted. Are you okay being used at bait? It's really dangerous."

Geordi was quiet for a moment but didn't take his eyes off mine. "Will it keep the others safe?"

"I think so, but it will make you very unsafe."

He swallowed hard. "I'll do it."

"You're a brave kid." I gave him a pat on the shoulder, then stood up and looked Kimberly in the eyes. "This is a big enough carrot that Gabriel should come running. That's when we'll start the assault, and while all eyes are trained here—"

"Molly and I will save the children," Kimberly finished for me.

"And hopefully, I'll be able to get Geordi out, too, before the end."

"This is a horrible gamble," Kimberly said with a loud exhale.

"All we're trying to do is buy Anjelica some time, right? Once they have God safe and Et'atal is neutralized, we can force Gabriel into the endgame."

Director Chapman approached. "We're in position."

I nodded to Kimberly and gave Geordi's shoulder a quick squeeze before he took a seat on Lucy's passenger side to meet with Bi'ri'thal.

"This is a lot of troops, Director," I said into my earpiece. "You really came through."

"I had to call in a few favors, but we pulled it together nicely, I think."

The four machine-gun-wielding demons standing guard eyed me menacingly as I approached the gate to the warehouse. I was more than a little happy to have the backing of Director Chapman's team behind my stupid plan.

I took a deep breath and put Lucy in park. I pulled Geordi into my arms once more before we exited the car. The doors to the warehouse slid open, and Bi'ri'thal stepped out, flanked by Fyathiel and Clereal. I didn't see Gabriel.

"Just the three of you. Where's your boss?"

"That's none of your business," Fyathiel scowled. "You've ruined everything with your meddling, but it's nice to see that our threats got to you."

"Oh, they didn't. What good is my book if the world is ending? I was just hoping to lure Gabriel here as well." I snapped my fingers, and floodlights painted the warehouse with a blinding light. "But I guess you three will have to do."

CHAPTER 38

Kimberly

In a career full of doing dumb things, infiltrating Gabriel's warehouse by myself was one of the dumbest I ever agreed to. I looked through a pair of binoculars. The Trident had doubled their forces since our last attack. I half-expected them to move their operation, but they were clearly too cocky to do that.

"They are almost in position," Lilith squawked into my ear. She was my only backup, as Molly was busy with preparations for summoning the Time Being's handmaiden.

"Did they start the attack?"

There was silence for a moment before she came back on the line. "It sounds like it, yes."

I looked into my binoculars again. For our plan to work, these demons needed to reinforce the attack on Bi'ri'thal's warehouse. They weren't moving.

"Why aren't these assholes taking the bait?" I hissed.

"Give it a minute."

It didn't take a minute for an angel to rush outside, grab a horde of demon and angel soldiers, and snap away. "Never mind, looks like that scooped up half of them."

"Oh, great," Lilith said flatly. "Now there's only the exact same number we needed a small tactile team to infiltrate last time."

"Let's just hope our friends can keep them busy for a little while." I had already scouted the place, so I was able to disappear to a small stack of crates fifty feet from the front entrance. "Tell me when I can move."

"Five seconds…four, three, two, go."

I ran across to another pile of boxes. I could have disappeared just as easily, but that came with a certain flourish of smoke and sparks when I needed to keep a low profile. That meant doing things the old-fashioned way.

Two guards stood watch at the side door. A wounded demon snapped onto the asphalt, bleeding green blood, and they rushed to her side. I took the opportunity to run toward the door, sliding it open and slipping inside before they could see me.

There were plenty of dark corners inside for me to hide, and I sank myself down into one, slowly crawling toward where the pentagram lay in the center of the concrete. The children were no longer tied around its edges.

A cursory glance around the warehouse revealed the two most likely places where they were being held: the shipping container across the room, guarded by a single angel, or the office up the stairs, which had a line of sight on the rest of the warehouse. Two guards stomped along the catwalk above, and Lilith didn't have eyes into the warehouse to see if anyone was in the office.

I clocked eight guards. The two on the catwalk, an angel at the shipping container, two demons in front of the hangar door, one angel pacing across the middle of the room, rotating his gaze along the interior of the building. Lastly, an angel and a demon sitting down at a table eating their lunch.

The angel in the center of the room's cell phone rang. He muttered something I couldn't understand and took off toward the shipping container.

"Exeter is being attacked by humans," he shouted. "Fyathiel called for more backup." He pointed up to the rafters. "Za'ir'thir." He turned to the one guarding the container. "Hilirael." He turned to the two eating their food. "You two, break is over. Let's go."

The five of them disappeared, leaving only three in the building. Success was looking possible. The soldier guarding the office moved down the catwalk and descended the stairs to take point on the shipping container…leaving the office unguarded.

I couldn't risk using my wings in the darkness since they gave off an ethereal glow, so I grabbed onto the nearest steel girder and shimmied up to the back of the catwalk. When I was sure there was nobody else there, I lifted myself up and rolled onto it.

"How is the attack going?" I whispered to Lilith.

"That all depends on how successful you are. The Army is taking a lot of casualties, but Ollie and the boy are still alive for the moment."

"At least that's good. If we lose Geordi, all of this will be just swapping one hostage for another."

I glared up into the office of the warehouse. There was an angel inside, but he was distracted by his phone and not looking at the container.

"I don't care how many casualties you're taking," he barked. "Get that boy now! And bring the Nephilim girl back here!" The angel slammed the phone down. I ducked down as I watched him walk out of the door and scream down to the angel in front of the container.

"Bunch of idiots! You would have thought it was a simple matter to open the gates of Hell. Right, Vithiel?"

One of the angels looked up at him. "Demons haven't been able to do it in thousands of years, Tomrael."

"Yes, but demons are morons. We, on the other hand, are not."

The demons at the other end of the warehouse cocked their heads. A yellow-skinned demon called out, "What did you say?"

"I said you were worthless!" Tomrael said. "I knew you couldn't read, but I figured you could at least understand the words coming out of my mouth."

"Hey!" a stout, red demon shouted. "We were born angels just like you!"

"Yes," Tomrael said. "And look at you now. Pathetic."

"Why don't you come over here and say that to our face?" the yellow demon spat back.

The red demon stomped his foot. "Yeah!"

"Maybe let it go, Tomrael," Vithiel said. "They are our brothers."

"Please. I will never back down from a demon." Tomrael unfurled his wings and bolted toward the demons. "To keep this fair, I'll let you keep your weapons. I'll fight barehanded."

This was my chance. Everyone was distracted, and I didn't know for how long. I threw a pinch of pixie dust and disappeared, rematerializing behind the angel nearest the container. Before he could react, I stabbed him through the throat. Blood spurted from his neck, and he slid down to the ground in a heap.

"Children?" I whispered. "Are you in there?"

I heard a whimper, then "Yes."

"Don't forget who is your better!" Tomrael screamed from the other room. "Pathetic."

I didn't have time to open the door and pull them out. Luckily, the basement safehouse had a high ceiling and a lot of space. I pressed my hand on the container and slammed a handful of pixie dust onto the ground. A moment later, we reappeared in the basement of the safe house. Molly jumped up from her computer and hurried over.

"You made it!" She practically squealed. "Did you get the children?"

"Ye—"

"I'm afraid not," I heard a familiar voice from inside. The door slammed open, and Gabriel stepped out, holding his flaming sword. "You are so predictable. All I had to do was let you walk right into my trap."

"Where are the children?" I asked.

"Oh, their blood should be opening up portals all over Hell right about…now."

CHAPTER 39

Anjelica

“So, you’re planning to just go in and ask Et’atal if he’s leading a revolution against his father?” I asked as I trekked across the streets of Dis alongside Akta. The streets turned from cobblestone back to dirt, and then back to cobblestone, and finally to asphalt when we had moved into modern construction, or at least, it wasn’t medieval. The buildings looked like they could have been built in the 1920s, or even the ‘40s, depending on the architect.

“That’s the long and the short of it,” Akta said.

“And you don’t think that’s dangerous?”

“Oh, it’s quite dangerous, but I am well versed in danger. Besides, I’m already dead. Evaporating from existence would be a boon to me.”

“Well, I’m not dead,” I replied. “And I would very much like to return to my life once I save my mother.”

Akta looked at me over her shoulder. “I know you want to save your mother, but I need you to stop talking about it, or I’m going to slap your mouth off your face.”

“Excuse me!” I tried to snap my response, but I was panting too hard from trying to keep up. “I will have you know that I am the consort of the queen of Forche. I will not be spoken to that way. I am only here to save my mother and—”

Akta stopped in her tracks and slapped me across the face, hard. "Say something about your mother again. I dare you."

"Bitch!" I said, seething and holding my cheek. "My mother"—Akta tried to slap me again, but I sidestepped her— "Hah! Try to hit me all you want, but it's true. She's the only thing I care about on this stupid planet."

"That much is clear," she replied. "Look around you. The entirety of Hell is under a metric ton of human souls. Untold numbers of monsters are buried under it, and all you can think about is your mother, who, from what I have heard, doesn't even want to be rescued. How obtuse can you be?"

I glared at her, my shoulders heaving with fury. "If you won't help me, then I'll do it myself."

She grabbed my arm, and I tried to jerk away. "I am helping you, Anjelica. I don't want Araphael taken prisoner, and I do not think it's right for your mother to be tortured. I am simply asking you to consider the big picture. Somebody is about to open a portal, letting these horrible things in Hell loose to terrorize Earth. I know it's not your planet anymore, but can you at least appreciate how absolutely terrible it would be if billions of charred souls and monsters were unleashed there?"

"Of course I can," I said, pulling free of her. "I'm not a monster. It's just that—"

"It's just that you have your head up your own ass, and that's okay." She took a step closer. "It's going to take some time for Clovis to get the mercenaries we need. Once he does, we'll save your mother, I promise."

I took a deep breath to steady myself. "Okay."

"I'm sorry for hitting you."

"You should be," I replied, rubbing my cheek again. "I will never forgive you for that."

"Fair enough." She shrugged. "Now, can we please continue trying to figure out what's happening here? It's too far along in this story for me to be this clueless."

I nodded wordlessly and followed her to a four-story apartment building. Painted a perfect white with Doric columns on either side of the front door, it was the nicest place around in an already posh area. Akta pushed through the door and headed up the stairs while an impish doorman rushed behind to try and stop her.

"Miss, no—you must be announced."

Akta smiled and waved him off as politely as one could wave someone off. "No, it's okay. I don't find it offensive for you not to announce me."

I slid past the imp and continued up the stairs with her, climbing to the fourth floor before stopping to huff for air. Akta worked to pick the lock to the penthouse, unsuccessfully.

"What do we do now?" I breathed, crouching over with my hands on my knees.

"Not a problem. I can fly, remember?" She opened a window in the hallway. "This will work. Grab on."

We floated out of the window and up to the roof, which was covered in red flowers that snaked along the ground, leading to the thick stone of the penthouse's courtyard. The view would have been spectacular if it wasn't for the blackened souls of charred humans smashing against the forcefield.

"Akta!" a gruff voice shouted. A dashing man in a blue robe and purple slippers stood behind us. He wore silk jammies beneath the robe, which he allowed to float open to show off his rippling muscles. "It's so nice to see you."

"I have to admit," she replied. "That wasn't the greeting I expected."

"Why wouldn't I be happy to see you?" He held a jagged dagger in his hand and cut into an apple with it. "Who else would I want to go through the Apocalypse with?"

"Anyone else, Et'atal." Akta spoke with a breezy tone, but I saw her body tense. "But since you're happy to see me, I guess you know why we're here."

"I can only assume you know of the Blue Trident and have come to stop my plans." He held up the dagger. "Do you recognize this dagger? I believe it was in your possession at one time."

"The Dagger of Obsolescence. I thought it was sitting at the bottom of Lucifer's lake."

"It was, but I reacquired it recently after it made its way to Dis. It is one of the few weapons in existence that can kill my dear father."

"And you're using it to cut an apple," I pointed out.

"Lucifer's castle has been warded from me, which makes it useless, for now." His grin was maniacal. "Not forever, though. I will find a way through, and I will stab him in the back with this."

"Like the traitor you are," Akta said.

"He is the traitor!" Et'atal shouted. "You know of the old ways, what this place used to stand for—back when demons had pride in their work. Look at what it has become. Join me, Akta. You would be a valuable asset to my cause."

"I will never help you, Et'atal."

He shrugged. "I thought as much but thought it would be kind of me to give you one more chance to get on board with the winning side."

"You have never won. Not one time in all our meetings, Et'atal. I have always stopped you." Her chest puffed out. "Always have and always will."

Et'atal tsked. "My, those are bold words."

"We're never going to let you start an Apocalypse," I chimed in. "You have to know that."

The demon laughed when he turned his eyes to me. "That's cute. As if you have a choice. I only allowed you to find me because I wanted to see the look on Akta's face when the portals to Earth opened all over Hell, and she realizes that she's finally lost."

Right on cue, bright lights rose in the ceiling of Hell, shining earthen light down upon us. Akta's mouth fell agape as the midday sun washed over her face. Fear filled her eyes.

"Yes, that is the look I was hoping for," Et'atal said with a smirk. "Delicious."

CHAPTER 40

Ollie

"It's over, Bi'ri'thal." Floodlights backlit my body, and my shadow fell over his face. "You're surrounded."

Bi'ri'thal didn't show any fear. He eyed Fyathiel and Clereal and then looked back at me. "You have made a powerful enemy today."

"Wouldn't be the first time, won't be the last."

"If you think we weren't prepared for this eventuality," Fyathiel added, "then you have miscalculated the depths of our infiltration of your planet."

Clereal stepped closer. "Do you know what it costs to buy an army?"

"No," I replied, backing away.

"Surprisingly little," he continued. "I thought your soldiers would be better paid, but it seems like to buy their loyalty away from flag and country, it only costs a few thousand dollars here, and a gift there. It was pathetically easy to turn them to our side."

I pulled Geordi close to my chest. "What are you saying?"

Fyathiel whistled, and the gate to the warehouse opened. Two soldiers walked in and tossed Director Chapman to the ground, beaten and bloodied.

"You have no idea what you have done! I'll have you court-martialed for this!" She tried to kick free. The soldiers did nothing but look up at Clereal and Fyathiel, which turned Director Chapman's gaze to them. "You!"

"Yes, us," Fyathiel replied. "I must say, Director, we had terrible trouble making inroads with your personal attachment of soldiers. They really are loyal. Luckily, to pull off an operation like this, you needed to involve other branches of the military, which alerted us to your aims. It was a simple process to embed our own people in your operation."

Clereal bared his teeth in a cruel smile. "And thank you for delivering so many fairy children into our care while you were at it. Whoever has been hiding them really is a genius."

The fairy children. I told Kimberly to bring them to the Army bases for protection. I led them directly into the Blue Trident's hands.

"You'll never get away with this," I said.

Bi'ri'thal cocked his head. "You don't understand. We already have. As we speak, portals to the underworld are opening all around the world. It's not a perfect solution, but it will do until we can get God and Lucifer to see the truth—a sanctioned Apocalypse is the only way to save the world."

"You're a monster." I crouched down to Director Chapman and whispered, "Are you okay?"

"No," she replied with a smile. "I think they cracked a couple of ribs when they took me in."

"Then why are you smiling?"

She chuckled lightly in response, causing her to wince in pain. "Because I always have a backup plan. There's an elite group of my most trusted soldiers standing by." She pulled a button out of her pocket and pressed it. Half a mile away, a rocket shot into the air and exploded like a firework. "When you fight demons, it always helps to think you're being deceived."

Her eyes rolled back in her head, and she fell back against me, unconscious. I heard another rocket fire, but this time it didn't go into the air. It whistled straight for the building, exploding against the side where Bi'ri'thal and the others stood. They flew into the air as the gunfire began behind us. Behind me, a hole burned through reality, and Aimee stepped through with a squad of soldiers who immediately surrounded Director Chapman.

"I can't keep it open for long!" Aimee shouted.

"I don't think so!" Bi'ri'thal growled raising his arms into the air.

She grabbed the director and rushed toward the hole, but they didn't get closer than five feet before a burst of brimstone crashed into the ground from high above, sending us all flying.

"Stick around a while," Bi'ri'thal growled.

Aimee skidded across the ground. I rose to my feet and held Geordi close to me while a group of angels and demons materialized around us. The world had exploded into gunfire and hellfire as soldiers dropped from the air, firing against each other.

Two more rockets fired on the building, rocking its foundation and sending bits of the walls down upon the demons.

I managed to drag Director Chapman behind a truck. Aimee's unconscious body lay in the middle of the asphalt on the other side of it. Angels and demons materialized all across the warehouse, and I only hoped their arrival meant Kimberly had given herself more time to save the children.

"We have to get out of here," I shouted at Geordi. "But I need to save my friend first. Stay here, okay?"

The boy nodded, and I rolled under the truck toward Aimee's unconscious body. The gunfire was directed at the warehouse behind me and the soldiers in front of the gate, which gave me just enough space to squeeze through and grab her. I dragged her across the lot until I felt a portal open behind me. I turned to see Fyathiel, smiling wickedly, wings extended.

"I have wanted to do this for a very long time," he said. His eyes were wild, and his face was covered in ash and soot.

His uppercut knocked me into the air, and then he kicked me into the fence, where I fell and dropped my wand. I scrambled for it, but he pulled me back to him and slammed his fist into my face again and again. I kicked and clawed at him, desperate to free myself. One of my flailing attacks connected with his chest, and he stumbled enough to drop me.

It was all I needed. I leaped for my wand and pointed it at him. "*Porth i begwn y gogledd*!"

A green portal opened, the bitter cold of the north pole breezing against my skin when I kicked him through it and closed it behind him. It wasn't going to hold him for long, but I didn't need long. I took Aimee under the shoulders again and dragged her behind the truck. All around me, the gunfire continued. Demons and angels materialized at every turn on my way back to Geordi and Director Chapman.

"*Porth i'r tŷ diogel*!" I opened another portal just as a demon aimed an automatic weapon at me. I tossed Geordi through the portal before turning my attention to Director Chapman and then Aimee, shoving them through as bullets peppered the air. Finally, I leaped through the portal myself and closed it behind me.

I slammed into the floor of the safehouse and caught my breath. I hoped that Kimberly could make it back with the children because that was about as big a distraction as we could give her.

"Oh good," I heard a familiar voice growl behind me. "You're just in time."

My heart dropped. Gabriel was standing, wings unfurled, in front of a shipping container. Kimberly lay unconscious behind him, along with Molly. He was calm and collected, with a triumphant smile on his face. This had been his plan all along.

"*Pelan T—*" I screamed, pointing my wand at him, but he kicked it from my hand before I could finish, then reached down and smashed his hand into my chest. I heard ribs crack, and I fell backward, drifting into unconsciousness. I had done my best, but my best wasn't good enough.

CHAPTER 41

Lizzie

"Holy sheep!" I shouted. Cannon fodder shot all around me, and angels fired brimstone at the oncoming demons. "Gosh dog bits!"

Of all the times and places I couldn't curse. It might have made me feel better, standing in the war zone that was the Elysian Fields. Agent Davis pulled me down just as a mortar exploded beside me, and we ducked behind a reinforced cloud.

Most of the soldiers on the battlefield didn't have wings, which meant they were just regular angels, putting their lives on the line in the protection of Heaven. This had been their paradise, at least until it was invaded by demons. Across the battlefield, angels and demons hurled fireballs and mortars at each other. The angels outnumbered the enemy, but the archangels and demons were slicing through their ranks. Soon Gabriel's forces would plow through Michael's.

"Lizzie!"

I turned to see a familiar face, and even in the chaos, I smiled. "Saturnius!"

He was covered in sweat and muck, the viscera of war. I threw my arms around him. "You're alive."

His sword hilt slapped against me as we hugged, and when he released me, there was a fire in his eyes I hadn't ever seen before. He had always been such a sweet soul, but now he knew the horrors of war, and that knowledge darkened his once pale eyes.

"What are you doing?" I asked. "You're not a fighter."

"None of us are, but when Michael came and said that rogue angels had taken God hostage and were trying to open the gates of Hell, what other choice did I have?"

I cupped his face in my hands. "You poor, sweet man."

"Not anymore, my dear," he said with a roguish smile. "You always rolled your eyes at my optimism, having never seen true pain in my life. After this, you will never be able to say such things again."

I smacked him on the back, laughing. "Even in the muck of war, you still see positive in it."

"Trying to, at least. And you?" He leaned back to study me. "You look like you have been Earthbound but that—is that where you have been?" He looked at Agent Davis, who was standing silently next to me. "Have you brought this strapping lad as reinforcement to our cause?"

"Something like that," I said. "I need to speak to Michael. Have you seen him?"

Saturnius pointed toward the middle of the battlefield. "He was leading a group of elite troops to break through the flank of the enemy's line on the left." He stopped for a second. "Look at me. I sound like a real soldier, don't I?"

"You are a real soldier," Agent Davis said. "Now, can you give me a precise location?"

Saturnius thought for a moment. "About three clicks north northeast of this location, you'll find a lake that was once filled with poppies but is now filled with the blood of the dead. Across that stream, Michael should be there if he is still alive."

"He's still alive," I said. "I have to believe that."

The old man smiled. "Then perhaps some of my optimism has rubbed off on you. Come, I will lead you."

"You don't have to do that," I replied.

"Nonsense. I know the battleplans like the back of my hand. I know where it is safe to cross. Without me, you will be gone in minutes."

I didn't argue. I couldn't show it on my face, but I was scared. I had never been into battle before. Even fighting Gabriel was nothing compared to the army bearing down on us right now. In our previous encounters, I was the strong one, the world-weary traveler who had seen things that Saturnius could not even imagine. Now he was the one guiding me.

"Watch yourself here. We have a last line of magical land mines dug into the cloud cover." He pointed to a ridge between the front line and the line of mortars behind him.

God's platform lay in the distance, not even two miles away. I remembered reading about World War Two when it would take weeks to gain mere meters on a battlefield. We didn't have that kind of time. We needed to save God in the next few hours if we had any hope of stopping this conflict and saving humanity.

The three of us leaped across the battlefield, trying to bounce low to stay out of the fray. Brimstone exploded on either side of us, and I watched it take out a squad of angels, vaporizing them to ash. Their screams chilled me to my bone. In the middle distance, a battalion of demons slaughtered a cadre of Michael's angels, who were only still standing because of the sheer number of their forces.

"Most of us had never handled a sword before," Saturnius said as he rushed across the battlefield and taking shelter behind a cloud formation. "And those that had were severely out of practice. Not much use of weapons training in Heaven, you know?" He looked at me. "Of course you know. Wasn't one of your big complaints about this place that there was never anything to do?"

"It was." I felt guilty saying it.

"That shouldn't be a problem now, right?" Saturnius said with a grin. I couldn't believe he could smile in the face of such destruction. "Perhaps this will teach you to appreciate the quiet times, yes?"

"Quiet is underrated," Agent Davis said.

"Yes," I said. "I would think this is like a Tuesday for you."

"We don't use those words to mark our days, but I get your meaning…and no, this is not an uncommon occurrence for me."

Saturnius poked his head around the cloud. "The lake is over that next ridge and looks unguarded. Michael must have taken out the squad of demons who held it. We need to go now while the coast is clear."

Agent Davis and I followed him as he leaped over the cloud and rushed toward the ridge. We were only a few yards out when a flurry of arrows blotted out the sun. We all held our breath for a moment waiting for the arrows to fly past. They lodged into the clouds behind us.

"Phew," Saturnius said. But he'd let his breath out too soon. Three demons rushed over the hill toward us. "Go!"

Saturnius gritted his teeth and held his sword close to his chest. He spun around and took out one of the demons before it could swing for him, and for an instant, Saturnius was victorious, but the other two demons did not let it last. I watched the light in his eyes extinguish as they sliced him in halves and then fourths.

I screamed and leaped toward him, but Agent Davis pulled me back. “Let me go!” I screamed.

He didn’t respond, just drew a gun from its holster and emptied half the magazine. The demons flew backward, their blood mingling with Saturnius’s. Still silent, the Godschurch agent bent down and pulled the sword from my old friend’s hand.

“Find a weapon. You’ll need it.”

“I don’t know how to use a sword, or a mace, or any of this stuff.”

Agent Davis placed his gun in my hand. “It’s a simple point and click interface. Watch out, though. It’s only got about ten bullets left.”

I bent down and picked up an axe, covered in the goo of the demon’s green blood. It was surprisingly light. “I’ll take this too. Just in case.”

After I murmured a quick goodbye to Saturnius, we ran forward, scrambling up the ridge. We found the lake just as the old man described it to us, and, just like he’d said, it was riddled with the bodies of angels and demons alike, its blue water swirling with green, red, and blue blood. On the other side of the lake, a small band of archangels fought against a mounting group of demons.

“That has to be Michael, and he’s in trouble!” I shouted.

Agent Davis was a natural, bouncing between the clouds like it was second nature. We made it to the other side of the lake in less than five minutes, which was just enough time for the archangels to have their position seriously compromised.

Agent Davis didn’t wait to join the fray and attack their flank. He moved with the sword like it was an extension of his arm, slicing one demon from nape to naval, separating another's head from its body. It was like a dance. I watched, mesmerized, as he singlehandedly took out six demons before they could even turn around.

When they did, I aimed the gun at one of the charging demons and emptied two rounds into its chest before turning to another and firing three times. I loosed my final bullets into a third's head.

"You're doing great!" Agent Davis shouted as we moved through the demons. However, without my protection, even he couldn't take on every demon. While he was occupied fighting, one of them broke off and bounded toward me, swinging a maul.

I braced myself for an attack, but who was I kidding? I wasn't ready to fight a war-hardened demon. I raised my axe to defend against the attack, but instead of the maul slamming into my face, I felt the goop of blood splatter across it. The demon fell in two halves at my feet, and Michael stood behind him, covered in blood and viscera.

"About time you showed up," he said with a smile. "We're just about to rescue God and could use all the help we can get."

CHAPTER 42

Anjelica

Akta stared at the open portal above us for a long time, her face showing a combination of despair and anger, before finally turning to Et'atal. "I don't understand. How do you expect your demons and charred souls to reach the top of Hell?"

Et'atal seemed genuinely taken aback by this question, blinking silently in response.

"Oh my god," I said. "You don't know."

"Yes, I do!" Et'atal stammered. "You just—wouldn't—"

Akta shook her head. "Even for you, this is a stupid plan. And what else can I expect from a demon, especially Lucifer's son?"

"It's not stupid!" Et'atal stamped his foot. "If God and Lucifer had just agreed to work with us to start the Apocalypse, we wouldn't have had to resort to our plan B."

"This was plan B?" I chuckled. "My god, what's plan C? You know what, I don't even want to know."

"Stop making fun of me!" Et'atal screamed, holding up the Dagger of Obsolescence. "Or I'm going to slice your throats!"

Akta put her hand on her own dagger. "You don't have the balls to do anything yourself, Et'atal. That's the problem with you. All your plans are circuitous and convoluted, with about a thousand failure points, and then you work with idiots who aren't smart enough to carry them out." She walked toward him until they were nose to nose. "If you really want the Apocalypse to start, why don't you go into that castle and slice your father's throat yourself?"

"I can't!" he shouted. "He's warded it against me!"

"Can't, or won't?" Akta held out her hand. "Come with me. I know he's sealed off the castle to everyone, but I can still get inside. If you really want to kill him, come with me and be done with it." Her gaze was steely. "Then, you can fix all the things your people bungled, and start your stupid Apocalypse."

Et'atal opened and closed his mouth a few times before finally managing to say, "Why would you help me? This is a trick."

Akta stepped back. "I don't need to trick you. I know you well enough to know you would never bloody your own hands. You'll cower in a corner and find some idiot to do it for you."

Et'atal held out the dagger again. "Watch it."

"Please," Akta replied. "Like we're scared of you."

"Yeah! We're not scared of you." I was actually quite frightened of both of them. "You're kind of pathetic for not taking out your old man yourself."

Et'atal grumbled. It was clear he sensed a trap, but I wasn't sure he cared anymore, and since I had no idea what Akta was planning, all I could do was watch and hope that it wasn't all for naught.

"All right!" Et'atal said, finally. "If you can get me to my father's castle, then I'll do just that. I'll stab this right through his gut."

"Wonderful," Akta said. "Now, hand me the dagger."

Et'atal laughed, looking at the dagger in his hand, its blade still dripping with apple juice. "You think you'd fool me that easily. If I give you the dagger, you'll fly away and—"

"Hold out your hand," Akta said, pulling out one of her own blades. When he did, she cut his hand with it and then one of her own. "I swear I will bring you to your father's throne room and return your dagger or be in your thrall for all time."

A blue light spun around their forearms as their hands met, squeezing and burning itself deep into their skin. Both of them gritted their teeth but neither broke the handshake until the light had disappeared. When it was finished, Et'atal smiled and handed her the dagger.

"You must really hate my father."

"I tire of Hell being mismanaged. I don't hate him any more than I like you." She held her other hand to me after putting away her dagger. "Grab on."

She threw a bit of pixie dust and we disappeared to the Black Gate. The red gem scanned all of us, then clicked forward to let us through. As I understood it, its purpose was to bar anyone who wanted to do harm to Lucifer, and yet, Et'atal was intent on killing his father, and it let him pass.

"You were not lying," Et'atal said when the gate latched behind us. "I have been trying to pass through that gate for centuries, but every time I was rebuffed."

"I take my contracts very seriously," Akta said, taking my hand again and having us reappear at the top of the stairs before Lucifer's castle. With some reticence, she handed the Dagger of Obsolescence back to Et'atal, then pushed open the creaking door.

We passed the musty suits of armor on either side of the hallway that led to the throne room, which was lit with blue torches. There were great gaps of space between the torches, as if great portraits had once hung there but had been removed. A humming sound came from inside the room.

Against the far wall sat a throne lifted high by the bones piled underneath it. On it, Lucifer sat humming to a skull he held with his claw embedded in the bone, puppeting the jaw to let it speak.

"There he is," Akta said. "Your greatest enemy, right in front of you. Do you see how pathetic he has become?"

"He has always been pathetic," Et'atal growled, holding the dagger at his side. "Today is the day he dies, and I become the true Devil."

Et'atal bounded toward his father, and I turned to Akta. "Are you sure about this? It sure seems like he's about to kill his father, which is kind of the opposite thing we're trying to do, isn't it?"

With a sly smile, Akta gestured for me to watch the scene before us.

"Father!" Et'atal said, his voice booming through the throne room. "You have been an absentee landlord for too long. It is time you relinquished control of this realm and allowed me to ascend the throne."

Lucifer's eyes moved from his puppet skull down to Et'atal. He frowned. "I thought I warded this place to keep you out."

Et'atal pointed the dagger back to Akta. "Your most trusted soldier has betrayed you and has sworn to help me destroy you."

Lucifer scanned the room, and his face dropped when he found Akta's. "I can't say I am surprised. I have mistreated her for far too long."

None of this made any sense. When offered the chance to kill Lucifer, Akta didn't take it. Why would she allow Et'atal to do so?

"And as for the underworld," Lucifer continued, "I never wanted to be its ruler. I have done my best—no. That is not true. I have done as well as I could, though it was nowhere near enough." He stood on his throne and began to walk down, his arms extended towards his son. "If it is your wish to rule Hell, then I will not stop you. Strip me from this eternal coil and let me see what is on the other side for me."

Et'atal stood before his father, his hand trembling. Tears filled his eyes as he pulled back to stab Lucifer, and that's when Akta made her move. She threw a pinch of pixie dust and reappeared in between the two demons. She kicked Et'atal across the room and sent the dagger sliding toward me.

"You fool!" Et'atal said, holding up his arm. "You have broken your vow. Now you are bound to me forever!"

Akta shook her head with a smile. "No, I said I would bring you here and return the dagger to you. I even gave you a chance to kill your father, but you failed. Our bond is broken, and you are finished."

"Why?" I asked, moving closer to the three of them. "Why bring him here?"

"He had his home guarded a hundred different ways. I needed to get him somewhere where he couldn't escape, like a castle warded to protect against him." She spun around and kicked Et'atal across the face, knocking him unconscious. "Well, that's one less thing to worry about."

She turned to me. “Now, get that dagger. I think we can use it to bargain for your god of Death.”

“I have no idea what just happened,” Lucifer said, staring at each of us in turn. “But I’m glad you are on my team.”

Akta began to speak when a leather-winged bat flew into the room and dropped a note. She took it and smiled after reading it. “Oh good, Clovis’s army is ready to protect the castle. I think I have a better way to use them, though.” She grabbed my hand. “Come, let us do our part to save the world.”

CHAPTER 43

Kimberly

When my eyes fluttered open, I was tied to a chair in the middle of the safe house. All the furniture had been moved away except for a basin where my feet were soaking in water. I glanced around the room and saw Ollie sitting on her knees, hands tied behind her back, mouth gagged. Molly sat next to her in the same position, though without a mouth gag, and Geordi sat in front of her, hands tied in front of his body.

"Oh, good." Gabriel sauntered into the room, drying his hands with a washrag. "We don't have a moment to spare."

"You're a psycho!" Molly screamed. "Let us go."

"No, I don't think I will," Gabriel said. "Not until you give me what I want." He turned to me. "You understand you've lost, right? My compatriots got sick of waiting for me and took matters into their own hands. The gates to Hell have opened. The children you tried to protect are dead. It's over. Your only chance now is to help me complete the formula so that I can talk to the Time Being and fix all of this."

"We'll never tell you anything," I shouted.

Gabriel laughed. "I thought you might say that. You are very tough, and just looking at your beloved, I can tell that she is, too. She can take torture, but it's much harder to watch someone you love get tortured."

"Idiot," I spat. "I'm immortal."

"So were my angel brethren and the demons you so easily dispatched, like they were nothing. There are limits even to immortality." He reached behind me and pulled out a battery with cables attached to it, taking the other ends in his hand. "It just means I can torture you longer."

He clasped the ends of the cord together and dropped them into the basin. A thousand volts of electricity coursed through my body, pulsating every muscle of my body. My jaw seized up, and my eyes rolled back in my head. It wasn't the first time somebody tried this torture on me, but that didn't make it less painful. There was nothing you could do to prepare yourself for being electrified.

"Stop!" Molly screamed.

A moment later, the pain subsided when Gabriel fished the cords from the water. I took choking breaths. The smell of charred flesh filled the room.

"Are you going to give me what I want?" Gabriel asked Molly. He spoke matter-of-factly like he was as comfortable torturing someone as he was taking a stroll in a nice meadow. "Or are you wasting my time?"

Molly didn't move for a moment, but when Gabriel lifted the cables to electrocute me again, she screamed and lurched forward. "Yes, okay! I'll do it."

"No!" I felt like I'd swallowed my tongue. "Don't!"

"What other choice do we have?" Molly said. "He's right. He's won. The only thing we can do is find Talinda and get her to fix this whole thing herself."

"That's my girl," Gabriel said. "Now, where can I find the files?"

"If you let me go, I'll get them for you."

"Please." He laughed. "I'm not an idiot. If I let you go, you'll delete them, trick me, or do something else that will only delay me further. Tell me where they are on your computer, and I will find them myself."

"Fine," she replied. She listed a complicated string of folders to click through, and Gabriel went to a computer in the corner of the room, tapping away. When he was turned away, she leaned toward me. "Babe?"

"I'm okay," I replied though I was still catching my breath. "I feel myself already healing from the attack. That was stupid, Molly. You can't let him get his hands on that formula."

"There's a password," Gabriel said. "What is it?"

"Alcatraz," she said, without taking her eyes off me. "Where Kimberly and I had our first anniversary."

"Gross," Gabriel said, typing into the computer. "Oh, good. It worked." He clicked around some more.

With him distracted, I whispered again to Molly, "What is your plan?"

"I don't have one," she said. Her eyes were wide. "He's already won. The best we can do is string this along until we find an opening to take him down. Can you get out of these ropes?"

"Please," I said, turning to Ollie. "You?"

Ollie nodded, and I turned to Molly, who turned slightly to wave at me with her already untied hands.

I nodded slowly at both of them. "We can't move until Geordi is safe."

"If it's between him and saving the world," Ollie said. "I'm choosing the world."

"I hope we don't have to make that decision." Molly winced as she tried to reposition herself. "My notes say that gods and angels can't get to Talinda, only humans. When the handmaiden comes and sees that he's an angel, well…with any luck, this will be over."

"Under normal circumstances, you'd be right, but I have found a loophole," Gabriel said, standing over us. "That is why little Geordi is so important. As a descendant of a god, he can protect me from Talinda's petrification spell, and as a human, the handmaiden will have to entreat with him. So, again, thank you for bringing him back to me." He ruffled Geordi's hair. "I could not have done this without the little guy."

***

Gabriel took the ingredients from a bag inside the storage container. There was palpable glee on his face, the kind you can only get during the final moments before a lifetime of planning comes together. It took half an hour for him to arrange the ingredients for the ritual. He drew a small summoning circle in the middle of the room and dragged me to one end of it, then ordered Molly into position on one of the edges.

"Once I've put these ingredients in the cauldron, everyone needs to chant '*virginem Talinda nos coget vos fundata est. Veni nobis et ne nos inducas in deam vestram.*' Understood?"

I scoffed. "And if we don't?"

"Then I will slaughter your girlfriend and torture you until the end of time. Got it?"

"Just do it," Molly said, sounding resigned.

"That's the spirit," Gabriel said, rubbing his hands together.

He poured some phosphorus into a measuring cup, which he emptied into the cauldron in the center of the circle. Next, he ground a piece of beryllium in his hands into a fine powder, placing it into the pot as well. Finally, he opened a canister of nitrous oxide into the cauldron. When he was finished, he stood up and brought Geordi to the edge of the circle.

"Now," he said. "Chant."

"*Virginem Talinda nos coget vos fundata est. Veni nobis et ne nos inducas in deam vestram*," he chanted. "*Virginem Talinda nos coget vos fundata est. Veni nobis et ne nos inducas in deam vestram.*" The second time we all joined in. "*Virginem Talinda nos coget vos fundata est. Veni nobis et ne nos inducas in deam vestram.*"

Just as I remembered, the fourth time there was a loud crack, and a light shot into the air, beaming through the floors above us into the sky above. After a moment, a glowing white leg stepped from the light.

It spoke in five different octaves at once. "I am a handmaiden of the goddess Talinda. Who has summoned me?"

The last time I was in this position, every bone in my body was frozen. Perhaps Gabriel was right, and Geordi's blood held some magic because this time, I could move.

"This child does," Gabriel said. "He has a wish for the Time Being."

The glowing woman bent down to Geordi. "Is that true, child?" She cocked her head and squinted. "No, it is not you who summons me." Her gaze fell on Gabriel. "It is you. But you must know that an angel cannot call on Talinda. She only answers to humans."

Gabriel's face turned stony, and he tossed Geordi aside. "I was afraid you might say that."

The flame sword appeared instant in his hand, and it was through her throat before I could warn her. Gabriel ripped her from the light and threw her dead body to the ground. She was nothing but a human being, dead as all humans eventually ended up. Gabriel disappeared inside the light just as it disappeared.

"NOW!" I shouted, and the three of us broke from our chains in sync and lunged for the light, disappearing into it as it puckered closed behind us. We vanished into the white, hot on Gabriel's tail.

CHAPTER 44

Lizzie

Michael lay prone on the edge of a cloud ridge as the rest of his squad, along with Agent Davis and me, waited for him at the bottom. The ragtag bunch consisted of two archangels, Saphiel and Ircheal, and four angels who had been warriors on Earth—back when that kind of thing could still get you into Heaven.

"So, this is how we're going to save God? Seems like a suicide mission," I muttered to Agent Davis.

Ircheal overheard me and whipped around. "Maybe, but we don't have many options. The enemy is bigger and more powerful than us, and they have more firepower with those guns surrounding God's platform targeting our men. The only prudent move was to distract them with a full-on assault while a small contingent tried to infiltrate behind enemy lines."

"That still sounds like suicide to me."

Saphiel joined her brethren in staring me down. "It's not far off. We started with three dozen men, and this is all that remains. It only takes one life to change the course of fate, though, and if only a single soldier survives to free God, then it will be worth it."

"And if we don't survive"—pain filled Ircheal's voice— "then we will have been vaporized from this plane of existence, and it won't matter much anyway."

Michael beckoned us to the top of the hill. We crawled on all fours to join him, forming a tight group on either side. He pointed to God's platform, which was surrounded by eight massive gun turrets. Moana sat at the top of the protective bubble that enclosed the platform, directing the turrets to fire across the battlefield.

Michael didn't take his eyes off of the offensive maneuver as he spoke, "The majority of the Blue Trident have pressed forward, leaving us an opening to squeeze through the gaps in their defenses." He pointed to six tents and a dozen guards patrolling the distance between us and the platform. "Don't get cocky, though. There are plenty of demons and angels on guard throughout that camp."

"How do we move forward?" Ircheal asked.

Michael thought for a moment. "It makes the most sense for us to split into three teams. If one of us gets caught, the others still have a chance to get through in the chaos." He looked at each of us in turn. "If they find you, cause such an end that they have no choice but to call in reinforcements. With the guards distracted, the rest of us have an opening to move through. Hopefully, Moana won't turn her guns on the camp and take out her own people, but she's just crazy enough to do it."

"How do we bring down the barrier?" I asked.

"Moana is a bureaucrat and a technocrat, not a warrior," Michael said. "Once we're at the platform, fly up and knock her down, and she should crumble quickly. Once God is free, he should be able to end this once and for all."

"I can't fly," I said.

"Me either," another angel said.

Michael nodded. "That's why each team will be led by an archangel. Ircheal, take Mota and Lawrence. Saphiel, take Gyu and Rebecca. I will take Agent Davis and Lizzie. Ircheal, flank right. Saphiel, take the left, and I will go straight up the middle." He paused, looking down. "May the gods protect us in this last stand for Heaven and for Earth."

The team silently broke apart. We watched the others go in their separate directions, and once they had taken cover on either side of the camp, Michael scampered down the cliff right toward its center. Agent Davis and I followed, sliding behind him.

He poked his head out from the edge of the tent we'd positioned ourselves behind, and a moment later, waved me forward to a crate of weapons across the way. I crouched the whole way over then slid under the crate. When I popped my head up, I saw a demon walking toward us. I turned back to Michael and pressed my finger to my lips, telling him to be quiet. I listened for the demon, but it was impossible to discern their position on the silent clouds. And then a shadow fell over the crate, and I saw a clawed foot on the ground in front of me.

My stomach churned as my worst fear was realized: the demon had seen me. His eyes went wide, and before he could scream, I rose up, swinging my ax upward through his jaw. He fell without a sound, bathing the clouds in green goo. Michael shook his head, and he rushed forward with Agent Davis.

"That's not very subtle," Michael said. "Somebody will find this body before too long. Let's hurry." He spent a minute pulling cloud cover over the demon, hiding it as best he could underneath the pristine white of Heaven's floor.

Agent Davis reached into his weapons cache and pulled out a studded mace. "Here, this is easier to swing than an ax."

We continued onward, moving from crate to tent throughout the encampment. I struggled to keep from bouncing too high on the clouds. Sometimes, Michael would send Agent Davis forward, other times, it would be me until we'd passed the outer reaches of the camp and entered its center.

The few demons on the outskirts of the camp were easy enough to evade, but with every step we took, they multiplied, some sharpening their weapons or forging them from black metal, others tending to injuries. By the time we reached the middle of the camp, every movement needed to be expertly choreographed to avoid the enemy's gaze.

"Once we make it through this clearing, the thick of demons and angels should clear up, and we can get to the other side of the camp."

We were less than a football field away from the great cannons, their shadow looming over us as their sonic booms quaked every inch of me. The smell of fire and salt followed each blast, but they came so quickly that the air became a thick fog of the stuff. "We need to go around," Agent Davis said. "There's no way through."

"That will give them more chances to find us," Michael said.

Agent Davis whispered harshly, "And if we just sit here, we're begging for them to find us. If we go arou—"

"Intruders!" The sound of the demon's deep voice sent a chill through me, but the demon soldiers were rushing to the right—Ircheal's contingent. The clearing was devoid of soldiers, Michael signaled us forward.

"Quickly," he said, rushing across.

How could he be so clear-headed, so callous, at the imminent death of his soldiers?

"More of 'em!" I heard from the left. They'd found Saphiel, too. "FAN OUT AND SEARCH THE WHOLE CAMP FOR MORE!"

"MOVE!" Michael shouted, standing straight and breaking out into a sprint. As I sped behind him, a contingent of demons and angels followed after us. He rose into the air and spun to them. "Go!"

A good person would protest in the face of Michael's noble sacrifice, but I bolted forward with Agent Davis without a second thought. While it was possible to walk on the cloud cover, slowly, running was impossible, and we only got a few feet before we were bouncing along, rising higher each time until we were a beacon of bouncing idiots for everyone in the camp.

"Christ." I heard Michael's voice behind me. He grabbed me around the waist with one arm and Agent Davis around the other. The angels were fast, but we were faster, rushing headlong toward the platform. For a moment, I thought we might get there, but one of the cannons turned on us. I found myself staring down the barrel of a weapon larger than all three of us combined. It charged up its gun to fire.

CHAPTER 45

Anjelica

"This is a pretty big risk," I said, standing on the cliff outside of Mephistopheles's castle. "How confident are you this is going to work?"

Akta shrugged. "About twenty percent."

"Twenty percent!" I threw my hands in the air. "You're about to gamble everything on a *twenty percent* chance of success?"

Akta chuckled. "You think I'm gambling everything? Please. Give me a little credit."

Below us, the charred souls had begun to shake off their daze and stand. Some of them climbed along the ledges toward the light of Earth. It wouldn't be long before the dead began to invade the living. Once the charred souls had risen to the surface, demons wouldn't be far behind. And yet, here we were, negotiating with the very demons who wanted the world to end.

"How much longer do you think we have until they break through to Earth?" I asked, my eye on the milling bodies.

"An hour, maybe," she replied. "Two at the most. It depends on how fast they climb." She turned back to the imposing castle. "But we need to focus on the task at hand. If we're successful, we can stop this before then."

There were no demons outside the red gate as we approached, but I heard their growls and disgusting grunts echoing from the parapets and windows above. They could be on us in mere moments if Akta's plan didn't work. She might have been comfortable with the situation, but I didn't like to gamble.

Akta was fearless, though, a benefit of being able to travel at the blink of an eye anywhere your mind could imagine. She walked with a confidence that I could only wish to have a fraction of—if I added up all the confidence I'd felt in my whole life, I doubted it would match what she had inside of her. Even with the world about to burn down, she still believed she could fix things.

Akta slammed her hand on the gate. "Mephistopheles! Open up! I have a proposition for you."

There was raucous laughter from inside, and a razor-toothed demon popped its head out, unhinging its jaw as it spoke. "The demon lord has no use for your deals. He only lives to see the world burn once again, as it was at the beginning."

Akta turned to me and raised an eyebrow. Though she had lived in Hell for thousands of years, she was not a diplomat. Meanwhile, I had spent my whole life negotiating with powerful people and coming to terms with them. Of course, Forche had more than a dagger and a prayer when it came to negotiating. Still, it made some sense that it would be up to me.

"That's bull, and you know it," I hollered back to him. "In the new order, Mephistopheles will do what he has always done, seek power. I've known enough like him. What he cares about is power and status. In the new world, there will be a struggle, and we have a secret weapon that will give your boss the upper hand."

The demon cocked its head as I spoke. "What could a human have to offer our great lord?"

"First, I'm half demon." I grabbed the dagger from Akta. "Second, we have this. The Dagger of Obsolescence. One of very few weapons known to be fatal to the Devil. We offer it to your master for the return of Araphael and my mother."

There was muttering inside. While the demons were busy, Akta grabbed my arm and twisted me away, walking down the steps of the castle.

"Where are we going?"

"That demon can do nothing, and you gain nothing by negotiating. However, we have done our job by planting the seed. Now, Mephistopheles's envoy will entreat us to come into his castle. When he does, we—"

"I know this part." I grinned at her. "Never go into a demon's castle."

She returned the smile. "You're learning."

We stood there in silence, staring ahead for what seemed like an eternity. Powerful men liked to make you wait, to show you that their time was more important than yours, that they were more important than you. Still, the longer they made you wait, the bigger a threat they considered you, and the more they were mulling your offer.

I never looked down, but I kept the walls of Hell in my periphery. The bodies were halfway up now, covering the red and orange rock with inky blackness. If Araphael came with us, I hoped we could make our way back to Earth and close up the portals. However, Mephistopheles must have made that calculation, too, which meant he would move cautiously.

The gates finally opened, and a lone woman came toward us. My heart dropped as I recognized her long tresses and soft face. They had cleaned my mother up and stuffed her in a black dress, but it was no doubt her.

She slowed as she reached me, careful to stay a distance away. "Daughter, it's nice to see you."

"Mom!" I rushed to her, but she pulled back. I frowned. "What are you doing?"

"I have told you before that I do not wish to be rescued. My sins are falling from me, and with every ounce of torture I take, I come closer to my eternal reward."

"They've brainwashed you, Mom. You can't believe anything they say."

"I am a grown woman." She spoke forcefully before collecting herself and clearing her throat. "I never asked to be rescued, sweetheart. But it is nice to see you again." She smiled. "I love you, you know. Very much. There wasn't a day that went by that I didn't think about you, and even now, you fill my thoughts. I am so proud of the woman you have become."

Tears filled my eyes. "Mom, please…"

She held up her hand. "That much is done, I'm staying right here. However, I don't like what is happening with the rest of Hell, either, so I have agreed to help. Mephistopheles will allow you in his castle to entreat with him."

It was a dirty trick to use my mother against me. I scanned her hard face for several long moments, and slowly, my resolve grew; my years of training took over. Finally, I let out a deep breath. "I'm afraid that's not possible. We will negotiate on neutral ground, and only after Araphael has been brought outside so that we can see that he hasn't been mistreated."

"I can assure you that he has no—"

"I'm afraid I can't budge on these points, Mother," I said, trying to keep my composure.

"You are two souls. You cannot hope to compete against our might," my mother said with a smile. "Please, come in, and we can settle this like civilized people."

I looked back at Akta, then straightened my shoulders, standing tall. "If we are so pitiful, then we serve no threat, and Mephistopheles should have no problem coming to us."

My mother turned her attention to Akta. "He will only agree to this if you give me your pixie dust for safekeeping to make sure you don't try anything foolish."

Akta pointed to her belt, which lacked the leather pouch where she kept her dust. "I've left it behind for that very reason to prove I am serious about doing this on the level."

"That was foolish." My mother's voice changed, her face contorted, and she morphed into Mephistopheles. The spritely demon hovered two feet into the air to replicate my mother's height. "Now, you have no way of escaping."

Akta smiled. "I never wanted to." She snapped her fingers, the sound echoing throughout the chasm. A hundred puffs of smoke flashed, and Clovis's demon army appeared all around us. Akta reached behind her and produced a pair of manacles that she slid over Mephistopheles's arms. "These will prevent you from using your magic to harm us."

Mephistopheles writhed, struggling against her. "You can't—do this."

Akta pulled him closer and spoke in a hiss, "I can. And I will do a whole lot worse if you don't release Araphael so we can stop this stupid Apocalypse."

"And my Mom!" I added.

"Yes, and her mother."

"I can't—everything is—curses…" He called over his shoulder to the castle. "GUARDS! Bring out Araphael…and the whelp's whore mother. NOW!"

"Now, now, now," I said, smiling at him. "No need for name-calling, just because you were beaten by two insignificant souls."

CHAPTER 46

Ollie

I leaped over Kimberly and scrambled into the white void just as its mouth closed around us. I could just make out Gabriel's toga in the vanishing light. In its original, heavenly white, it would have been impossible to see, but the muck and grime of Earth had turned it a muddy brown.

I clawed at the toga as it swishcd past and latched onto the hem. Once I had hold of him, I pulled myself closer and clasped my other hand around his ankle. Gabriel noticed something was wrong when he took another step, but he lost his balance trying to shake me off, stumbling backward. We fell together and rolled. By the time we landed, we were completely entangled together in a pastoral field with a shimmering white castle in the distance. I could see every light in the night sky, even though it was the middle of the day and the sun beat down on me.

"Get off me!" Gabriel shouted, kicking and shoving me until I lost my grip. I rose to my feet as he brushed himself off. "You!"

He lifted his hand, clearly expecting a fiery sword to appear inside of it. When it didn't, he growled, and I laughed.

"Not so tough without your sword, are you?"

He balled up his fists. "I am still plenty strong even with my bare hands."

As he advanced, I pulled my wand from my pocket. "*Mudlosgi.*"

It might have been a little presumptuous to assume that my wand's magic would work when Gabriel's didn't, but it never hurt to try things. When my wand didn't so much as sputter, it gave Gabriel more time to advance. He clobbered me with a right cross that knocked me off-kilter. I tripped over my trench coat, tumbling to the ground again.

I pushed myself to stand and slid off my coat. It had been a while since I had been in a true bare-knuckle brawl, and I had always counted on my superior strength to save me. Something told me I wouldn't have that advantage this time.

Gabriel threw a jab, which I blocked. "Why can't you see what I'm trying to do here?" he said as he took another swipe. "This is for the good of the whole universe."

"Yes, you've said that before." I swung at him, but he ducked and caught me in the side. I winced and faltered, and he backed off as if he was toying with me. "Why can't you see what you're doing is frigging bananas?"

"The world is already over. The Blue Trident has opened portals to Hell all over Earth. Any minute now, the charred souls of Hell will leak out, and the only way to save everyone is by resetting the timeline."

He knocked me three times in the side of the head, and I just barely pushed him off before he cleaned my clock with a vicious uppercut.

"You sound like an abusive husband. You destroyed everything, and now the only way to fix it is doing things your way? What kind of sales pitch is that?"

He sighed. "I really thought I might be able to talk some sense into you, Oleander. But maybe your mother was right about you. Maybe you are poison to everything and everyone you touch."

Invoking my mother was a sure way to get under my skin. It didn't take a genius to figure that out, to dig into my insecurities and get me swinging wildly. I screamed as I went on the offensive. I knew he was goading me, and yet it was as if I had lost control of my body. I played right into his trap, swinging recklessly until I was out of gas. It felt like I'd landed a fair few punches, but when I was done, Gabriel smiled the kind of smirk that told me things were going exactly as he'd planned.

"I didn't want to hurt anyone, but I must admit I do look forward to destroying you, Ollie."

His muscles twitched, and the barrage started. It felt like I was being hit by a half dozen people at the same time as he peppered my face and body with punches. I lost count of how many times he struck me before I fell to the ground, unable to move.

He didn't follow me to the ground. If he had, that would have been the end of me. Instead, he spat on my bruised body, shaking his head. "Pathetic." He turned to the castle. "When I see the Time Being, and my wish is granted, it will be like this never happened. Savor the feeling of pain because it is the last you will have before I wipe you from existence."

I clawed at the grass to follow him, but as he crested over the hill and out of sight, all I could do was let out a gurgled gasp borne from the fluid filling my punctured lung.

"Here, drink this." The words were muffled through my cauliflower ear. I moved painfully and slowly to see a young girl, silhouetted by the sun that streaked through her perfect blonde hair. She knelt down, holding a waterskin toward me. I took it and greedily sucked down what remained from it, though I only realized that after I'd finished it.

"Sorry for drinking it all," I said, panting when I handed it back to her.

"It's okay," she replied. "I offered. Besides, the more you drink, the more it helps."

I didn't understand what she meant at first, but then my body began to jerk uncontrollably. My broken bones cracked and contorted until they no longer dug into my lungs. My arms slammed into my shoulders, popping them back into place, and my breathing was no longer labored. I wasn't quite in any condition to fight, but at least I didn't feel at the edge of death.

"Thank you," I said, stretching my limbs. "What's your name, kid?"

"Hadiya." She gave a shy smile. "I'm in training to be one of Talinda's handmaidens."

"Oh," I replied, thinking about the dead woman we'd left bleeding out on the ground on our way to follow Gabriel into the white abyss. "I see. I think there was one of you when we called to you."

She nodded. "Juniper came for you. She's one of my favorites."

Shit. Now she had a name. "She seemed very nice."

"What happened to her?" Hadiya stood expectantly. When she didn't see her friend, she must have put two and two together. "I see. You aren't supposed to be here, are you?"

"No, I'm not."

"What is your wish for Talinda, then?"

"I don't have a wish. I just want to stop Gabriel, and—"

"Yes," Hadiya mused. I wasn't sure she was talking to me. "That must have been why Talinda told me not to go with Juniper today. I hope her death does not cause an anomaly in the time stream."

I raised my eyebrow and sat up, immediately regretting the movement. The fire in my belly still ached from Gabriel's thrashing. "You don't seem too broken up about it."

She smiled. "Time doesn't work the same way here. When I go back to the castle, I will see Juniper again, in the walls of time, if I look hard enough. Nothing is ever dead in the flow of time."

"That's…pretty nice." I pointed to the castle in the distance. "So, that's where Talinda lives. I have to get there before Gabriel does."

"It will take him forever to get there without Talinda's permission." Hadiya held out her hand. "Come. If you are truly a friend, I can show you the way."

CHAPTER 47

Kimberly

I lost Ollie in the handmaiden's light, but I would not lose Molly. She barely made it through the white gate before it closed, and then only because I pulled her through with a great heave, as though she were a sack of flour. The force of her weight sent me careening to the ground, tumbling through the whiteness until we landed in a dewy meadow, her on top of me and then something else on top of her.

"Can you get off me?" I struggled to speak through the great pressure on my chest.

A wet stickiness fell on my face when she pushed something off of her body and then rolled off of me. I wiped the goo off my face and found that it was blood.

"Are you okay?" I scrambled over to Molly.

"I'm fine," she replied, though her voice was thick. Her eyes were focused on something in the thick grass. It was a dead woman in a white toga, her blank eyes staring.

"I think this was the same woman who came for Lizzie," Molly said. "I thought…I thought she was an angel or some sort of light spirit. In the end, she was just a woman, like you or me."

"We'll get him." I squeezed her shoulder.

"It doesn't really matter, does it? There's still going to be chaos and carnage, whether we kill Gabriel or not." A shudder went through her body. "It's like nothing we do even matters."

I knelt beside her. “Don’t say that. Of course, it matters.”

“How? There’s just some other horrible tragedy that will come in a week, or a month, or a year, and we’ll be right back here chasing our tails, trying to save the world, with people dying all around us.”

“I don’t mean to be callous, but that’s the job. It’s what we signed up for whe—”

“No.” Molly turned over her shoulder to face me, her eyes filled with tears. “It’s what you signed up for. I went along because I loved you.” She sniffled. “I think about that day at the lake where we had our first mission—with that kelpie. I wonder what would have happened if I had decided not to go with you.” Now her tears fell down her face in wet streams. “How many more dead bodies will I have to kneel over?”

I didn’t know how to comfort her. In all the years we had been doing this, she had never shown an ounce of wavering doubt. “How long have you felt this way?”

“I honestly don’t remember not feeling this way.” She swallowed her tears and looked at me again, her eyes red from crying. “I can’t do what you do, stuff it all down like that. I don’t know how you do it.”

“It’s a trauma response, basically.” I sighed. “I’m completely broken.”

“No…” She started, but it was half-hearted at best.

“It’s okay. I know it. It’s how I’m able to do the work. Part of me is happy that you don’t feel the same way. It means, somehow, I’ve been able to protect you from this terrible mess of a life.”

"We don't have to keep going," Molly said. "I know it's not much, but we could start a life here or anywhere. We don't have to keep saving the world."

I chuckled and poked at a piece of grass, speaking slowly. "I do, though. It's part of who I am. I understand if it's not the same for you, but you asked how to keep going. For me, knowing there is injustice in the world, I can't sit idly by. It wouldn't sit right with me—it eats at me. I do it because I can't not do it, but I never want you to feel like that. So, if you need to sit here and grieve for this woman, then you can." I stood up. "But I can't. I won't stop while there's still something to save and somebody in need of saving. Right now, the whole world needs saving." I smiled sadly at her. "I'm not going to let him blink us out of existence. I swear to everything that is holy, I will stop him. And then I'll go back to Earth and save whatever I can, for as long as I can."

"Goddamn it, Kimberly." Molly wiped the tears from her eyes. "You always know what to say, even when you have no idea what to say. Did you know that?"

"I'm sorry," I said. "I'm not trying—"

"Oh, hush up." She held out her hand. "And help me up. We have work to do."

I didn't argue. I grabbed her hand and yanked her up, taking her in a tight embrace for a long moment. "You don't have to do this. I can go on my own."

"No," she whispered. "You're right. We have a job to go." She pulled away from me and looked at the handmaiden. "I want to bury her, first, though."

"Okay," I said. "Okay."

The soil was soft from the rain but digging through the clay underneath the topsoil wasn't easy using only our daggers. When we were satisfied that the hole was deep enough, we closed the handmaiden's eyes, covered her chest with her hands, and laid her in the ground. Without the blood-stained clothes, she would have looked like she was sleeping. We worked quickly to cover her and stuck one of my extra daggers into the earth to mark the grave.

"When we reach Talinda, we'll tell her where to find the body," I said, staring at the grave alongside Molly. "Do you want to say a few words?"

"I didn't know her," Molly said. "But I feel like we should." She cleared her throat. "I have not spoken to Lizzie much about her experience where you're from, but from what she told me, you were kind and strong. You didn't deserve what happened to you." She began to cry again and pressed her hand to her mouth. I stood by silently until she regained her composure. Finally, she took a deep breath. "It's horrible that bad things happen to good people, and if I had my way, that would never happen. But that's not the universe we live in. The universe we live in is cruel, and you were a shining light of hope. There's not much more that any of us can aspire to be but a beacon of hope in the darkness. Though your light has faded, you have touched many and will shine in their hearts for years to come."

"Those were lovely words, intruder." Words not spoken by either of us and followed by a bright light in front of us. A short woman emerged, her dress the same white the handmaidens wore, though her eyes were dark purple and her dark, olive skin shimmered in the light. "My mistress has seen what you have done for her handmaiden and is pleased." She turned to the castle. "Follow me, and she will entreat with you."

"We have—Gabriel is coming to—"

She held up her hand. “We are aware of what is coming for us. Believe me when I say that angel will not come until we are ready for him.”

CHAPTER 48

Anjelica

The world moved in slow motion while I waited for the gates of Mephistopheles's castle to open. The charred bodies climbing the walls of Hell had slowed to a crawl, and every turn of the heads around me happened at half speed. I watched the beads of sweat form on Mephistopheles's head one at a time as Atka held the Dagger of Obsolescence to his throat.

"If one single charred soul makes its way out of Hell, I will send you to oblivion," she hissed before the world ground to a halt around me.

I tried to keep a straight face, not betraying my worry despite feeling every thump of my chest in my ears. The hardest part of a negotiation was after your demands were made and before they were fulfilled. Anything could happen in those moments, and we had no promise that my mother or Araphael would be returned unharmed.

It couldn't have been longer than half an hour, but it felt like four by the time the gates cracked open, and two demons flew out of the castle and dropped my mother on the path. I ran out from the crowd of soldiers to embrace her, ignoring the demons on either side of us.

"Mom," I sobbed. "You're okay."

She cracked a smile. "Of course I'm okay, my love. I feel lighter now that my sins are washed away from me."

It was the same thing that Mephistopheles said when he impersonated my mother, and it made my blood boil. I spun around toward the tiny demon floating nearby. He grinned, his jagged, yellowed teeth glistening in the fires of Hell.

"What did you do to her?" I said. "What did you do to my mother?"

He laughed. "You don't understand anything. I've done nothing to her but show her the truth."

"Torture is not the answer. You've brainwashed her. I want my mother back."

He laughed. "You are so naïve. You've spent, what, a couple of days in Hell, and you think you know everything."

"I am a demon, just like you."

"You are nothing like me!" His voice boomed. "I am a demon lord. I have been here since the first days, since before the fall of Lucifer, since Hades ruled this land. You may not believe that I have her best interests at heart—"

"I don't even believe you have a heart, you evil bastard."

He shrugged, and the movement of his neck caused Akta to nick his neck slightly. He sneered in pain. "I take my job very seriously. I was made to absolve sinners of their sins before they move on. We all were. It was God that twisted our purpose when he sent angels to Hell and made them look like us. If I were in charge, I could fix this place because I know its ways."

"You will never get the chance," Akta growled.

"No, I suppose I won't, which means Hell will burn." He smiled. "You may have won this day, but with Lucifer in charge, the Apocalypse is inevitable. If you give me the knife, I will end this. We can save everyone."

I lunged toward Mephistopheles and knocked him over, smashing his face into the ground and punching him until my fists bled and my hands were numb.

"Don't hurt him on my account," I heard a low voice growl behind me. I spun around to see Araphael standing next to my mother.

My bitterness fell away immediately. I ran to him and hugged him just as tightly as I had my mother. When I did, I realized just how rail-thin the god of death was, nothing but skin and bones—possibly not even the skin.

"You're okay," I said.

"Of course," he replied. "They would never torture me. They fear death too much, even here. It seems like the only one not afraid of me is you." He nodded toward my mother. "And you, of course, my dear."

Mom's eyes filled with tears, and a big smile spread across her face. "I never thought I would see you again."

He let me go and took my mother's hands. "Yes, it is my great shame that I wasn't here to carry you to the afterlife myself." They looked at each other for a few seconds, and though Araphael's orange eyes showed no sign of emotion, there was a depth of love I saw in my mother's that I'd never ever seen before, even when she looked at me as a child. It was then I realized the connection they had was more than admiration; it was more than friendship. It was everything.

"NO!" Mephistopheles screamed behind me. I turned in time to see him grab the knife out of Akta's hand and leap toward Araphael's heart. "You won't stop me!"

My mother's eyes went wide, and she pushed me out of the way. Before Mephistopheles could find Araphael's heart, he found my mother's and plunged the dagger deep into it. She gasped silently and fell to her knees.

In the commotion, the demons pulled Mephistopheles off of her, and I dropped to the ground beside her.

"Mom, Mom, Mom. Stay with me." Her hands flecked away, turning to black ash, disappearing into the sky. I whipped around to Araphael. "Do something!"

"I can't," he said, his head lowered. "That dagger is too powerful. Were I to give all my power to her, she still could not hope to survive."

"That's not true—" I tried to grab on to her, but her body was nearly disintegrated already, just pieces of ash. "Please, Mom. Don't go."

She smiled. "This is what I wanted, my love, to be free. And now I am. No more torture. No more hatred." She looked back at Araphael with tears in her eyes. "No more love. No more anything." She turned back to me. "It's okay. I'm not afraid."

I grabbed her around the shoulders, which were already fading, and squeezed her tightly until I felt her disappear under me, and I was only holding air. I had done all of this to save my mother and ended up killing her again. Now there was nothing left to save and no hope to see her again.

When the last of my mother had vanished, the dagger fell to the ground and rested against my knee. Its hilt was warm against me, and when I took it in my hand, a gust of heat pulsed through me. I held it before me and turned to Mephistopheles, seething.

"I'll kill you!" I shouted.

Araphael put his spindly hand on me. "You will not!"

"How could you say that? He killed my mother. Didn't you care for her at all?"

"I loved your mother like I never loved another mortal in the whole of the cosmos. Killing this demon will not stop the pain. It won't bring her back."

I held the knife up toward him, my hand quaking. The trembling reverberated through my whole arm, and then my whole body, and when the emotion had washed over me completely, I fell to the ground. Araphael took me in his bony arms, letting me cry.

I hadn't yet collected myself when movement caught my attention—the charred bodies making their way to the tip of Hell. They would soon be through the holes, crawling over Earth.

"You're right," I said. "The best revenge is stopping this Apocalypse before it can get started."

"That we can do," he said. "That we can certainly do."

CHAPTER 49

Lizzie

"TURN!" I screamed as we looked down the barrel of Moana's gun turret. The yellow from the brimstone attack glowed brightly, and the three of us covered our faces. We barely cleared the barrel when the heat exploded and nearly blew us apart. Even dodging the main blast, the heat burned my arms, and the afterburn sent us spiraling down into the clouds below.

Michael screamed, unlatching us from his bosom as he writhed in pain. I had to work to stand up, and that's when I saw the extent of the damage. Half of Michael's left wing was charred black and smoking. Immediately, I dropped to my knees again, madly shoveling cloud cover over it to put out the fire. He cried out in pain as the fire sizzled away and the smoke dissipated into the air.

"Don't wait for me," he breathed. "I'll be fine."

All around us, the low sounds of growls inched closer. Demons and angels popped up from every side and moved in on our location. I thought it would be over for us, then I remembered something—something from far back in my memory.

"Wait, clouds are water, right?"

"Theoretically," Agent Davis said, facing the oncoming enemy, preparing himself.

I smiled. "Well, I'm a water nymph." I stood up and moved my hands around my body in a clockwise motion. "*Amnis aqua*!"

Water leeched from the clouds until I'd shriveled them up to nothing. The stream of water crashed into the onslaught of demons and angels. I kept them at bay while Agent Davis pulled Michael to his feet, and we stumbled through the streets, keeping the onslaught of demons behind us.

"Move faster!" Agent Davis shouted at Michael. "Your legs aren't burnt!"

They hobbled forward together, and I stayed slightly behind, throwing water whips and streams of water toward the attacking army.

"*Fluctus magni*!" I shouted, bringing the water from all the clouds around us. I lowered my arms, and the water came crashing down upon the far side of the clouds. The deluge knocked back the angels and demons. With the battlefield clear for a moment, I turned to catch up to the others.

I slipped myself beneath Michael's arms, and we picked up the pace as we neared the platform. The guns were too big to find us while we passed under them but when we reached the base of the platform, they spun around, just as they had the first time.

"Stay where you are!" Moana shouted from atop the protective bubble around God. I could see him trapped within the fizzling blue forcefield. "Or you will die."

"Already dead, ash face," I shouted back.

"You need to get up there," Michael said. "I can't—and I don't think Ircheal or Saphiel are coming either."

"I can't fly," I said. "Unless you're going to make me an archangel."

Michael grimaced with his eyes closed. "That's exactly my plan."

“Really?” I couldn’t help the smile from spreading across my face.

“Really. Now, kneel.” I did, and he pulled a flaming sword from nowhere. “Elizabeth, I name you an archangel, guardian of the realm of Earth, bearer of the flaming sword of vengeance. Rise and take your position in the hallowed halls.”

A great swell of pride flowed through me, followed by a tremendous pain as two enormous wings ripped through my back. “This is awesome,” I said when they spread out behind me in full glory.

“I’m not supposed to do that,” Michael said. “But if anyone’s earned the title, it’s you.” He looked up. “Now, get up there and finish Moana. That’s an order.” The demons and angels following us had now surrounded us.

“Agent Davis, shall we?”

Agent Davis turned his attention to the Blue Trident rushing toward him. “Let’s go.”

I bent my knees and soared into the air. The wings moved with me like they had been part of my body for my entire life. Before Moana could get a beat on me, I clapped my hands together.

“*Fluctus aestumque scabant*!” Focusing on the base of the turrets, I leeched more water from the clouds and sent it crashing toward them. The turrets cracked and wobbled until they tipped over, exploding as they fell toward the Earth.

“NO!” Moana screamed.

“Yes,” I replied, bringing my hands together and sending a tidal wave upon her. The water knocked her backward, off of the bubble and into the cushion of the cloud cover. She skidded to a stop, knocking into a crate of weapons.

She popped up, cradling the controls in her hands tightly. I called forth another torrent of water and smashed them from her hand. She was defenseless and drenched.

"You ruined everything," Moana howled. "Everything! You have no idea what you've done!"

"Sure I do." I nodded, pulling the controls away from her hand and kicking her backward. "I'm saving the world."

I dropped the controller to the ground and smashed it with my foot. Another howl burst out of Moana as the barrier fell from around the platform. God stepped forward, free—and pissed. He disappeared, and, in a flash, hundreds of demons exploded out of existence. At the same time, Gabriel's angels began to fall to the ground, their arms and legs bound in electric blue shackles.

In minutes, the fighting was over, and God appeared in front of me. "Thank you."

"My pleasure."

He turned his attention to Moana. "What have I done to anger you so?"

She wept. "I'm sorry. I'm so sorry. I was just doing what I thought was right."

He sighed. "You put your judgment before mine. Perhaps I gave you too much power." He touched Moana, and she was bound in the same way as the other angels. God sighed. "I'm so disappointed in all of you."

"In all honesty," Moana replied, her head lowered, "I'm disappointed in myself."

“Yes.” God shook his head. “But not for the right reason.” He turned to me, and his frown turned to a smile. “I owe you my thanks.”

I shrugged. “I was just trying to help.”

“Your valor will be rewarded. For now, I have a lot of cleaning up to do. If you’ll excuse me.”

There was an ominous tone in his voice, and part of me dreaded what he meant by cleaning up, but he was right about one thing: There was a terrible mess, and it needed to be repaired.

CHAPTER 50

Ollie

Every step we took toward the castle brought us impossibly closer to it. For every ten steps we walked, it was as if we'd traveled a mile. Gabriel, meanwhile, struggled to move even an inch. The young girl was right. You couldn't move toward the castle without a handmaiden and whatever magic they possessed.

"How long have you been in training, Hadiya?" I asked.

"Two hundred years," she replied. "Though that doesn't matter."

"I think it does," I replied with a smile.

With a few more steps we were at the door to the castle. Hadiya pushed open a wooden door that led us into the courtyard, an oblong area with dozens of towers converging impossibly at a point in the sky high above us, as if the laws of time and space there were warped and twisted.

Hadiya didn't seem to even notice. She pushed open another door, taking me down a hallway and into a room where thousands of red and white threads crisscrossed at the top. She walked across the stone floor to another door, this one copper. Hundreds of the threads fed into a small window above the door, continuing into the next room. There they split paths toward two separate looms, one on either side of a platform where a spindle sat.

Four women in white togas, with golden bands pulling back their long hair, weaved the string into the loom. They looked intently into the rafters, watching a red string move closer to them. The dread on their faces grew until the thread began to vibrate. When it turned white, they looked relieved.

Another woman appeared, dressed in a ragged blue dress, pockets sewn up and down its sides. Her hair was thin and white, and her face looked as if it had been pulled like taffy. Her nose and cheeks drooped low, and the bags under her eyes were puffy, like she hadn't slept in ages.

"My gods, they are getting harder and harder to catch." She sighed. "Are you all right, my girls?"

The women all nodded as she used her knobby cane to hobble back to the spindle.

"Mistress Talinda?" Hadiya said meekly.

The woman turned to her, squinting. "Ah, yes, Hadiya. You have brought her to me. Excellent." She moved faster than before, bobbing her head as she approached me. "You are Oleander White, are you not?"

"I am."

Talinda looked me up and down, then examined me a second time with more verve. "I thought you would be bigger. Can you take off your sunglasses for me, sweetie?"

"No," I replied. "I don't take them off for anyone."

"It's perfectly safe, my dear. We're not here to hurt you. We won't laugh at you. You're safe here."

Something about her voice soothed me, and I believed her. Before I realized what I was doing, my glasses were off, revealing my blue eye swirling along with the red one. When I caught wind of what I had done, I scrambled to put my glasses back on, but Talinda stayed my hand.

"I don't—"

"They're beautiful. A very rare gift you have, even among angels." She pointed to my blue eye and then my red one. "And among demons. To be gifted like this and to waste it on petty criminals."

"Who are you, my mother?"

She tsked, though there was a smile on her face. "Just an interested party. Now, you were here to tell me something?"

I nodded. "Gabriel, an archangel from Earth, makes his way here to demand you—" I stopped, seeing her polite smile. "You already know this, don't you?"

"Of course, I do. That's my job. It's very hard to know everything that will happen and not do anything about it."

"It seemed like you were doing something about that red thread."

She nodded. "Yes, yes, yes. I am doing something about that, but I admit, I am getting old, and my creaky bones are not what they used to be." She searched my eyes, not daunted by them in the least. "Which is why, as of late, I have considered bringing in some help. Somebody who could run around and fix all the anomalies in the timeline."

"Like Lizzie did?"

Talinda stared hard at me. "Yes, but on a more permanent basis."

My eyes narrowed. "Are you offering me a job?"

"So to speak. This was a bit of a trial, and you've passed. You made it here before Gabriel, and even though it would have been easier to just give up, you never did."

The woman had to be crazy. I was an angel and a criminal, not some sort of time agent. Even if she were serious, I hadn't had a boss since I could remember, and certainly wasn't looking to start now.

"I'm not sure I'm looking for a job," I said, finally.

"If I remember correctly, you have burned every bridge on Earth and have nothing to look forward to except being on the run from criminals for the decided future."

"But I'm rich, so there's that too."

She raised her eyebrows and spoke like she was dangling a carrot in front of me. "Did I mention you get to travel through time?"

"I assumed as much, but that—"

The door opened, and another woman came forward. "The two pixies have arrived, ma'am."

"Thank you," Talinda said before turning back to me. "Let's put that off for the moment. Are you ready for the endgame, my dear? I like seeing the ending of things, almost as much as I like new beginnings."

"Gabriel is very dangerous," I said.

"And so am I. There is a reason I do not let angels, or even gods, into my domain. They follow my wishes because they fear me as much as they respect me." A shadow passed over her face. "I do not like when people hurt my handmaidens. When Gabriel reaches this castle, the laws of time and space bend to my will." She took a hobbling step toward the door. "And I will rain down my vengeance upon him."

"You never needed our help, did you?" I asked, staring after her.

Talinda paused and looked over her shoulder at me. "No," she said. "But it was very sweet of you to try. So few people try these days. It always warms my heart when they do."

CHAPTER 51

Lizzie

While God stopped the incursion in a matter of seconds, it took some time for Michael and Agent Davis to round up the treasonous angels for processing, especially with Michael nursing a lame wing. When they were finished, all the Godschurch agent could do was shake his head.

"You realize this is over 70 percent of the archangels in Heaven, right?" He asked. "If I take all these angels in, there are going to be questions." He glanced over at me. "We already discussed how bad that would be for Earth."

"Yes, we don't want the Godschurch knowing, if at all possible."

Michael took a deep breath, rubbing his chin. "They would be no use to us, and if we imprison them here, there is too great a risk of them escaping and wreaking havoc again." He cleared his throat. "Isn't there anything you can do?"

"We have a penal colony on Zabaric 13. It's in a remote area of the universe where the gods rarely look and ask questions even less often. I could take them there. I'd need help, though, as it requires working outside of the realm of the Godschurch."

"Take whatever you need," Michael replied. "And thank you. If Zeus ever found out about this, it would be the end of us all."

"I only need one archangel, and I already know which one." Agent Davis stepped toward me. "What do you say? Will you help me?"

"Me?" I stammered. "I don't—I can't—" I gave Michael a pleading look, and he raised his eyebrows in question. "Are you sure?"

The archangel nodded. "You have earned a life bigger than what can be offered in Heaven. Before you make a decision, though, God would like to have a word with you."

I looked back at Agent Davis, but he waved me off.

"Go," he said. "Think about my offer. I need to have words with Michael in private anyway."

Thoughts of traveling through the galaxy swirled through my head. I had to admit, the idea of staying in Heaven was a melancholy one, even if I had seen behind the veil. There was too much sadness here. I would do my duty if it was what God required of me but being able to travel beyond the stars had my heart aflutter as I climbed the stairs to the platform at the center of Heaven.

God was staring off into space when I reached the top of the stairs. His face was covered in yellow powder from a plastic case of cheese puffs in his lap, and a bottle of mead hovered next to him.

His eyes snapped to focus as I walked closer, and he smiled, flakes of cheese falling from the edges of his mouth. "Elizabeth, my savior." He clapped his hands together, and yellow dust peppered the air. "I am so proud of you. Imagine, saving our planet twice in the span of just a few decades. Even the greatest of my archangels could not say the same."

I bowed my head. "I am happy to be of service to you."

God moved forward and placed his crusty hands under my chin, raising my face to meet his eyes. “You bow your head to nobody.”

I wiped the crumbs from my chin. “Thank you.”

He turned from me then and looked out on the vast smoldering battlefield. “I’ve made a real mess of things, haven’t I?”

“I wouldn’t say that. Gabriel and the others are the ones—”

“Who turned on me because of the choices I made.” God sighed. “In truth, I never wanted to be put in charge of this planet. It was foisted on me. Still, I did try to do a good job.” He shook his head. “I was ill-prepared in the end, it would seem. Maybe I should have yielded to the Blue Trident. Perhaps they were right, after all.”

“No,” I said firmly. “Don’t say that. They were definitely in the wrong.”

“Their methods might be wrong, but their ethos wasn’t completely incorrect. Something must be done to ease Lucifer’s burden, or the entirety of the underworld will collapse upon itself.”

“Well, I don’t know the right answer, but I do know it’s not to start an Apocalypse and put all of humanity at risk.”

His eyes narrowed. “If the Apocalypse were to come to pass, I would face judgement for it, that is certain. Perhaps I deserve it.”

I placed my hand on God’s shoulder. “You’re talking like somebody who has lost, instead of someone who just won a great victory.”

“Was it a great victory? Almost all my most trusted advisors turned on me, and I am left with the burning wreckage of their aftermath.”

"I say it's time to rebuild. Allow more people into Heaven, make it better than it was before."

He smiled at me. "I might just do that." He looked down from his platform at Agent Davis. "And you will go off with the Godschurch, I presume?"

"I—only if you don't need me here," I replied.

"Oh, I need you here, but I cannot deny you this opportunity. It might never come around again. If anybody in this galaxy has earned the right to follow their dreams, it is you."

"Thank you." I didn't know what else to say.

God smiled and squeezed my shoulder. "No, thank you."

With that, he clasped his hands around mine for a final time and bid me goodbye. When I reached the bottom of the stairs, Agent Davis and Michael were finishing their conversation.

Michael turned to me first, giving me an appraising look. "Those wings suit you."

I spread them out a little farther and grinned. "You should have given them to me a long time ago."

"I agree. I'm glad I could rectify that mistake, even if it took the end of the world to do it."

"Have you decided?" Agent Davis asked.

"I have." I took a deep breath and let it out, not yet fully believing the idea of it. Me, traveling in the stars. "I would like to come with you."

"That's what I wanted to hear," he replied with one of his handsome smiles. "It won't be glamorous work, you know."

I laughed. "I'm okay with that. I can't wait to get started. Before I go, though," I said, looking at Michael, "when you find my parents, please let them know I love them."

"You have my word."

"Thank you." I nodded, more to myself than anyone else, and then said, "Agent Davis, I think I'm ready."

CHAPTER 52

Anjelica

"Thank you," I said, shaking Akta's hand. "You have been a true friend and companion. I'm sorry I ever doubted you."

She shrugged. "It happens. Are you sure you don't need any help?"

Araphael shook his head. "It is simple enough to close the portals, though it is nasty business."

"Then go."

I turned to Araphael. "Grab on tight."

We had both lost so much in the bowels of Hell, and I had no interest in losing more. When I clutched onto his cloak, I did it for keeps, digging my fingers in until my knuckles were white. We rose off from the ground quickly and smoothly, heading directly for the nearest hole in Hell's ceiling. The charred bodies were dangerously close to making their way through the portal.

"Grab that one!" Araphel shouted as we neared.

I took hold of one of the blackened souls and got ready to hurl it downward. Araphael turned on a dime and sped through the opening, carrying all three of us.

"What are you doing?" I screamed. We appeared back on Earth, in the middle of an Army base that had been invaded by demons and angels. "I thought we were preventing them from returning to Earth."

"I need its blood," he said, slicing the body along the neck and dribbling it on the edge of the portal. As he did, the portal quaked, collapsing down upon itself. The demons and angels guarding the portal lunged in attack, but Araphael turned their bodies to ash in an instant, and they blew away in the wind.

For the first time, I saw clearly the reasons for keeping Araphael locked up. He could have ended this incursion in an instant. The Blue Trident couldn't hope to match his power.

Araphael dropped me to the ground. "Wait here for me."

I didn't have time to respond. He was gone a second later, and I was alone on the Army base. Most of the buildings had been destroyed and what few soldiers remained didn't dare show their faces. Without a watch, it was hard to tell how long I sat there. As far as I could figure, the sun had barely tracked across the sky for an hour when Araphael returned with a crackle.

"It is done," he said. "And I have initiated a cloaking spell which should provide any fairies on Earth with the ability to remain hidden for a while. It won't last forever, but I am considerably powerful, in my way."

"Thank you," I said, staring at my feet. "Not just for doing this and saving the Earth, but for loving my mom."

His voice was thick when he responded. "I'm sorry I couldn't protect her. I will regret it every day of my life, which is a considerable length. She was an incredible lady."

There were things I had never really understood about my mother, apparently. She had always been just "Mom" to me, but there must have been something pretty incredible about her to ensnare a god. "Can you tell me about her?"

“I would like that. Perhaps we can talk more as I return you to your planet if that is your wish.”

I nodded. “It is. There is nothing for me here, and Margaret is waiting for me.”

He held out his bony hand. “Then let us be away. Let me tell you of my first meeting with your mother.”

I smiled and took his hand.

***

Araphael returned me to my room at the castle and took his leave. Though he promised to return soon, he could not guarantee exactly when. I took it as the platitude that it was and never expected to see him again. I moved through the room in darkness, taking off my tattered dress and yellow headband and easing into a nightgown.

I brushed my teeth and slid into bed, only to hear a groan coming from a lump in the blankets next to me. I scrambled to my feet and flipped on the light to see Margaret roused from sleep, blinking.

“You’re back!” She sat up straight in the bed.

“And you’re in my bed,” I said, stunned. “What are you doing in my bed?”

“I had no idea where you went. We have had people looking for days.” She trailed her hand over the top of the blankets. “This…well, it smelled like you.”

“My mother died,” I replied. “And I had to see her one last time.”

“Oh, no!” Margaret reached her arms out to me. “I’m so sorry. Come here and tell me all about it.”

I slid under the covers, melting against her. “What are people going to say?”

"I don't care," she whispered. "It's long past time that we lived our truth."

I squeezed her tightly and fell back against the pillows. "That sounds nice."

"Now," Margaret said. "Start from the beginning."

CHAPTER 53

Ollie

Talinda led me back into the courtyard, where Molly and Kimberly were seated at a small concrete bench.

"I hope you didn't have any trouble finding the place." She smiled at the two of them. "I appreciate the grace you gave to my handmaiden."

"It was our pleasure," Kimberly said. "But it was mostly Molly's idea."

"It was all Molly's idea if I recall." Talinda tapped her forehead, then winked. "It's a gift and a curse."

Molly nudged Kimberly with her elbow. "It was a joint effort, like most everything else in our lives."

Talinda's smile grew. "Yes, I love that about you two. Always in concert, even when you are not in sync. I have enjoyed watching your path. If I didn't know how much you had to return to after this, I would have given you the same offer I gave Oleander here, though we all know you wouldn't have taken it."

The offer Talinda gave me, to join her flock and help her write the wrongs of time, rattled around in my brain. The idea filled me with a sense of wonder and dread. It was true that I had nothing to return to on Earth, that, in fact, I had burned every bridge I ever built. But to uproot myself completely and join the Time Being? That was even scarier. There was no way to predict what my life would become.

Kimberly and Molly exchanged a look, then Kimberly said, "I have no idea what you're talking about."

"Me either," Molly added.

"Oh! I apologize. That often happens in conversation with me." She gestured toward the door. "I think you have earned the right to see how this plays out."

"We're ready to fight." Kimberly squared her shoulders.

Talinda held up her hand. "There will be no need for that, I hope. I haven't been in a fight in a long time, and I don't intend to have one now."

She snapped her fingers and waited. It didn't take long before the door to the castle opened, and Gabriel stumbled inside. When he saw the three of us, he tried to call his sword from thin air but failed.

"It's okay, Gabriel," Talinda said. "There is no need to cause a scene."

"You—you know who I am?" He bent down on one knee.

"I do, and I know what you seek. I also know that you will feel more comfortable telling me yourself, so please, go ahead."

Gabriel stood up, his head still bowed. "Thank you for an audience with you, your grace. My planet, Earth…it has been besieged with incompetence and ignorance, all due to the god that rules it. Long ago, we had a chance to end his reign and bring about a golden age, and I chose the wrong side in that battle. With my defection, the rest of my people threw down their weapons, and the insurrection failed. I wish to go back and choose the right side this time."

"I see." Talinda narrowed her eyes. "You would like for me to send you back in time, creating a time paradox that will destabilize the whole universe so that you can rise against one of my brothers and take control of a planet?"

"I do not wish to speak out of turn, but I know that you have the ability to nullify time anomalies if you are so inclined. If you would just—"

"You forget yourself." Her eyes went white. "And now, you presume to tell me my business?"

"No, my goddess. I am only saying that if you wanted—"

"I must obey the rules like any other. If I didn't, then I could resurrect the handmaiden you so callously butchered." Gabriel started to shake, and Talinda towered over him somehow. "Yes, I know all about that little incident, and what you have done to get here."

He pointed at me, shouting wildly, "She has turned you against me! They have all turned you against me! If you would only—"

"NO!" Talinda's voice boomed through the courtyard. "You have turned me against you. Do you think I need these three to tell me the business of the universe? That I have not seen everything, in every way, that I don't know the very depths of your immortal soul? I am time eternal!"

Gabriel cowered, his eyes wide with terror. He knew there was a reckoning coming. "I only wanted to serve the gods," he pleaded.

"You wanted to supplant our logic with your own! That is not servitude. That is blasphemy." Talinda took a giant step forward. "I have judged your soul, and I find you wanting."

Gabriel wasn't going down without a fight. He balled up his fist and swung at Talinda, but obviously she saw it coming. She caught his hand in midair, and where she touched him, he turned to stone. The effect extended through his body, encasing him in an eternal shriek as the granite fell down his throat and froze him in place.

When it was finished, Talinda brushed her hands and turned to us. “I’m so sorry. I wish you did not have to see me like that. People who wish to affect the timestream irritate me so.”

“What if he was right?” I hesitated to even ask, knowing it might piss her off. After seeing what I’d just seen, I definitely did not want to piss her off.

“It doesn’t matter,” she said, leaning on her cane. “My job—our job—is not to judge right or wrong. It is to protect the flow of time, to make sure that no one, human, angel, or even god, weakens it by taking time into their own hands. We all have moments of regret, but just because he believed things would be better doesn’t make it so.” She turned to Kimberly and Molly. “In fact, every day is a chance to turn it around, as long as we try.”

Molly frowned. “Then…we do have free will?”

“I didn’t say that.” Talinda shook her head. “You have the right to make any choice you would like, but you must live with it, always. Every choice can only be made one time, which is what makes it precious.”

Everyone might have only one chance to make a choice, but Talinda had dominion over time itself, which meant she had dominion over choice itself. I had made many bad choices in my life and taken a thousand wrong paths. I couldn’t pass up a chance to help people fix theirs and maybe get a chance to redeem some of my own in the process. Even if I wasn’t looking for a boss.

I took a step forward. “All this talk of choice helped me reach a decision. I choose to stay here, with you, and fix what is broken in the timestream.”

Talinda smiled gently. "I hoped you would say that."

"You didn't know it would happen?"

"I knew there was a very good possibility, as I know that if I gave the same choice to Kimberly and Molly, they would most likely choose to return to Earth." She turned to them. "Isn't that right?"

The two pixies looked at each other and wrapped their fingers together, then Kimberly said, "Yes, it is. We have work to do, and it's the kind of work nobody else can do but us."

"But first," Molly added. "I think we're going to take a vacation."

Talinda let out a laugh. "You deserve it."

"I hope we see each other again." I walked over to them and took their hands in mine.

They both wrapped me in a hug. Even though we had never been close, we had saved the world together—multiple times. As painful as it was to watch them go, I knew it was the right thing. The moment I made my decision, it was like a weight lifted from me. The path forward was clear.

When we had all broken from the hug, Talinda snapped her fingers. Kimberly and Molly were gone into the ether. We were alone, and Talinda turned to me.

"Are you ready to begin?"

I hesitated. "Honestly, I feel like I could sleep for a week."

"You can do that, and then we can get started in a few minutes."

"Wait, what?"

"It's best not to think about it," Talinda said, opening the door to the castle. "Time is weird."

CHAPTER 54

Kimberly

"Are you sure you're ready to give up everything?" I asked Malika, Geordi's mom. We were standing in front of her house in Vancouver. She'd put it up for sale and packed everything she needed in her car. "It's not an easy life."

"Anywhere without my Geordi isn't a life at all." She smiled at me. "Thank you for bringing him back to me."

"Of course," I said.

Molly was playing with the young boy on the lawn. They were kicking a soccer ball together when I approached.

"You're getting good," Molly said.

"I'm on a team. We made the championship last year." Geordi stopped the ball with his foot and looked at me. "I'm not going to be on that team anymore, am I?"

I shook my head. "No. You're not. Usually, I wouldn't have you and your mother stay together at all, but she is a very forceful woman, and you will be a very powerful protector."

I held my arms out, offering him a hug, and he ran to me.

"Is it going to be okay?" he asked.

"You have a long life in front of you, kid. Everything's going to be just fine."

***

Molly and I reappeared in our San Francisco apartment. With all the commotion, I had forgotten about the explosion. Luckily, we had the floor reinforced, along with all the walls, so nothing was destroyed except for our stuff.

Molly put her arm around my shoulder and gave it a squeeze. “It’s just stuff.”

I smiled. “Yeah, and the good stuff is in Mallorca anyway.”

“Oooh, I could really go for a week in Mallorca right now.”

I took her hand that was resting on my shoulder and leaned into her with a sigh. “How about two weeks?”

Molly scoffed, then laughed. “Now you’re just talking crazy. Besides, you’ll probably get a call and be off in a couple of days anyway.”

“I think my phone has been fried, and I have no plans on activating another until we get back.”

“Wow,” Molly said. “Two weeks of unimpeded Kimberly time. How long do you think until we get sick of each other?”

I kissed her on the nose. “I will never get sick of you, ever.”

“Gross,” she said, then kissed me. “I love it.”

***

You have just finished *Heaven.* Stay tuned after the author’s note to skip forward twenty years into the heart of the Apocalypse with Katrina’s stories in *Death.*

AUTHOR'S NOTE

This is it! We've finally wrapped around to *Death*! I know these author notes are very weird if you have started from book 1, but this is actually the 11th book in the Godsverse I've written. It was super tricky because I had to do two things: Give these characters satisfying endings and explain why you don't see them in the rest of the series.

Originally, Talinda was going to die, and Lizzie was going to become the new goddess of time, but these last two books (*Time* and this one) haven't worked like I planned in the outlines. I'm not somebody who strictly holds to an outline, but usually, I at least hit the major beats by the end.

In these last two books, I didn't follow my plan at all. By the beginning of book 2 in both stories, I was completely off the rails and in uncharted territories.

Perhaps it's because they both dealt with time, or just because we've been doing construction in my house during the writing of both those books, but they veered wildly from what I had written. It wasn't until I reached the end of the book that I even considered Ollie joining Talinda. It honestly came out of left field, even for me. In the original outline, she was supposed to join Anjelica on Onmiri, so I knew she wouldn't stay on the planet, but I never thought she would join Talinda, of all people.

Lizzie was another one whose ending completely changed during the book, especially with the introduction of Agent Davis. Agent Davis was supposed to pair with Ollie, not Lizzie, but when it came time for them to break apart, it just made more sense to send Lizzie with him, and that sealed her fate. Lizzie really came into her power during this book, and I'm glad she got her reward from saving the Earth—twice. It always sat in my craw that she didn't become an archangel in the last book, so I was happy to rectify that.

As far as Anjelica, I'm going to be honest. I didn't love writing her as an adult. She was one of my favorite characters in the whole Godsverse Chronicles in the first two books, but I wish I had brought her back younger before the world beat her down, and she lost that childlike wonder from the first two books of the series. But isn't that what it's like to grow up?

I always knew she would return back home in the end, though, and her role was more of a catalyst than anything. I needed a reason for the story to start right then for each character, and I wanted to bring all four characters into an Avengers-style team-up. I thought maybe this would allow her to regain her innocence…but when she ended up in Hell for most of the book, I knew that was out of the question.

For Kimberly, since I've already written *Darkness*, I knew exactly what happened to her before, during, and after the Apocalypse. She had to be on Earth, still doing her thing, which meant that in the end of the book she needed to return to neutral. This was the easiest thing to accomplish because it just meant getting her back to San Francisco with Molly by the end of the book.

By the way, Molly was supposed to be sucked into Hell when the portals opened, but that's another thing that just didn't happen.

Most importantly, I needed to get everything set up so that *Death* made sense. This was the hardest part because I had already not only written myself into a corner but into about seven books' worth of corners. While the other books could play with the world, and tell stories set several decades from the Apocalypse, this is only a few years before it happens in the next book. Since I had already written that book, I couldn't do anything that would break the universe that I've spent ten years creating.

One thing I love about this book is that it sets up the potential for lots of spin-off books: Ollie with the Time Being, Lizzie with the Godschurch, Kimberly saving fairies, and Anjelica on Onmiri. I don't know if I will ever write any of those, but I do have some ideas in my head.

If you've already read all the subsequent books, I hope you'll read through them again with this new information. It might bring a new perspective to the world. If you haven't yet, then you have seven more books full of action, adventure, and magic waiting for you. I hope you loved this book and all the other books I have in store for you.

***

And now for a preview of *Death.*

DEATH

Book 5 of The Godsverse Chronicles

By:
Russell Nohelty

Edited by:
Leah Lederman

Proofread by:
Katrina Roets & Toni Cox

Cover by:
Psycat Covers

Planet chart and timeline design by:
Andrea Rosales

Dedicated to every fan who read the Katrina Hates the Dead graphic novel and hounded me for years to make more stories in this world. You're to blame for all of this.

PROLOGUE

Two years ago, the world went through the end of times, the Apocalypse, or whatever the religious types call it. God beamed all the good boys and girls up to some giant orgy in the sky and left the rest of us asking one question: Why not me?

A rift opened in the desert. Hellspawn poured out onto Earth. They ravaged humanity, ripping us apart for their own pleasure, torturing us in the most grotesquely creative ways possible. They looted our towns, raped our bodies, and slaughtered us at will. It was bedlam; Hell on earth. And there was nothing we could do to stop it.

Then, one day, the monsters got bored and opted for a quiet life in the suburbs. They squatted in the homes of the people they once brutally murdered. They were neither pleasant nor polite neighbors. They threw raucous parties late into the night and played their guitars too loud. They shot off fireworks in the dead of night. They lived like frat boys. We lived in constant fear and a state of perpetual loneliness, expecting to die and scared to live. We tried to get along any way we could, even after we'd lost everything.

CHAPTER 1

"Stay out of here, man!"

The metal door of my apartment shook and shuddered over and over as a zombie slammed against it. Wooden doors broke too easily. They splintered and sheared during even a light zombie attack. Metal doors lasted forever if you could find a few suckers willing to lug it up a flight of stairs for you.

The door slammed again. The zombie on the other side wouldn't give up; I had to give him that. "I told you I'm not letting you in, so piss off!"

Zombies were a nuisance more than anything. Their spongy flesh barely held against your fist. They were only intimidating as a horde, and there haven't been zombie hordes for months. At most, you got a few zombies huddled in a group.

As far as monsters went, zombies ranked at the bottom of the Apocalyptic monster scale. There were all sorts of demons around since the Rapture, not to mention ghosts, and minotaurs, and these three-headed dogs, and seven-headed hydras, too. It's a complete mess. It's what you deal with during a full-blown Apocalypse. The kind the Bible warned us about for all those wasted millennia.

Also, most zombies talked, and not just "we eat brains" either. They were lucid, just like anybody else on the planet. Well, some of them anyway. If they rose from the grave before their brains rotted, they could speak. Otherwise, they were the shuffling stupid zombies like in old horror movies. But that's just science.

I slammed my weight against the banging door. “Go away!”

“I’m not going anywhere, Katrina!” the zombie shouted back. “I have squatter’s rights!”

“Go away!”

This particular zombie might or might not be, but definitely was, my old roommate.

He’s a dick. Not because he’s a zombie, either. That just doesn’t help the situation. No, he’s a dick because he hasn’t paid rent in six months.

I was making headway getting the door actually closed and locked when my phone rang.

Yes, there was still cell phone reception two years into the Apocalypse. No, I didn’t know why it still worked, but you don’t have to be a genius to figure out that the corporate shills who ran the cell companies weren’t churchgoers. Otherwise, they would’ve been raptured. Weird how that caveat worked, where you could escape damnation just by going to church. Lotta rapists went to church. Lotta good people didn’t.

We found all sorts of good men and women God left behind after the Apocalypse began. Men and women who did the Lord’s work, even if they didn’t go to church or praise his name. God was a vindictive bastard. The Devil was worse, though, for unleashing this Hell upon us.

I flipped open my phone. “What do you want, Ronald?”

Ronald was my boss at the only job I could find after the Apocalypse. Yes, there were still jobs. We’re not savages. People gotta make a living. They gotta eat. We’re not marauders. Well, some of us were marauders, but not most of us.

"Katie!" Ronald shouted into the phone.

"Don't call me that!" I screamed. I hated when people called me Katie.

His shrill voice pounded against my eardrum. "It's loud over there. Somebody tapping that ass or something?"

The door slammed again. I braced against it with all my weight. "You think I would pick up the phone if I was getting nailed, Ronald?"

"I'd like to think so. I mean, I imagine it often enough, Katie."

"Imagine me ramming my fist through your skull if you ever call me Katie again."

The zombie slammed against the door again. I pressed my ass against it to prevent him from coming in. "Look, Kate. You gotta come in."

"Screw you, man. I've worked for the past three weeks straight. This is my day off."

"Don't know what to tell you, Kat. Gary and Melissa both caught the Plague. They can't come in since they're dying."

"Can't you find somebody else?"

"Who else is there, man? I guess I could pull a couple of zomboids off the street. They're always good for a shift."

"No! Do *not* do that. I'll come in, alright? Just do *not* hire any zomboids."

"I knew you would."

"I hate you."

The door slammed again. I'd had enough. I ripped it open and glared at the jaundiced zombie smiling back at me. "Screw off, Barry. I kicked you out two weeks ago."

He scratched his red hair. Flecks of skin fell to the ground. "I know, Katrina, but I just found a copy of *Donald in Mathmagic Land*. I wanna watch it, so I'm gonna need my TV."

"I haven't seen a dime from you in six months. Consider the TV my payment."

"Alright, alright. That's fair. But you know I'm just gonna keep coming back for it, right? I mean, it's not like there's a whole lotta functional TVs left in town, aside from the Black Zone, and I ain't crazy enough to go there. I've been salvaging around and looking for one. So, like, you *could* keep it, and then you'll have to keep seeing me, or you could let me take it, and I'll be outta your hair forever."

I sighed. His zombie logic was sound. "Take the TV, and you're outta my life forever, agreed?"

"Scout's honor. Now let me in. I'm freezing my nerps off."

I stepped aside and let Barry into the apartment. "Fine. Grab it and go. I'm late anyway, and I gotta shower to get the stench of you off me."

"Fair enough. Hey, can I walk with you? It's not safe out there."

I grumbled to myself on the way to the bathroom. "Fine! Just wait for me out here."

"Thanks, Katie!"

"Don't call me that!"

***

I winced as the cold water hit my shoulder. We haven't had hot water in a year, but my body never acclimated to that moment the cold water first hit my naked body.

Hot water was a luxury, and we didn't get luxuries anymore. Some businesses still had access to hot water, but only if it was critical to their operation, like water treatment plants.

There wasn't much we could hold on to these days, but clean water was one of them. It was one of the few things that kept us human, one of the few things that kept us going even on the worst days.

On special occasions, I gathered kindling and boiled water the old-fashioned way, but this wasn't a special occasion. This was just a run of the mill Thursday.

I rubbed the remnants of my last bar of soap over my aching shoulder. Trucks didn't deliver soap anymore. Luckily, there was always plenty of human fat to turn into soap, and there was always an industrious person willing to harvest enough to make more, but it took time. Another batch wasn't due for a couple more days.

Scars covered every inch of my body, save for my face. I wore long jackets and pants to cover them up, but as the soap rode against my skin, it told the story of every battle I ever fought in Braille, from the first days of the Apocalypse through last night, where I beat back seven zombies with a hatchet. Every scar was a reminder that nowhere was safe.

"Are you almost done in there?" Barry shouted to me.

"No!" I screamed back. "Go away!"

The less civilized zombies still terrorized the countryside. The more docile ones lived in apartments and kept to themselves. The most enterprising demons hired less industrious monsters to flood the streets with terror, and zombies were their weapon of choice. You could go without a zombie attack for days, forget that life was a constant struggle, then face four attacks in an evening. Once the zombies tired us out, the demons would come and finish the job.

Anybody still alive could fend off a zombie attack on their best day, but it's harder to have your wits about you after you've been up for a hundred hours straight. That's where people got slaughtered nowadays. Everybody left was covered in scars, mentally and physically. We could all handle ourselves, but sometimes…you just lost your faculties. Other times, you lost the will to live.

Everybody lost the will sometimes. Hopefully, you got it back before you did anything stupid, cuz there's a mighty crappy price you pay for death.

Hell.

If I died, I went to Hell. There were no ifs, ands, or buts about it. God already beamed the good boys and girls up to some giant orgy in the sky, and I wasn't one of them. Which meant there was only one way out. Hell on Earth was bad enough, but Hell in Hell was an unbearable thought.

I ran the soap over a deep scar across my thigh, received in the first days of the Apocalypse when Barry was still a human. Back then, and even before the Apocalypse, we were roommates. We met through his sister, Connie, and hit it off well enough. After high school, neither of us wanted to go to college. We just wanted to chill out and smoke weed all day. Barry sold enough dope on the side to make his half of the rent. I worked for mine.

Once the Apocalypse hit, the world erupted into endless flames. If you've ever seen the pictures of a forest fire engulfing Los Angeles, with the Holly Hobby homes in the foreground and the blaze burning inches from it, you know what it looked like.

The entire city of Overbrook caught flame at the same time. Our neighbors ran screaming through the streets. Great demons with swords and scythes indiscriminately hacked down everybody in their path.

That's where I got the scar. I turned a corner and came face to face with a big demon, like Andre the Giant on steroids. It swung its scythe at me and sliced across my thigh. I bled out on the street, losing consciousness. Barry found me. If he hadn't dragged me to a hospital…let's just say they took good care of me there.

Overbrook hospital did good work until they were overrun with demons. Like the big box stores and malls, they were easy targets for marauders and demons. There weren't hospitals anymore, but clinics existed sporadically around the city. Everything in Overbrook existed haphazardly. There's a doctor over here, a laundry over there, and a restaurant wherever there is room. People found little pockets of safety in the nightmare and hunkered down.

***

I dressed the same every day. I didn't have the energy to agonize over my closet. I needed that brainpower to stay alert. Long pants to cover my scars with a white t-shirt and leather jacket.

I rocked workout gloves, too, because they helped me grip poles and other weapons. They are a top-five must-have item for any Apocalypse. I've been saved from so many blisters with those gloves. The last thing you want is an open wound when the monsters come out of the woodwork and attack.

I put together my look to be part utilitarian and part badass. I would be lying if I didn't say that part of my schtick was to look the part. People left you alone if you walked with a snarl, combat boots, and workout gloves. Even after two years, there were lots of people who ran away from a fight unless it was necessary, even though we could all handle ourselves. You don't get this far without having some serious survival skills.

I didn't much work out anymore, but I didn't need to, either. Just living was enough of a workout. Back before the Apocalypse, Connie and I did Krav Maga with our friends Peter Li and Chad Bowden so we could protect ourselves from her horrible father. It came in handy after the Apocalypse when I had to break way more than noses. For us, at least. Peter and Chad barely lasted a month.

Ironically, you needed those skills less now than you did at the beginning. The monsters were softer now than when the Apocalypse first started. A function of living on Earth, I suppose. They got a little doughy around the midsection and decided playing video games was better than ripping people apart.

Those that enjoyed the heat and violence of Hell returned to the brimstone to torture billions of new victims. The runty ones remained. They didn't have the same killer instinct. Most of them just wanted to be left alone.

Finally dressed, I walked out of my bathroom and saw Barry on the couch watching the TV, manspreading like he owned the place, with his hand down his pants. Men never change.

"Let's go!" I shouted to him. "Quit dicking around."

CHAPTER 2

Barry walked behind me as we made our way through the rusted gate and out of my apartment complex. He'd started banging on my door at twilight. It was dark by the time we left the apartment. Night was the worst time in Overbrook. The dead came out at night.

I don't usually take that long to get ready, but I did drag a little bit. I didn't want to go to work. The job sucked. The people sucked. Not that anybody wanted to work, but slinging moldy pizzas on a Thursday night in Overbrook was bad by any job standard.

Overbrook used to be the nicest little city in the Pacific Northwest, surrounded by trees and cut off from the world's evils. We were content to be left alone. We didn't need much, and we didn't ask for much.

New movies didn't come to Overbrook, except for stuff like *Star Wars* and *Transformers*, and we liked them just fine. Nobody opened trendy new restaurants, but that was okay. Maximillian's had the best pie in Oregon and ice cream sundaes as big as your head. We had a hospital, but most of us just went to the doctor down the street we'd been going to for our whole lives. Mine was Dr. Call. He got raptured up. Deservedly so. One of the few who deserved it, by my estimation.

It was the kind of sleepy, little town Norman Rockwell painted. I was perfectly happy living in my quaint little hamlet, working a sleepy, little job, and living a sleepy, little life. It was peaceful in Overbrook.

Main street was the only place in town where it ever hustled or bustled. Most of the shops and restaurants were there. On the Fourth of July, everybody gathered in the square to watch fireworks. Great joy existed there once.

Not anymore.

When Barry and I walked past it now, on cracked and slanted sidewalks, it was a shell of its former self. Mud and soot turned the white-washed buildings an ashy gray; vandals had smashed through the windows years ago. Huge trees grew straight up through the asphalt on the street. Only a ghost town remained.

Years ago, I walked blissfully ignorant through the town square high out of my mind. I remember wandering around after school completely blasted with my friends Dave and Swayze, laughing and joking without a care in the world. That was before they went off and got married and then dead.

Now, I looked warily around every corner. Streetlights flickered as we ambled through the main drag. The hydroelectric dam still delivered us power, and people manned it at all hours to make sure we had electricity at night. We protected it with our lives. It was the only thing separating us from the creatures living in the darkness.

I probably should have just driven around instead of always walking. After all, there was an abundance of cars in Overbrook. You could have your pick, but cars made noise, and noise attracted monsters. Also, cars are only great until you roll one. Then, they become a liability. Even though I fought too many monsters walking around, it was still less of a gamble than driving. Besides, gas was precious in Overbrook. People fought and died for it. Cabals made their fortunes hoarding it.

I turned up a blind alley at the end of the main drag. Barry huffed and puffed behind me, fumbling his TV with every step. I didn't like using alleys. Alleys were prime spots for an ambush, but this one cut ten blocks off my walk, and those ten extra blocks were a harrowing affair. The sooner you got inside at night, the better.

"Wait up!" Barry shouted. "This thing is heavy."

"You're the one who wanted to walk with me," I said. "Remember that?"

"You're a real asshole. You know that? Sound just like my sister."

Connie. She used to be my best friend until I let Barry die. Since then, she'd been cold as ice. Really, it's a bit of a misnomer to say I let him die. That boy was a glutton for pain and a magnet for misfortune.

"How is she?" I said. "Haven't seen her around for a while."

"She's been avoiding you."

"That'll pass, eventually. She still sacrificing goats to the Dark Lord?"

"I don't think it's goats anymore. I think she moved up to cows."

"Is that an upgrade?"

"I think so. She's still pissed our douchebag dad got blue lighted and not her. Won't stop trying to summon the Dark Lord until he brings her justice."

Blue lighted. It's what we called it when people got raptured up to Heaven. Connie's dad was a real dickhead, but he was a churchgoing dickhead. That seemed to be the only criteria. You could be a child molester, but if you went to church, you'd still get blue lighted.

"Well, that does eat up a lot of time," I said.

"She still finds time for Dennis."

I frowned at her boyfriend's name. "Well, they both need to get over it. Life isn't fair."

"I'll pass on the message. You're all heart, you know."

"Hey, I let you move back in, even though you were a zomboid, didn't I?"

"Yeah, you're a saint, Katie."

"Don't call me that."

"You pitied me and felt guilty for letting me die. It's not like it was out of the goodness of your heart. You coulda just given me a handie and called it a day."

"If I ever touch your dick, it'll be to rip it off."

"See, like I said. Cuun—"

Shook! A five-foot-long stake smashed through the front of the television, shattering glass everywhere, and sliced through Barry's chest. I spun around to see the wooden stake protruding two feet in front of him.

"Aw, come on!" Barry said, looking down at the stake. "Uncool!"

"Relax! You can't feel pain. It's just an inconvenience." I latched onto the stake with both hands. Next time people laughed at me for wearing gloves, I would tell them this story.

"Get it out. Get it out!"

"Hold still, you big baby."

I dug my combat boot into Barry's chest and heaved. With one hearty yank, the stake slid through him and onto the ground. Blood, pus, and mucus spurted from Barry's chest.

"How does it look?" Barry asked.

I knelt to check out his chest. There was a massive hole where his heart should be. “You'll survive.”

Zombies didn't need their insides. They didn't seem to need anything except a functional brain. I was skeptical that one rattled around inside Barry's skull, but if it didn't, then he'd be gone. “You think?”

“I've seen better. I've seen worse. You'll live.”

Barry stuck his hand inside the hole. “Gross.”

I grabbed his wrist. “Don't touch it.”

He slapped my hand away and poked at the hole again. “What do you think that was all about?”

“I don't know, but it can't be good.”

Groaning rose from the end of the alleyway. I'd heard it before, dozens of times. A small band of zombies lurched toward us. These weren't zombies like Barry. There were braindead ones, the kind that a demon could easily control. These types of zombies rotted in the ground for years before they dug themselves out.

Unlike zombies in the movies, these ones weren't motivated by brains, and they didn't have some great sense of smell, or sound, or whatever allows for zombies to perfectly track down groups of humans. Mostly, these zombies just stood around, gathering dust, until something found them and took control. It was usually a demon ready to take on a middle management position.

I sighed. “I wish they would just get here already. The longest part is watching them amble over here, you know?”

Three zombies emerged from the darkness. One was tall and lanky, like Keith Richards, except less gaunt. Another looked like a fatter, uglier, Danny DeVito. A third crawled along the ground with its legs missing and looked just like my uncle Ramsey.

"Can we go now?" Barry asked meekly.

"It's just a couple of zomboids, Barry."

Cracking my knuckles, I readied myself, even though I really didn't want to fight. I had tweaked my shoulder last night, and just clenching my fists made the pain vibrate up my right arm. I had intended to ice it but never got the chance.

Like I said, that was how people died. They fought too hard for too long, and then a zombie horde found them at the right moment.

"What are you doing?" Barry asked.

"Fighting. What does it look like?"

His head lolled back. "Oh god. We're gonna die!"

"Please. They're the dumbest, slowest monsters on the planet."

The zombies ambled forward.

"They're gonna rip us apart. We should run."

"I'm not running, Barry. Then they'll just terrorize somebody else. I can't let that happen."

"Fine. Fight them. What do I care? Just remember to stab them through the—"

"The brain. I know, Barry. Barry?"

Barry slumped over against a chain-link fence, a wooden stake through his left eye. He was dead. For real dead this time. I'd staked enough zombies to know a perfect kill when I saw one.

"That's it!" I shouted. "If anybody was gonna kill that annoying prick, it was gonna be me!"

The legless zombie croaked when I dropkicked it fifty yards into a parked car. It crashed through the windshield, twitched for a moment, and then fell down dead, a piece of glass embedded in its stupid head.

I spun around to pick up Barry's TV and used it to cave in the Danny DeVito-looking zombie's skull. He fell to the ground, and the television landed on top of him. Blood oozed out from under the TV as the zombie fell silent.

I crouched down in front of Barry. His dead, lifeless eyes looked back at me. "Sorry, buddy."

Pressing my hand against his shoulder, I yanked the stake out of his eye. I clutched it in my hand and thrust it up into the Keith Richards zombie's jaw, sending it shooting out through the back of its skull.

They were all dead. For real dead. They fell within a matter of moments. That's all it took to kill a pack of them on a good day. Last night, it took ten minutes, and I'd almost died four times. Tonight, I was on fire. Every move I made was the right one. But it doesn't always end up like that.

I crawled over the spear that had pierced through Barry's chest. It was still damp with his blood. Poor Barry. He didn't deserve what came to him. He was a good guy to the end, even if he was a deadbeat, and now he died twice, making him the ultimate deadbeat.

Back before we got the lights back on, the night was even more dangerous. Massive minotaurs and three-headed demon dogs roamed through the streets, ripping humans apart. I stupidly refused to stay inside.

I had this grand plan to get out of the city and head to the mountains. Nobody lived in the mountains, and it was cold. Hell monsters didn't like the cold. I tried to convince them all for weeks; Stephanie, Kenny, Linda, John,

Emerson, Eric K, and the others whose names faded from memory long ago.

It took two weeks of planning, but we finally loaded up four trucks of survivors and headed out. We were supposed to leave at daybreak, but logistical nightmares forced us to delay until nightfall. Connie told me to wait until the next day, but I didn't listen. I had to get out of Overbrook ASAP.

We didn't get five blocks from our place before a monstrous minotaur smashed into the lead truck and rolled it. Two of the three-headed demon dogs attacked another truck. It was bedlam. I tried to turn them all around. I tried to get back, but demons blocked our exit and forced us to scatter.

Barry and I barely got off the trucks with our lives. We were battered, bruised, and in pain. They wounded Barry the worst. He bled from his forehead and wobbled from a concussion.

I pulled him down an alley with a minotaur rushing after us. Of all the monsters Hell threw at us, the minotaur was the toughest I ever dealt with personally. There were worse ones, like hydras, but not in Overbrook. Demons could be reasoned with, zombies could be killed, ghosts could be evaded, and imps could be punted, but minotaurs never stopped.

We ran until we couldn't run anymore. We turned corners and jumped over fences, but the minotaur just kept coming.

Finally, we reached a dead end. The only way out was a broken picket in the fence. Barry couldn't get through, but I could.

"Go!" he shouted to me.

I wanted to say that I fought him or at least screamed at him, but I didn't. I left him there. I just left him. At that moment, I knew why I wasn't raptured. No good person would have left Barry to die.

Now I'd let him die a second time.

Clapping echoed from the end of the alleyway. I gripped the spear tightly, feeling Barry's blood ooze over my hand. I gritted my teeth and waited for the son of a bitch who controlled the zombies to show himself.

"Bravo, my dear." I heard from the darkness. "Thank you for disposing of them. They really were the worst mouth breathers I ever had the displeasure of overseeing. Thank you for sending them back to Hell. I doubt they'll be back any time soon."

Out of the darkness came a dapper demon, red as blood, horned, and dressed in an elegant three-piece suit. He was immaculately put together, down to his perfectly polished black shoes that shone like mirrors.

"What are you doing here, Thomas?" I snarled. If there was a demon in the world I hated more than any others, it was Thomas.

"I want you back, my love. You are an exquisite specimen."

I held my spear up to his throat. "You never had me, Thomas. You can't trick somebody into sleeping with you and then get pissed when they wanna cut off your dick."

"Trick? I don't like that word."

"What else would you call it?"

"I don't know. It is my way." Thomas took slow steps toward me, his palms turned up. "I'd call it…Tuesday, I suppose."

"Of course that's how you feel. You have no soul."

"That would be accurate, Katrina, as you well know."

"I'm going to stab you through the throat if you take another step." I shifted into a ready stance.

Thomas grabbed the spear and punctured himself through the throat. He grinned maniacally as blue bile from the wound dripped down his neck. "My dear, I'm not a mortal, or even a zombie. Your weapons have no effect on me. There's nothing you can do to harm me."

I smiled back at him. "Maybe not—" I pressed my combat boot into his groin. A painful moan escaped his lips. "But I'll bet that, horndog as you are, you manipulated your nerve endings so they're concentrated in your cock, just in case I wanted to screw you again."

I pulled the spear out of Thomas's neck and jammed it into the gap between his pants. His confident bravado fell away, and he doubled over. "Now, I'm no expert, but that looks like harm to me. Now, leave me alone, or I'll cut your head off. Got that?"

Thomas's blue blood spurted from the fresh tear in his pants onto my jacket as he collapsed onto his side. "Got it."

I looked down at my jacket. Thomas's bile stained the perfect leather. "Man, I love this coat. This stain is never gonna come out."

For good measure, I kicked Thomas in the face as I walked away because screw him and his beautiful face.

***

If you enjoyed that preview, make sure to pick up *Death* today.

ALSO BY RUSSELL NOHELTY

NOVELS

My Father Didn't Kill Himself
Sorry for Existing
Gumshoes: The Case of Madison's Father
Invasion
The Vessel
The Void Calls Us Home
Worst Thing in the Universe
The Marked Ones
The Dragon Scourge
The Dragon Champion
The Dragon Goddess
The Sleeping Beauty
The Wicked Witch
The Fairy Queen
The Red Rider

COMICS and OTHER ILLUSTRATED WORK

The Little Bird and the Little Worm
Ichabod Jones: Monster Hunter
Gherkin Boy
How NOT to Invade Earth

www.russellnohelty.com

1000 BC – BETRAYED (HELL PT 1) /PIXIE DUST

500 BC – FALLEN (HELL PT 2)

200 BC – HELLFIRE (HELL PT 3)

1974 AD – MYSTERY SPOT (RUIN PT 1)

1976 AD – INTO HELL (RUIN PT 2)

1984 AD – LAST STAND (RUIN PT 3)

1985 AD – CHANGE

1985 AD – MAGIC/BLACK MARKET HEROINE

1985 AD – EVIL

1989 AD – DEATH'S KISS (DARKNESS PT 1)

2000 AD – TIME

2015 AD – HEAVEN

2018 AD – DEATH'S RETURN (DARKNESS PT 2)

2020 AD – KATRINA HATES THE DEAD (DEATH PT 1)

2176 AD – CONQUEST

2177 AD – DEATH'S KISS (DARKNESS PT 3)

12,018 AD – KATRINA HATES THE GODS (DEATH PT 2)

12,028 AD – KATRINA HATES THE UNIVERSE (DEATH PT 3)

12.046 AD – EVERY PLANET HAS A GODSCHURCH (DOOM PT 1)

12,047 AD – THERE'S EVERY REASON TO FEAR (DOOM PT. 2)

12,049 AD – THE END TASTES LIKE PANCAKES (DOOM PT 3)

12,176 AD – CHAOS

Milton Keynes UK
Ingram Content Group UK Ltd.
UKHW032325121024
449589UK00011B/542